The Chamomile

OTHER BOOKS BY

Susan F. Craft

FICTION

A Perfect Tempest

NONFICTION

A Writer's Guide to Horses

*Puzzles, Pictures and Paper Airplanes:
What We Do When Our Parents Get Sick*

*Reporting on Mental Illness Fairly, Objectively, Sensitively:
A Guide for Journalism and Mass Communications Students in
South Carolina*

The Chamomile

A Novel of Revolutionary America

by

Susan F. Craft

To Kitty,

Hope you enjoy!

Susan F. Craft

INGALLS PUBLISHING GROUP

INGALLS PUBLISHING GROUP, INC

PO Box 2500
Banner Elk, NC 28604
www.ingallspublishinggroup.com

copyright © 2011 Susan F. Craft
Text design by Ann Thompson Nemcosky
Cover painting by Susan F. Craft
Cover design by: Aaron Burleson

Library of Congress Cataloging-in-Publication Data

Craft, Susan F.
The chamomile : a novel of revolutionary America / by Susan F. Craft.
p. cm.
978-1-932158-94-6
1. Young women--Fiction. 2. United States--History--Revolution, 1775-1783--Fiction. I. Title.
PS3603.R343C53 2011
813'.6--dc22
2010053489

Acknowledgments

Among countless other things, writing a novel requires persistence and encouragement. I have so many to thank for holding my feet to the fire, for stoking the waning embers when I became discouraged, and for fanning the flames of inspired moments.

I offer my deepest and most heartfelt appreciation to: my loving and supportive family--my husband, Rick; daughter, Allison; son, Donovan; son-in-law, Doug; and granddaughter, McKenzie, who made a sign for my door, *Shh! Grandmother is writing*; Paula Benson, my dear friend and intuitive sounding board, who insisted I write *the letter;* Marion Chandler, historian, for invaluable assistance with historical facts; Ingalls Publishing Group, especially Senior Editor Judy Geary, who have made me feel like family; The Inkplots, my writers critique group, who helped me hone my craft and inspired me to keep writing; Susan Lohrer, editor and host of my inspirational writers' blog; Karen MacNutt, history buff, and Carole and George Summers of the Francis Marion Symposium, who have forgotten more about the Swamp Fox than I'll ever know; Rudy Mancke, naturalist, who so generously shared his knowledge of South Carolina's wildlife, terrain, flora and fauna, saving me hundreds of hours researching in the library; James McCord on whose website (www.mccordclan.com) I discovered the picture of the Charlestown Harbor we used for the book cover; Basha and CuChullaine O'Reilly, founders of the international Long Riders' Guild, for assisting with an accurate portrayal of horses (visit www.thelongridersguild.com for information about their World Ride and also www.lrgaf.org to view my project, *An Equestrian Writer's Guide*); Susan's Tribe, my sweet sisters in Christ who lifted me up in prayer--Rhonda Baker, Sara Cheek, Lisa DeKruif, Brenda Lyles, Kathy Richards, Karen Shipp, Evelyn Stewart, Linda Weed, and Lynne Westra (you'll see these names again).

Above all, thanks to my Lord from who all blessings flow.

A British Army officer noted for his cruelty and relentless persecution of those opposed to his political views was one day walking with Mrs. Anna Elliott in a garden where there was a great variety of flowers.

"What is this, madam?" he asked, pointing to the chamomile.

"The rebel flower," she replied.

"And why is it called the rebel flower?" asked the officer.

"Because," answered Mrs. Elliott, "it always flourishes most when trampled upon."

Noble Deeds of American Women
by Jesse Clement

I, Lilyan Allison Grace Cameron, do hereby solemnly promise in the presence of Almighty God to bear allegiance to his present MAJESTY, KING GEORGE THE THIRD, AND HIS Successors, Kings of Great Britain, to be a true and faithful servant and to strictly observe and conform to the Laws of England without any Equivocation, mental Evasion, or secret Reservation whatsoever.

Chapter One

November 16, 1780
Charlestown, South Carolina

A MUFFLED THUMP PLUCKED Lilyan Cameron from a pleasant dream. She rose on her elbow and peered around the bedchamber enfolded in darkness except for the glow from the fireplace. She glanced over her shoulder at Elizabeth, whose chest rose and fell in restful sleep. Seeking her unfinished dream, Lilyan snuggled back under the covers and closed her eyes. Another thump sounded, and she sat up again. The noises were coming from her brother's makeshift bedroom in the attic.

What's he up to now?

Lilyan slipped out of bed and draped a wrapper around her shoulders. Nerves scraping like charcoal across a taut canvas, she lit a betty lamp, sliding the wick deep into the whale oil to keep the flame low. She tiptoed across the room and cracked open the door in time to spy her brother creeping down the stairs; fully dressed except for the boots he clasped in his hand.

She slipped into the hall as he reached the bottom step. "Andrew Cameron, where do you think you're going at this time of night?"

"Shush! Not so loud." He edged beside her. "You'll wake

Captain McKenzie."

Lilyan craned her neck, barely making out his scowling face in the dim hallway, and then glared toward the captain's bedroom. The last thing she wanted to do was wake the British officer who had been billeted in their home the past three months. She grabbed Andrew's sleeve and pulled him into her room, closing the door behind them.

She placed the lamp on a chest of drawers and jammed her fists onto her hips. "Tell me what you're up to."

He pushed back his shoulders. "It's not something I can talk about."

"You're involved with the militia again. I know it." Fear curled into a lump in the pit of her stomach. "But what about your wound? It hasn't had time to heal. Look at you. You weigh a full two stone less than you did when you ran off the first time."

Andrew rolled his eyes. "It's been three months, and my shoulder's fine."

"And what about your promise not to take up arms again? You'll be breaking your word."

"Blast my parole!" His words exploded in a barely controlled whisper. "Why should I be held to a promise I made to the bloody redcoats? Raiding up and down the coast forcing women and children to watch as they burn their homes. The parole means as much to me as the oath of allegiance you made to the king."

"There *is* a difference." Lilyan jabbed her finger into her chest. "*I* took the oath so we wouldn't lose our home. Our business."

"That's exactly what I mean. Both pledges were forced on us."

"What's wrong?" Elizabeth called out, her voice raspy.

Elizabeth threw off the covers and slid from the bed. The lamp cast shadows across her angular features and made her copper-colored skin glow. When she drew near, as always, her serene manner lessened the tension that often crackled between brother and sister.

"I caught him trying to sneak out of the house. He will not tell me where he's going, but I know it has something to do with the militia. Tell him he can't go, Elizabeth. He's too young."

"Too young! I fought in the battle of Camden, didn't I? That makes me more of a man than most fellows I know."

"But what if you're caught? What if they put you on one of those horrible prison ships—assuming they let you live? Andrew, you simply cannot do this."

"Keep your voices down," Elizabeth warned. "Lilyan, this time I think Andrew is right."

Lilyan gasped.

Elizabeth patted Lilyan's shoulder. "I understand what you say, but this is something Andrew feels strongly about. It's something I agree with. We cannot ask him to stand by and watch as other Americans fight and die."

Lilyan clasped the lapels of her brother's blanket jacket. "Once before, when I thought I had lost you, the pain was unbearable. Don't put me through that again. Please, dearest, you're all the family I have."

"Understand me." Andrew spoke firmly, curling his hands around hers. "I must do what I've been called upon to do."

Defeated, Lilyan dropped her forehead onto his chest.

He gently pushed her away and grasped her forearms. "Will you give me your blessing?"

Lilyan tensed. He would not make that request lightly. She looked into his eyes, the same fern green as her own, and his earnest expression disarmed her. Brushing back a lock of his dark auburn hair, she nodded. He hunched over, and she kissed him on his right eyelid and then his left.

"God be with you, Andrew Cameron," she said and then kissed his lips. "While we are apart, one from the other."

Andrew spoke the last words with her. When he wrapped his arms around her, Lilyan winced as she felt his shoulder blades through his coat. Before the war he had been a strapping young man with the full, muscular frame of a true Highlander. He seemed so frail now.

He opened the door, stuck his head out, and then glanced back. "Take care of each other," he said in a gruff voice and then hastened away.

Lilyan's knees gave way and she sank to the floor. Her shoulders shook as the tears she had been holding back rolled down her face. Aware that they were not alone in the house, she pulled her mobcap from her head and pressed it to her face.

Elizabeth eased the door shut and knelt. Lilyan sank into her arms, giving herself up to grief, rocking back and forth until her sobs subsided into deep shuddering breaths.

"Come." Elizabeth helped her up. "You're freezing. Let us get back into bed."

While Lilyan crawled onto the four-poster, Elizabeth threw kindling on the embers.

Lilyan held the covers open for Elizabeth, who slipped in and put her arm around her. Lilyan dropped her head onto Elizabeth's shoulder. "I don't know which aches most, my head or my heart."

"Would it help if we prayed?"

"Oh, yes. I think it would."

Lilyan closed her eyes and listened as her friend beseeched the Lord for mercy and strength. Her words and manner, so confident and assured, spread as a balm over Lilyan's pain.

Lilyan sat up and drew her knees toward her chin. "I do feel a little better now. I'm so thankful you're here with me. But then, you've always seemed more like an older sister than a servant."

She laced her fingers through Elizabeth's. "Although servant ceased to have meaning for me quite some time ago. You are family."

"I feel the same." Elizabeth pressed Lilyan's hand to her cheek.

"Elizabeth? Do you ever regret leaving your home and coming to Charlestown to be with us?"

"Never. When Mr. Cameron came to my village and heard that my dear eww-nee-t che and oewh-doe-dah—my mother and father—had died of smallpox, he became my friend. We had something in common, you know. He still grieved for your mother."

"Yes, he was never quite the same after she left us."

"In time, he asked if I would care for his children. He made me feel needed, and I could not resist."

Lilyan chuckled. "He was quite a charmer."

"When he pledged to my aunt that he would guard my life with his own, even she realized the promise for a better life he offered." She shook her head. "No. I have no regret."

"But what about a husband...children? Are we keeping you from those?"

The idea pained Lilyan, and she suddenly felt selfish for never before giving it a thought.

Elizabeth leaned forward. "Lilyan—"

A door shut, and they froze.

"The captain!" Elizabeth sprang from the bed and gathered her clothes. "I'll go out to the kitchen and prepare breakfast. You stay here, and I'll bring you something to eat after he has gone."

"But I should help."

"You hide your feelings like sun through the wings of a dragonfly. One look at you and he will know something is awry. This way, he can't ask you how Andrew is, and you won't have to lie. I am much better at that than you." She smiled, taking the edge off her words.

After Elizabeth left, Lilyan dragged herself from the bed, sat at the dresser, and loosened her braid. Trying to ignore the thoughts crowding her mind, she scraped the brush through her waist-length hair until her scalp hurt. She completed her morning toilet, donned a dress, and secured her hair under a sheer, white mobcap. Feeling wilted, she splashed cold water on her wrists and pinched her cheeks. After slipping on her shoes and polishing the buckles with a damp cloth, she rose from the chair to view herself in the mirror.

Her dress was blue, the favored color of the colonials. It was certain to raise the hackles of Tories who showed their loyalty to the king by wearing green.

At least in this small way I can show my support for Andrew.

As she knotted a lace scarf around her shoulders, she rehearsed the responses she would make to anyone who dared reproach her. After all, if folk said anything to her at her shop, she could ask them to leave if she had a mind to.

What if someone asks after Andrew? How will I answer? To bolster her courage, she attached the clan Cameron crest pin to the side of her cap. *Will I ever see him again? Will this band of the Camerons die out with me?*

Unable to bear such thoughts, she hurried from the room. Downstairs, she met Elizabeth carrying a tray into the dining room from the outside kitchen.

"Did Captain McKenzie leave already?" Lilyan asked.

"Yes. He seemed to be in a hurry."

Lilyan sat at the table, and Elizabeth placed a plate of toast and a mug of cider on the table before her.

"You're not eating?" Lilyan spread a napkin across her lap.

"I had something already. Excuse me for a moment, would you?"

Elizabeth left the room for a few minutes, but returned to stand with her arms folded behind her as she watched Lilyan spread fig preserves on the bread.

Lilyan nibbled on the toast, licked the sticky, sweet fruit from her fingers, and wiped them on her napkin. "This is so good, Elizabeth. But … I'm afraid I don't have much of an appetite."

"I know. But please finish it. You need to keep your strength up."

Lilyan took another bite and sipped some cider. "Do you think Captain McKenzie suspected anything?"

"No. He was as pleasant as usual."

"For the enemy, you mean."

"Somehow I cannot think of him that way. And you like him as well. He did much to help Andrew recover as quickly as he did."

Would Andrew suffer another wound? A wound that will not heal this time? Lilyan fought the queasiness invading her stomach. "Yes, I know, and I hate being so mean-spirited about him. War is so vexing. People you thought were friends no longer speak to you, and people who are supposed to be the enemy become your friends."

Lilyan dropped her toast and pushed her plate away. "How friendly do you think the captain would be if he found out Andrew has joined the fight again?" She slumped back in her chair and stared at the napkin she twisted in her fingers.

Elizabeth remained so quiet Lilyan glanced up. "What are you hiding behind your back?"

Laughing, Elizabeth held out a package. "Happy birthday."

Lilyan leapt up and hugged her. "My goodness, I had quite forgotten." She tugged on the blue satin ribbon and unwrapped the brown paper to reveal a pair of moccasins. "How beautiful."

"You are pleased?"

"I adore them. Thank you so much. This beadwork must have taken you weeks." Lilyan traced her fingertip along the toe of the moccasin. "It's the same design as your belt, isn't it?"

"Yes. It's an ancient Cherokee pattern my mother taught me."

"I don't think I've ever received anything so lovely. You must teach me how to do this."

Elizabeth nodded. "I would be proud to teach you, little sister."

"Little sister. I like the sound of that." She glanced out the window at the people passing by. "It's time to go."

"Wait. You're not going alone?" Elizabeth followed her to the entryway.

"It's such a short walk. I'll be fine." Lilyan slipped her cape from a hook on the wall. "After all, I am officially a spinster now."

"Do not talk such foolishness. You have had several offers. Even so, I thank God you had the wisdom to refuse them. To wait for someone who is worthy of you."

"Someone who will put up with me, you mean?"

"Well, that too."

They shared a smile, and then Elizabeth helped Lilyan put on her cape.

Lilyan opened the door and stepped outside and then turned to hug her friend once more. "Thank you again for remembering my birthday."

Elizabeth nodded. "I'll pray we hear from Andrew soon."

As the door closed behind her, Lilyan vowed to give her brother two days, and then she was going after him.

Donovan Lewis begs leave to acquaint his Friends and the Public that he has resumed his business of PAINTING and GLAZING and that orders sent to him at his shop in St. Michael's Alley will be punctually attended to.

Chapter Two

Outside on the stoop, Lilyan paused to breathe in the cool air, rich with salt from the sea and the pungent odor of loamy soil settled atop centuries-old layers of oyster and clamshell shards.

She pulled her cape tighter against a blustery wind that whipped in from the Ashley and the Cooper, twin rivers that flowed on either side of Charlestown. At the tip of the peninsula, the rivers joined together in a rush to the sea, forming marsh-lined inlets and tiny islands that peppered the bay areas, ripe with oysters, shrimp, loggerhead turtles, and myriad species of waterfowl and wildlife.

Lilyan had been born in this thriving port city that now boasted a population of fifteen thousand. Her house was situated at the junction one of the busiest streets in town and a three-block thoroughfare leading to the river. From her bedroom window she often peered through her spyglass to watch dockworkers and sailors loading and unloading cargo from the ships moored at the wharfs. Lilyan's wallpaper shop sat at the water's edge between a cooperage and the northernmost wharf.

As Lilyan quickened her pace, she nodded greetings to friendly passersby and glared back at those who sneered at the color of her dress. She tread across slippery cobblestones that had served as ballast in the bottom of ships sailing from faraway ports; places she knew Andrew longed to see. The thought that he might never have an opportunity to travel spawned such resentment she kicked one of the rocks, sending it skipping across the road. She watched, mortified, as a man jigged to avoid the unexpected missile, but not before it bounced off his shin.

Ignoring the pain spreading up her foot, Lilyan hurried toward the gentleman. "Pray, sir, do forgive me." She glanced up in time to catch a hint of irritation in a pair of eyes that were the most unusual golden brown she had ever seen.

"You are hurt?" she asked, noting his slightly aquiline nose and his full bottom lip now curling up at one corner. A niggling ache permeated her big toe, and she rubbed her shoe across the back of her other leg.

"Mayhap not as much as you," he said in a voice warm with good humor.

Despite proper decorum, Lilyan continued to stand there taking in his six-foot frame and the sooty curls that strayed from the buckskin cord tied at the back of his neck. She studied his deeply tanned face once more, intrigued with his eyes. Topaz, she mused. More golden than brown.

When he grinned so wide a dimple popped into his right cheek, Lilyan felt her face grow hot.

"Forgive me for staring. I am an artist. I have a terrible habit of treating people as subjects. Always on the lookout for an interesting face, you see. And yours is quite interesting."

The man lifted his right eyebrow and met her gaze with twinkling eyes.

"Not ... not, that that makes it any less rude," she stammered.

I am chattering like a magpie. And to a complete stranger. What must he be thinking? Judging by his quizzical expression, she was not certain she wanted to know.

The gentleman swooped his hat from his head, and bowed in a grand gesture. "Not at all, miss. I'm rather enjoying myself."

Embarrassed with her behavior, Lilyan adopted a demure look. "If you are sure you are not hurt, I will bid you good day, sir." She bowed and then dashed away before he could say anything else.

Trying not to seem a scared rabbit, she adopted a normal pace, but she could feel his eyes still trained on her. Curiosity overcame better judgment, and she turned around to find him where she had left him, his arms folded across his broad chest. And yes, he was quite brazenly starring back at her. He smiled and nodded, sending her scurrying down a lane that took her out of her way. Two blocks later and back on track, she approached a row of shops, waved to the baker, and skirted past him to avoid the cloud of flour he swept into the street.

The buildings in this mercantile area of town mirrored each other—three stories high, measuring about fifteen feet wide and thirty feet long, with servant and slave huts crowded into long, narrow backyards. The businesses took up the first floors; the merchants and their families lived on upper floors.

One could purchase almost anything on Elliott Street—gauzes, muslins, satins, and silks from the fabric shop at No. 8; mantuas from the French seamstress at No. 12, whose modest sign read, "Plain needlework done faithfully, with expeditiousness;" and hats and gloves from the snooty milliner at No. 14, whose patrons visited her shop more for her gossip than for her wares. The apothecary offered salts, camphor, opium, spirits of lavender, James' powders, and Stoughton's bitters.

As Lilyan passed the soap and candle maker's, she made a mental note to purchase some of Elizabeth's favorite lemon zest castile. She slowed her pace to catch the tantalizing aromas floating out from the sundry store. The mixture of nutmeg, cloves, and cinnamon evoked a vivid memory of her mother's spice chest and its contents so treasured they were kept under lock and key.

At the end of the street, Lilyan joined a group of people reading the handbills tacked to a public message board.

"I see old Chamber's Negro has run away again. He's offering three guineas reward this time," said a gentleman who rested his hands on his rotund stomach.

"Yep, and look, he's got two saddle horses for sale. Six guineas each. Thinks more of his horses than his Negro fellow," said another man, who snorted his derision.

"Well, look at that, Donovan Lewis is back in business," commented a woman standing next to Lilyan, who stood on tiptoe to read his notice.

"Old hardhead almost lost everything, refusing to take the king's oath," the woman continued. "Finally buckled under, though. Came to his senses." The woman turned her attention to Lilyan and stabbed a finger toward her dress. "Speaking of sense, have you lost yours, young woman?"

Lilyan straightened her back. "I—"

"Mistress Cameron," a voice called out from behind her.

Lilyan turned and watched her apprentice, Gerald Snead, lope toward her. When he raised his hand to tip his cocked hat, Lilyan noticed rings of stitch marks on his sleeve. Despite the fact his mother must have let the hems out several times, his wrists still stuck out from under the cuffs.

"Sorry I missed you at your house," he said, breathless from his sprint. He took her arm and pulled her across the street, tugging firmly as she glared behind her at the people who had knotted together obviously gossiping about her.

Gerald and his identical twin, Herald, were the same age as Andrew. As youngsters the three had been inseparable—combing the marshes for wild geese, gigging frogs, and seining shrimp in pools deposited by the ebb tide. The boys shared their bounty with Mrs. Snead, who cooked it into succulent stews and gumbos, which drew customers in droves to the tavern she and her husband ran. Some of Mrs. Snead's patrons swore she could make the sole of a shoe taste good.

Since coming to work for Lilyan two years ago, Gerald had given up his boyhood ramblings and had become a serious student whose paintings and print-block carvings rivaled his teacher's. Not so with Herald, who had talked Andrew into running off and enlisting in the colonial militia. Although the brothers shared the same wheat-colored hair, cornflower blue eyes, and handsome looks, the similarities ended there. Where Gerald was shy and well mannered, Herald was boisterous and loud. Gerald was happiest in the shop sketching murals and designing wallpaper patterns. Herald seemed more at home trudging through the forests with a musket slung across his arm.

"Pardon my saying so, mistress, but are you baiting for trouble this morning?" Gerald draped her arm through his, setting a brisk pace.

Lilyan ignored his question and, when they stood at the entrance to her shop, she withdrew her arm and turned to stare at the ships in the bay.

19

She chewed her bottom lip. "Where are they?" she demanded, training her eyes on the largest vessel.

"I can't say," Gerald answered without hesitation as if he knew full well who *they* were.

"Can't or won't?"

"A little of both."

Lilyan reached into the slit at the side of her dress and pulled a key from the apron pocket underneath her skirt. She unlocked the door, waited for Gerald to enter, and then closed it behind them.

"Can you not offer me some hope for their safety?"

"All I can say is Herald said he would be back tomorrow."

Tomorrow? By then I'll have plenty of things stored up to say to one Andrew Cameron.

Lilyan walked around the front counter toward the back of the shop. She continued through the workroom, a rustic barn-like area covered on three sides with shelves stacked high with paper and cloth samples, paints and brushes and blocks of wood, and carving knives. A thick layer of stucco plastered the third wall, which she used as a canvas to design murals. She opened the back door and stepped onto a deck jutting over the water. A gust of crisp, cool air lifted her skirts as she walked to the edge of the platform and leaned on the railing.

"Mek you duh rarry so?" a voice called out in Gullah.

She leaned over and spotted Lancaster, a slave who belonged to one of the local merchants, sitting in a canoe near the shore. Though he spoke in the parlance of slaves, Lilyan understood him well. As a young girl, she had loved to mimic the language, delighting in the mixture of Portuguese and English mellowed with the essence of the African Rice Coast.

"I'm worried about Andrew. He's run off again."

The young man, his face as shiny as polished onyx, doffed his felt hat and then continued weaving a shuttle loaded with twine through a tear in one of his nets. *"Dat one gunna rarry you to the grabe."*

"That's so. If he keeps this up, he will be the death of me."

He folded the net and grabbed the oars. *"Best leabe, now, missy. Timma to fetch me some wurrums."*

One of a band of Negroes whose masters allowed them to roam the rivers and the channels to catch fish and market them to the townspeople, Lancaster often chose this section of the banks to hunt for worms and to seine.

"God go with you," she called out.

As he paddled away, Lilyan was reminded of when her father, Douglas Cameron, used this building for his profitable trading business. Playing pirate, she would often climb up on the roof with her spyglass trained on the ships anchored in the bay and she would watch traders and their slaves dock their boats laden with deerskins.

What a sad irony, she thought. Patriots were fighting to free themselves from what they considered the yoke of tyranny, and yet some remained blind to those unfortunate people who lived in real bondage.

She thought again of her father whose life had ended so suddenly and tragically.

"Oh, Da. Has it really been two years? I miss you so," she whispered.

Would you have controlled Andrew better than I? No, you probably would have gone with him and left me to worry over the both of you.

"Mistress Cameron, Mrs. Coatsbury has arrived for her appointment," Gerald called from the workroom.

"Thank you, Gerald." She stepped back inside, took off her cape, and hung it on a hook. "Would you ask her to join me? I have a design for her to view."

"Oh, my!" Mrs. Coatsbury exclaimed from the doorway and hurried to the mural Lilyan had painted. With her eyes dancing, she perused Lilyan's interpretation of a Japanese woman standing in a grove of cherry blossoms. She clapped her hands like a child rejoicing over a Christmas present. "It's brilliant. You've captured it perfectly."

The woman's obvious delight touched Lilyan's heart. "I'm so pleased you like it."

Lilyan motioned her toward a chair and sat beside her. "It's a much smaller scale, you realize, and it's in sinopia. I would enlarge it considerably if we are to apply it above your dining room fireplace. And there will be many rich colors—especially in the kimono. I envision deep oranges and vibrant yellows."

"This is all so fascinating," said Mrs. Coatsbury. "How is it done?"

For the next half hour, Lilyan explained the process, answered her customer's questions, and then set a date for the project.

After seeing Mrs. Coatsbury to the door, Lilyan rearranged a stack of wallpaper patterns and checked the inventory. Tightening the cork tops on some of the crocks of paint, she reminded herself to replenish her supply of pigments. She joined Gerald, who sat at a table behind the front counter, and stood behind him to watch him carve a block of wood.

"Excellent, Gerald." She ran her fingers across the smoothed edges of the stencil block. "Wonderful detail. A daisy?"

"No, a chamomile."

"It reminds me of the decoration your mother carves into her pies."

Gerald's knife slipped, and he jerked his head around. "I—I suppose it does."

"Well, I hate to interrupt you, but I need you to fetch Callum. I want to visit the paper mill, and he insists on taking me there himself. Last time I went by myself he threw a grand fit."

"Yes, ma'am. I know right where he is. Where he always is most mornings—in the tavern, drinking cider by the fireplace—"

"Waiting for your mama's pies to come out of the oven," Lilyan finished his sentence.

Grinning, Gerald wrapped the stencil block in a piece of gauze and tucked it onto a shelf under the counter. He threw on his hat and coat and knotted a crocheted scarf around his neck. As he stepped across the threshold, a gust of wind rushed in from the bay, and he struggled to keep the door from slamming behind him. He hurried away, clasping his collar around his neck with one hand and clamping his hat to his head with the other.

Lilyan shivered as the icy wind cut a swath through the shop, fluttering the drawings on her desk. She stoked the lumps of coal Gerald had ignited in the Franklin stove, happy with herself for having made the decision a year earlier to make such an extravagant purchase. She filled a teapot with water and had just placed it on the stovetop when the door to the shop opened.

Lilyan curtsied to the two women and managed to put a cordial smile on her face. "Mrs. Melborne. Mrs. Stafford," she greeted, hoping she didn't sound as halfhearted as she felt.

Mrs. Stafford nodded, but Mrs. Melborne stared at Lilyan's

dress and tilted her head.

Can her nose go any higher without making her fall over backward?

"How may I assist you?" Lilyan motioned them toward the seating area by her desk.

Mrs. Stafford, in a pumpkin-colored satin dress and matching demicape lined with fur, perched on the edge of her chair as if ready to take flight.

The moss green silk of Mrs. Melborne's skirt swished as she slid gracefully into the chair nearest Lilyan. "Well, Mistress Cameron, as you may know, my family now owns Violet Plantation."

Lilyan knew a lot more than that. Mrs. Melborne was cousin to the infamous Lt. Colonel Banastre Tarleton, the Butcher of Waxhaw. Because of that connection, her husband, a captain under the command of General Cornwallis, had received Violet Plantation as a prize of war, sequestrated from its owner, who had refused to pledge his oath to King George.

The owner had been a particular friend of Lilyan's father, and the thought of his cruel treatment left a bitter taste on Lilyan's tongue. Her hands itched to toss the women out on their richly attired behinds, but the repercussions of that action would prove extreme. Thoughts of Andrew and Elizabeth held her in check.

"Yes, I had heard of your … good fortune," Lilyan said.

Mrs. Melborne fingered a curl at the nape of her neck. "We have a lovely dining room there—"

"Truly lovely," Mrs. Stafford emphasized, and they nodded to each other as only the privileged can do.

"But unfortunately," Mrs. Melborne continued, "it has only one window. So, I'm considering a mural covering the longest wall, across from the fireplace. Similar to a painting I saw at the Queen's House. A pastoral scene of the English countryside."

Lilyan nodded. *Could I bear to be around this woman long enough to finish such a task?*

"You have been to the Queen's House?" Mrs. Stafford simpered.

The silly woman is going to fall off her chair.

"I've had several occasions to attend Her Majesty. Fourteen of her children were born in that house. Used to be called Buckingham's House, you know. But it's more of a palace now."

As the relative of Tarleton, the son of a moneylender and slave trader, you may have been in attendance. Though probably as a maid.

Lilyan cringed at her own ungracious thoughts. "I may have something that will suit. Give me a moment, please."

In the storeroom, Lilyan sorted through a stack of sample drawings and breathed deeply to help calm her nerves.

Lord, forgive me for my ugly thoughts. But trying to remain civil to these people is difficult. They represent everything we're fighting to change. Grant me patience, please.

She found paintings she thought might interest Mrs. Melborne and headed with them to the front when she overheard part of a conversation that made her stop short.

"Yes, I do so worry about my dear husband," whined Mrs. Melborne. "He is preparing as we speak to join with cousin Banastre at a place called Ninety-Six. Seems there is some fort the barbarians are trying to take away from us. Then he will be off to track that notorious ruffian Francis Marion."

"I have heard of him," Mrs. Stafford replied, "a vile man who lives in the swamps like some sort of animal. Totally ignores the proper rules of warfare."

"Humph. If you ask me, none of these colonials know how to do anything properly."

Lilyan had heard enough and, squaring her shoulders, she strode into the room. As she passed the stove, she noticed the water boiling. She put the paintings on her desk, grabbed a potholder, and picked up the kettle.

"Oh, my," said Mrs. Stafford, "how I would love a cup of tea."

Lilyan braced herself. "I am afraid we have no tea here. Our drink of choice is coffee."

"I beg your pardon." Mrs. Melborne stood and took a few steps toward Lilyan. "I would be very careful about talk like that, young woman."

"I should say so," said Mrs. Stafford, slipping her arm around her friend.

"Have you not taken the oath, Mistress Cameron?"

"I have." Lilyan slammed the kettle back onto the stove.

"And where is your certificate?" Mrs. Melborne demanded, nostrils flaring.

"Where it is mandated to be." Lilyan pointed to the window

24

display by the entrance.

Mrs. Melborne stomped across the room and grabbed the piece of paper. "It says here you promise to be 'a true and faithful subject to His Majesty the King of Great Britain.'"

Lilyan's stomach muscles quivered. She yanked the certificate away and shoved it back in the window. She dropped her arms stiffly to her sides and clenched her fists.

"I must inform you, ladies, I was incorrect. I do not have any samples to suit your needs. Besides, I have more business than I can manage. I am afraid all I can offer you is a strong cup of coffee."

"Well—I—" Mrs. Melborne's face flushed to the roots of her hair. "Come, Rowena, let us leave this place. I should have known to expect such uncouth behavior from a *tradesperson*." She drew up her nostrils as if smelling something unpleasant. "Especially one who roams about the streets without an escort and works all hours of the night without a chaperone. I imagine one cannot expect anything different from these colonials."

Lilyan remained stoic as the women flounced from her shop and slammed the door behind them. She watched them hurry away, the feathers in their hats bobbing wildly as they carried on their animated conversation. She wrapped her arms across her chest and, irritated with her awkward handling of such a volatile situation, she paced the room. Flustered, she hurried out to the deck, where, as usual, the balmy aromas and the sunlight dancing on the green water slowed her thundering pulse—until she focused on the prison ships.

Would they be Andrew's final destination?

A chill slid its way across her arms, and she stepped back inside.

My Dear Mistress Cameron,

It is with profund exultation that I inform you of a fortuitous happenstance. Without particularizing, it is my belief that I have discovered after many trials & attributable upon your most excellent idea a Wonderous New Method of fabricating panels for your wallpaper designs. I humbly invite you to view this Discov'ry at first hand & wait upon your reply.

Your Most Obedient Sev't
Pierre Dessausure
Proprietor

Chapter Three

LILYAN WAS SEATED at her desk, hard at work with her correspondence when Gerald and Callum entered the shop. Gerald sat at the counter and continued his carving, while the stocky, craggy-faced Angus McCallum began his incessant grumbling.

"I dinna know why in this world you want ta go gallivantin' up to the paper mill in this weather. Catch your death of cold, you will. And what about all them British crawling about town? Murderin', thievin' varmints." Callum slapped his coonskin cap against his leg, wafting the aroma of a hundred pinewood campfires across the room.

Angus McCallum had strong feelings about most things and did not mind letting people hear them—loudly and often. He had a hot Scot's temper that had drawn him into many fights during his sixty years, evidenced by a badly repaired broken nose and a scar that streaked his face from his ear to his chin. After Douglas Cameron's death, he became Lilyan and Andrew's self-appointed guardian; a task he fulfilled with the fervor of a crusading knight. Callum was a man you either hated or loved. Lilyan adored him.

Lilyan cupped Callum's face in her hand. "We all know I will be safe with you by my side."

"Don't go tryin' out them feminine wiles on me, lassie." Callum looked up at her with watery eyes barely visible underneath his droopy lids.

"You bundle up good, now." He helped her with her cape, lifting the hood over her hair and tightening the drawstrings.

"I should not be but a couple of hours, Gerald," said Lilyan.

"Yes, ma'am. I'll take care of things," he called out, already intent on his carving.

Lilyan and Callum walked out the back door, across the deck, and down the stairs. At the bottom platform, Callum stepped into a dinghy and helped Lilyan aboard.

"Don't go fiddlin' around too much," he grumbled.

He untied the mooring rope from a ring buried deep in the tabby seawall, a barrier made of lime concrete and oyster shells, which curved around the tip end of the city. He waited for her to settle on the plank seat in the prow before locking the oars into place.

"Don't want to go havin' to fish you out of the water."

Lilyan did not respond to the warning he had repeated to her since she was a child. Instead, she peered at the prison ships. Curving a hand over her brow, she could barely make out the names of the two closest vessels, the *Torbay* and the *Success-Increase*.

"Is it true what they are saying about the prisoners?" she asked.

Callum cleared his throat. "You know, lassie, I could tell you not to worry over it, but I know it wouldna do no good. I'll tell you a little, but not all. There's just some things not fit for a lady to hear."

"It's that bad?"

"Aye, that bad. There are more than a hundred and thirty men aboard the *Pack Horse*—the one farthest away—a schooner built to hold eighty. Most of the prisoners fought in the Battle of Camden and have been on them ships ever since. Not much food, no coats or blankets or shelter from the cold nights. And that's as much as I'm gonna' tell ye."

"And that is where Andrew would have been if you had not made him take the oath."

"Don't remind me of that dark day." Callum pulled hard on the oars as they headed north against the currents.

"But it saved his life."

"Ach! You don't know what a hard thing it was. What good is a man's life if he lives it under the yoke of another? But when I saw the condition of the poor wee lad, I felt hard pressed by the promise I made to your da to keep the two of you safe."

Lilyan gripped the seat on either side. "Well, it may have been all for naught. Andrew has run off. And I know it's to fight with the militia again."

Waiting for a reply that never came, Lilyan twisted around and glared at him. "You know something, don't you?"

Callum skimmed the surface of the water with one of the oars, causing them to swerve starboard. "Current's mighty strong, or else I'm just gettin' too old," he mumbled.

Callum slammed his jaw shut tighter than a rusty beaver trap.

Stubborn old mule. Irritated, she turned her back on him.

A seagull floated past, pushing against the cross currents to join others as they foraged through garbage strewn along the shore. Lilyan wrinkled her nose as they neared a part of town that seemed to have lost its decency. Filth coated the streets marred with more alehouses and shanties than ever before. Two years had passed since a fire had destroyed the businesses and homes in the area, but due to a shortage of materials, nothing had been rebuilt. She watched two women, one white and one colored, clad in only their shifts and stays, entice two sailors into a one of several shacks dotting the shoreline.

Lilyan had no sure knowledge of what went on inside the ramshackle hovels. Once as a young girl, she had broached the subject with her father, but his vague explanation had left her with more questions than answers. That conversation had occurred during the only time her father allowed her to accompany him on a trading mission.

What a special time that was. Traveling from the ocean to the mountains and back, the magical adventure, packed with amazing sights, sounds and smells, had dazzled Lilyan so she christened it her *wonder time.* She had celebrated her tenth birthday on that trip, a year after her mother's death.

Lilyan recalled how one night, while pushing a glowing pinecone back into their campfire, she asked her father how babies came to be. Blushing a brilliant red underneath his auburn beard, he had explained to her in very broad terms what the Bible said about God's command to "be fruitful and multiply." Although he kept insisting that it was a joyous thing when it occurred between a man a woman who loved each other, Lilyan came away with a less than favorable impression of what that joyous occurrence might involve. Not long after returning from their trip, Mr. Cameron brought fifteen-year-old Elizabeth home to take care of Lilyan and her brother and no doubt to explain the many questions his daughter would pose as she became a woman.

Lilyan glanced back at Callum, and still smarting from his refusal to reveal what he knew about Andrew, she seized the opportunity to tease her old friend.

"Callum," she said, all innocence, "who are those women?"

"Wha—? Ne'er you mind who they are." He rowed faster.

"But from what I've heard, I understand they are selling wares. What kind of wares?" she pressed on.

"And just where have you heard about such things?"

"In my shop. You would be surprised what one can overhear."

"Well, then, look out to sea or straight ahead. Don't matter which, as long as you're not looking over there. And another thing, nothing good ever comes of listening in on other people's conversations."

He continued mumbling so low Lilyan could not make out his words. Pleased she had succeeded in teasing him, she leaned over the side of the boat and drew her hand across the surface of the water that was changing from blue-green to coal black as they neared the marshlands.

"It's freezing," she said, drying her hand against her skirt.

"Best keep your hands out of it, then."

"Oh, look." She pointed to a white egret wading among the emerald green reeds that popped out of the water in thick patches.

When they entered a tidal creek, Lilyan breathed in the loamy smell and surveyed the landscape that never ceased to touch a chord deep within her. Channels of water, furrowed by the ocean's raking fingers, splayed out like silver ribbons, tapering off into strips of tall grass and cattails with tops that had burst into their autumn attire of gray-brown feathers. The ebbing waters exposed dead reeds scattered across the shoreline in thick piles that crackled in the wind.

"So many shades of green," she murmured, wondering how she could capture them all on canvas. "When can we go foraging again? I have some ideas for new colors."

"*We* can't." Callum maneuvered the boat to shore and braced his hand on Lilyan's shoulder as he moved past her to jump onto the sandy beach.

"But I'm just about out of some of my pigments, and the next shipment isn't due for two months. If it makes it here at all." Lilyan allowed Callum to grasp her under her arms and lift her out of the boat.

Held in his iron grip, she was reminded that, despite his age and recent years of town living, Callum retained the strength that had allowed him to survive decades of trapping, hard living, and fighting Indians.

Depositing her onto the narrow path leading to the paper mill, he looked into her eyes and, as if sensing her disappointment, he acquiesced, "I said *we* can't go. But *I* can. Give me a list of what you need, and I'll see if I can fetch it."

Lilyan patted his shoulder. "You're a dear man."

"Ach." He stared at the mill about sixty yards away. "How long will you be?"

"Maybe an hour, maybe less."

"I'm gonna bide a wee here. Catch a few winks."

"Don't let the alligators get you," she called over her shoulder.

"They wouldna want none of me. Too leathery," he said, causing Lilyan to giggle.

She picked her way through knee-high bulrushes and spartina that whispered and teemed with birds and bugs. Her skirt brushed across a patch of rust-colored grass, disturbing a couple of lizards that darted across her path. She stopped midway across a wooden bridge spanning a narrow rivulet and scanned the mounds of oyster beds and gleaming black mussels.

The mill sat at the end of the bridge, nestled among a hammock of palmetto trees, wax myrtles, and live oaks. Although only two years old, the exterior of pine planks had already faded to gray alternately bleached by the scorching Carolina sun and battered by salty gales that whipped their way across the channel.

When Lilyan entered the building, Pierre Dessausure, the proprietor, hurried toward her. *"Bonjour, Mademoiselle* Cameron. So good to see you." He wiped his hand across the front of his apron and bowed. "Come see what we have done with the gauze you brought."

Lilyan followed him toward a row of barrels. Stopping in front of one, *Monsieur* Dessausure grabbed a long paddle and stirred the mucous liquid, wafting up a foul stench Lilyan had never gotten used to.

"See how white it is? I used rags made from only the finest cotton. Now, come see what happened." His eyes danced with excitement. He tugged her elbow, drawing her toward several racks from which large squares of paper had been hung to dry.

"Feel this." He ran his fingers over one of the sheets.

Lilyan followed suit. "Smooth, yet flexible."

"Now. For the *pièce de résistance.*"

He hurried toward the back of the mill. "We took the bolt of gauze you brought, moistened it with a thin coat of gesso, and then attached sheets of the paper in a row. And, *voilà!*" He motioned toward a table that ran the length of the room.

Lilyan stared at the continuous strip of wallpaper stretching across the entire bolt of cloth, almost twelve yards long. "I cannot believe it."

Suddenly, the delight left *Monsieur* Dessausure's face. His expression darkened as he stared at something behind her.

Lilyan spun around to find Gerald standing a few feet away. "Gerald? What—?"

"Excuse us one moment, please." *Monsieur* Dessausure led Gerald out the side door.

Lilyan dashed to a window and spied Gerald pulling a letter from a leather pouch slung across his chest. With their heads bent together, the two of them talked several minutes, and then *Monsieur* Dessausure darted back inside.

He handed Lilyan a piece of paper that looked as if it had been torn from a recipe. It was a note from Mrs. Snead pleading with her to come quickly.

"You must leave now." He grasped her elbow and led her toward the door.

"What has happened?"

"Please. Do as I ask. You must go quickly with Gerald to the tavern."

Pulse racing, Lilyan followed him outside and up a sandy hill to the road beside the mill. When she spotted Gerald holding the reins of his horse, a terrible premonition seared her mind.

"Is it Andrew? Is he—?"

"You will know more soon," Gerald said. He mounted the horse and reached to help seat her up in front of him.

Lilyan balked. "We can go much faster if I ride behind you."

"That you cannot do. You're a lady." As if sensing her frustration, he smiled. "Mother would skin me alive if I allowed you to ride straddle. Besides, it's important we take our time. Avoid suspicion."

Lilyan allowed the two men to assist her onto the horse. Gerald drew his arms around her, clasped the reins, and kicked the horse forward. As Lilyan clutched the horse's mane in one hand and leaned back against Gerald's rail-thin body, she wondered if he could feel her heart slamming through her shoulder blades.

"Callum is down by the boat," she shouted over her shoulder to *Monsieur* Dessausure.

"I will tell him," he called back.

Lilyan twisted her head around to look back at Gerald. "And will you tell me?"

"I am to leave the details to Mother, but I can tell you Andrew is alive. He and Herald both. Alive, but in trouble."

Relief wilted her shoulders, and she sucked in a deep breath.

Gerald released the reins long enough to pull the hood of Lilyan's cape up over her head. "You must keep your pretty face covered so as not to tempt the redcoats we'll be passing. I—I mean, that's what Mother said. That your face is pretty, I mean."

Mrs. Snead's advice proved sound as they neared a detail of British soldiers patrolling the outskirts of the city. Lilyan lowered her head, pulled her hood across her face, and leaned into Gerald. Her cheek pressed against the scratchy wool of his jacket, and even through the thick fabric, she could hear his heart race as the men trudged close enough for her to reach out and touch them.

"Hold up there, boy," ordered one of the men.

She felt Gerald's body tense as he reined in.

"State your business."

"Taking my sister to the doctor, sir."

"What's wrong with her?"

"Real high fever and vomiting. Mama says it could be anything."

Lilyan moaned and made her body tremble.

"Get along with you, then," came the gruff reply.

Lilyan and Gerald remained silent as they passed several more groups of soldiers.

"We're beside the British hospital," Gerald whispered a few minutes later.

Although the trip from the mill to the outskirts of town was only a half an hour, to Lilyan it felt as if they had been traveling four times as long.

"You can uncover your face now," said Gerald. "Won't be long before we're at the tavern. You've done well. Andrew would be proud."

"I don't know how you can say that. I was scared to death."

"My father says it's a sign of true courage; doing what needs to be done, even though you feel like you're going to leap right out of your skin."

As they entered a main thoroughfare, Lilyan perused the silent rows of houses on either side. "Where is everyone?"

Mistress Lilyan,
        Make all pos'ble Haste.
    Annabelle Snead

Chapter Four

$\mathcal{G}$ERALD DID NOT ANSWER, but kicked the horse's sides and propelled him to another road. Outside his parents' tavern, he slipped off the saddle and reached up to help Lilyan. When they stepped onto the porch that stretched across the front of the two-story building, the door flew open.

"Come in. Come in," said Mrs. Snead as she hurried toward them.

A buxom woman as wide as she was tall, Mrs. Snead clasped Lilyan to her. Making little cooing noises, she gently patted Lilyan's back. Wrapped in Mrs. Snead's ample arms, Lilyan breathed in the aromas soaked into her apron—apple pie, peanut soup, and lemon zest. For the first time in a long time Lilyan felt safe. But as much as she wanted to stay where she was, she knew she had to find out about Andrew. She stepped back and looked into the woman's soft brown eyes.

Mrs. Snead touched Lilyan's cheek. "I will answer what questions I can. There's no one here now. They've all gone to the jail. But we still must be very careful." She stepped over to Gerald and, rising up on her tiptoes, she gave him a peck on the cheek.

"Well done, my fine brave lad. You keep a watch out and let us

34

know if anyone comes in."

Lilyan followed Mrs. Snead behind the counter and into the back of the kitchen. She waited as the woman took a betty lamp from its hanger on the wall, lit it with a straw from the stove, and opened a door leading to the cellar.

"Close the door behind you." Mrs. Snead proceeded down the flight of stairs. She placed the lamp on a rough-hewn wooden table and motioned for Lilyan to sit in one of the chairs.

Lilyan took a seat and glanced around the cellar filled to the ceiling with barrels and crates bulging with straw. A musty smell hung in the air, and the dim light of the lamp made the room even gloomier. She clasped her cape closer and tucked her hands into its folds.

Mrs. Snead lowered herself into the chair facing Lilyan. "I know you're worried, so I'll get right to it. Andrew and Herald and about ten other men have been arrested. They've been taken to the city jail."

Lilyan's stomach muscles tightened. "Gerald says Andrew wasn't hurt. Are you sure?"

"Positive. Mr. Snead has already been to see them."

Lilyan let out the breath she had been holding in. "Why were they arrested?"

"They were caught making plans to move a shipment of very special supplies from the city."

"Supplies?"

"Uh-h, well, I can't really go into detail."

"Mrs. Snead, I assure you. I can be trusted."

"I know. But we have to be so careful."

"We?"

"A group of Patriots, trying our best to defeat the British."

"I want to see the last of them too. I want this awful war to end. Above all I want my Andrew back home again." She placed her hands on the table. "These supplies. Would they be the powder magazine hidden in the basement of the Exchange Building?"

"Glory be! How do you know about that?"

"From Andrew. After he came home from Camden, for days he suffered a fever and often he would ramble on about things. Some did not make sense, but the magazine was one thing I picked up on. So you see I can keep a secret."

35

"That might be a valuable thing in the next few weeks."

Lilyan stared at the black plume of smoke rising from the lamp wick, and her nose twitched at the smell of burning whale oil. She dreaded hearing the answer to her next question. "What will happen to them?"

"The Board of Police will decide. Mr. Snead thinks they will send the prisoners to the Exchange dungeon." She gave a thin smile. "They might be locked up right next to the brick wall that hides the very thing they were trying to steal away."

Tears stung Lilyan's eyes.

"There, now. We'll find a way to get them back safely. I just know we will." Mrs. Snead dabbed her eyes with the hem of her apron.

Lilyan reached for the woman's soft, plump hand. "I am sorry. I've been so worried about Andrew I forgot how you must be feeling."

"Since he came into this world, my Herald has found his way in and out of trouble. I pray with all my heart he will find his way out of this. And poor Gerald. I told him he had to stay away from the jail until his father can come back and let us know what is happening. But he's about to go mad. Wanting to do something—anything—to save his brother."

"Could I stay here until your husband returns?"

"Of course."

"And would you ask Gerald to fetch Elizabeth? I would feel so much better if she were here with me."

"I'll send him straightaway." Mrs. Snead pushed herself up from the table. "Let me lay the wick out farther. Light up the room a little more for you."

Lilyan watched Mrs. Snead climb the stairs and close the door behind her.

What can I do, Lord? What would You have me do? Why is this happening?

As Lilyan waited in the dusky cellar, the thoughts whirling around in her mind grew so heavy she dropped her head and pillowed it on her arms. Emotionally spent and deeply frustrated, she sat up and pressed her cool hands against her eyes. She did not know how long she had remained that way before she sensed she was no longer alone. She looked up to see two men on the stairs.

They stood so still and quiet, for a moment they did not seem real.

Once during her *wonder time*, Lilyan's father had taught her how to stand like that; to control her heartbeat and breathing so as to become one with her surroundings. These men had obviously mastered the skill. Feeling trapped, she jumped to her feet, but before she could take a step, one of the men put up his hand, rippling the fringe dangling from his buckskin sleeve.

"Don't be alarmed, Mistress Cameron," the man said softly. "We are here about your brother."

Lilyan's heart tripped. "You have news of Andrew?"

"Yes." He stepped closer. "Please, allow me to introduce myself. I am Captain Nicholas Xanthakos, and this is Samuel Harris."

The man behind the captain took two steps, stood against the wall, and crossed his arms in front of him. Like many Indians, he wore moccasins, buckskin leggings, and a coarse linen shirt underneath a wool coat. But this was no ordinary Indian. The two turkey feathers standing straight up from the back of his head, the shell dangling from the cord wrapped around his ponytail, and the carving of a black snake on his powder horn identified him as a Catawba—the fiercest and most feared warriors in the Carolinas. This reputation meant so much to them some even bound the heads of their male infants to make them flat. In battle, the sight of their distorted heads and their faces painted completely black except for a white circle around one eye terrorized their enemies. Mr. Harris had such handsome features, Lilyan was glad he had been spared the head-binding.

"Please, Miss Cameron." The captain motioned to the chair.

She sat back on the edge of the chair. The captain leaned on one knee in front of her and rested his arm on the table, his face level with hers. Lilyan wondered why he looked so familiar. She studied his strong square jaw, long chiseled nose, and coal black hair, but when she looked into his eyes, she realized he was the man she had met on the street earlier in the day.

"What can you tell me?" she asked.

"We don't have much time, so I will be blunt. I was the officer in command of a mission to move the powder magazine from the Exchange—Mrs. Snead told me that you are aware of the hiding place."

Lilyan nodded.

"Someone—who will no longer be among us when I find him—informed the British. They ambushed our men at our staging area on James Island."

"You and Mr. Harris? You got away?"

"We weren't there. We were out trying to muster up more militia. They come and go as they please, you know, not like the regular army."

"I know. Like my Andrew." Lilyan sighed. "What's going to happen to him, Captain?"

"One of three things. The prisoners could be taken to the barracks at Shutes Folly. Or the police might decide to keep them in the cellar at the Exchange. Or they could be sent to the prison ships."

"Which do you think?"

"Andrew broke his oath. I fear it will be the ships for him."

"That has been my fear too. My nightmare."

Lilyan stared into the captain's eyes. Tiger eyes. No, too commonplace a description. If she were to paint them, she would use amber—soft, warm, golden amber. The captain stared back at her with an expression so honest and full of kindness, she knew he was a man she could trust with her life and with her brother's.

The cellar door creaked, and before Lilyan could give it a thought, the captain had sprung to his feet and shielded her with his body.

"Lilyan?" Elizabeth called softly.

Lilyan jumped up and slipped around the captain to find Mr. Harris poised on the stairs, knife in hand.

"I'm here," she responded.

Elizabeth flew down the stairs, and they held on to each other a few moments.

"Mrs. Snead told me what happened." Elizabeth glanced at the men, who had sheathed their knives. "And these men?"

"This is Captain Nicholas Xanthakos, Andrew's officer in command. And this is Samuel Harris."

Elizabeth curtsied to the captain, but barely acknowledged Mr. Harris.

"An honor, ma'am. Most assuredly." Captain Xanthakos bowed.

Mr. Harris nodded to Elizabeth. "Greetings, daughter of my mortal enemy."

Elizabeth glared back. "Greetings to you, son of the flatheads."

Although Lilyan knew about the terrible, bloody history between the Catawba and the Cherokee, she could only stare in amazement at hearing such a rude reply from her usually gentle, sweet-natured friend.

Mr. Harris spoke something in a low, singsong language, and Elizabeth responded in kind.

"Ha!" the captain exclaimed. Clearly he understood what they said and enjoyed the exchange.

"I am surprised. A daughter of the Cherokee dog people can speak my tongue," Mr. Harris prodded.

Elizabeth stood straighter and snarled back at him, "It is not a pleasant experience, for it leaves a foul taste in my mouth."

"Elizabeth!" Lilyan exclaimed. "These men are here to help us."

Elizabeth blanched. "Do forgive me. This man opens old wounds."

"Maybe we should leave." The captain started toward the stairs.

Lilyan grabbed his arm. "No, please. We must talk about what we will do. How we will free Andrew."

"That is something best left to others." The captain patted her hand.

Lilyan stiffened at the patronizing gesture. "To men, you mean? Oh, if only I had my pistol."

Mr. Harris smirked. "And what would *you* do with a pistol?"

"She can shoot the eye out of a squirrel at twenty paces, river man." Elizabeth wrapped her arm around Lilyan.

"And you, cavewoman," Mr. Harris snapped, "you claim this too?"

"No. But I *can* throw a knife and chop the head off of a turtle at twenty paces."

Elizabeth's deliberate insult to the animal revered by the Catawba as part of their trinity astonished Lilyan, but she determined she could not let it bother her. She had enough to worry about.

"Ee-yah!" Mr. Harris exclaimed and then sprinted up the stairs.

"I do think it's time for us to go," the captain said.

"But what about the prisoners?" Lilyan held out her hand palm upward.

"Don't worry, my dear. There will be a better time for us to talk. Be patient. I will contact you soon." He bowed and quickly ascended the stairs.

When Lilyan heard the door thud behind him, she felt more bereft than ever.

Quartermaster Abington,

The bearer of this Note, is Due recompense for Lodging and Board for one Captain Stephen McKenzie of the Forty-Second Regiment of Foot, Royal Highlander Regiment, in the amount of 15/-

By Order of Lt. Colonel Nisbet Balfour
Commandant, Charlestown, South Carolina

By hand of Matthew Whitby, First Clerk
Office of Deputy Secretary

Chapter Five

THE NEXT MORNING, Lilyan and Elizabeth barely waited for the sun to rise before hurrying to the jail to visit Andrew, but the jailor turned them away. They did the same the next day, the next, and the next.

"I cannot bear this waiting," Lilyan complained after their fifth unsuccessful attempt to see her brother. She had not slept well in days, and her temples throbbed from the stress of trying to avoid the nightmarish thoughts her mind insisted on conjuring up—Andrew in chains, in pain from his shoulder, wracked with fever, hungry.

"Captain Xanthakos told us to be patient." Elizabeth folded Lilyan's arm around hers as they walked away from the jail.

"Fancy him telling us such a thing. I do not see him following his own advice."

"He made an impression on you, though. Didn't he?"

"He has a very pleasant smile." It did not take much effort for Lilyan to form a picture of that smile along with the warm, topaz eyes. Aware that Elizabeth was grinning at her, she changed the subject. "If only Captain McKenzie would come back. He would help us."

41

"He *has* been gone longer than is his custom."

"Let's stop by the headquarters office. See if they will tell us anything."

Lilyan quickened their pace. Two blocks away, they walked up the marble steps and onto the portico of a building that had once been the home of a friend of Lilyan's father. Within a week of conquering the city, the British had commandeered the house and driven the family out.

Inside, Lilyan and Elizabeth approached a soldier seated at a desk at the foot of a curved staircase that swept gracefully up to the second floor. The young man stood and greeted them with a broad smile.

"Ladies." He bowed his head. "How may I assist you?"

Lilyan curtsied. She could not help but smile back at the man so handsomely dressed in a red and black uniform. His chestnut brown hair had been brushed to a sheen and tied back with a black ribbon—unlike Captain Xanthakos, whose sooty curls sprang free from the rawhide string he used to contain them.

Elizabeth stepped forward. "Could you possibly give us some information about Captain Stephen McKenzie? He is lodging with us, but we haven't seen him for over a week. Do you know when he is expected back?"

"I say," a voice called out from behind them. "Why would you want Captain McKenzie when I would gladly offer you my services?"

Lilyan turned to find a British officer dressed in a uniform made from the finest cloth she had ever seen. She could not tell which had been polished most, the buttons on his waistcoat or the tips of his boots.

He swept his body into a low bow, showing the top of his immaculate white wig. In another grand gesture, he seized Elizabeth's hand. "And who is this creature?"

When he bent to kiss her hand, Elizabeth jerked away.

He clucked his tongue and smirked. "How delectable. Quite the *sah-vage*."

The way he intonated the word with an oily French accent pushed a chill up the skin on Lilyan's arms. The lascivious look in his eyes and the protruding false mole near his upper lip repulsed her. She knew Elizabeth felt the same way when she saw her slide her hand into the underpocket of her skirt to touch the knife that never left her possession.

"Bradenton," another man in uniform called out sharply before descending the stairs, "the colonel wants you."

Bradenton pulled a lace kerchief from his sleeve and made an exaggerated bow. "Duty calls, my beauty. But I do so look forward to making your acquaintance." At the bottom of the steps he paused long enough to nod to the naval ensign who passed him and approached Lilyan.

"Is that the kind of behavior one can expect of Britain's finest?" Lilyan asked him.

The ensign gave a curt bow and then looked at her as if amused by her challenge. "Do beg your pardon, ma'am. Bradenton's the son of an earl."

"And that excuses bad manners?"

The man's eyes twinkled. "Quite."

"You honestly believe that?"

"It is the way of the world we live in."

"Then perhaps it is time to change our world."

His expression sobered and he addressed the man at the desk, who had slipped back into the room. "Are you assisting these ladies?"

"Yes, sir."

"Continue on, then." He turned to Lilyan. "Good day, miss. And you," he said to Elizabeth, tapping a two-fingered salute to the tip of his hat.

When the ensign left, closing the door behind him, Lilyan turned to the soldier and waited while he scribbled something on a piece of paper.

He folded the note and handed it to Lilyan. "I've written Captain McKenzie's regiment number as well as the purser's name and address. The captain left instructions allowing for payment to you for his accommodations."

"But that is not why I came. I would like to know when you think the captain will return to Charlestown." Lilyan attempted to hand back the note, but he refused it.

"I cannot say. And even if I knew, I would not be able to give you that information."

"Thank you for your time." Lilyan could barely squash her frustration.

There has to be someone, somewhere, who can give me answers.

Trying to think of who that someone could be, she turned and followed Elizabeth, who was already on her way out.

When they reached the street Lilyan muttered, "Well. How unsatisfactory."

"And unsavory. The man Bradenton—there is something evil about him." Elizabeth rubbed her arms.

"You felt it too? His eyes especially. Such a cold, almost transparent blue. And his lips. They are so … full. Fleshy."

Elizabeth shuddered. "To think he almost kissed my hand with them. When I get home I'm going to wash. He made me feel unclean."

"I am headed for the shop. I don't know how well I can concentrate, but I have to try."

"Are you coming home for dinner, or do you want me to bring you something?"

Lilyan shook her head. "I can manage."

"Good. Try not to worry so much."

Lilyan walked briskly, quickly covering the four blocks to the shop. When she turned the last corner, a gust of wind pushed open the sides of her cape. As she clasped them together she looked out across the ocean. In the distance, shards of rain emptied from a dark gray cloud inching its way toward the city. The grayness suited her mood; the impending storm, her temperament. Thoughts of a steaming cup of coffee hastened her steps.

Inside the shop, she set about lighting the Franklin stove and putting a pot on to boil. She was ensconced at her desk, halfheartedly thumbing through swatches of material, when two women entered through the front door.

"Good morning, Mrs. Cheek." She smiled as she rose from her chair and made a bow.

"Good morning, Mistress Cameron. May I introduce my friend, Lady Katherine Richards? She and her husband recently purchased the Willows plantation on the Cooper."

Lilyan curtsied to the diminutive woman with bright red hair and laughing sapphire eyes. "Welcome, Lady Richards."

"It is such a pleasure to finally meet you. Sara has done nothing but sing your praises. I am interested in having a mural painted in my home and I cannot wait to see your work."

Lilyan motioned toward the chairs by her desk. "I would offer you a cup of tea, but all I have is coffee."

"Coffee, Lilyan?" Mrs. Cheek spoke the words as if gently scolding a child, but her warm brown eyes twinkled.

"I do have some apple cider."

"Cider sounds lovely," said Lady Richards.

"I have samples for you to look through while I put the cider to boil," said Lilyan, leading the way to a table laden with selections of wallpaper, drawings, and paintings.

Lilyan went to the back room to fetch the crock of cider and a pan. When she returned, the women stood beside the table, deep in discussion.

"Miss Cameron, may I ask why so many of the samples are predominantly blue? Is this a popular color?" Lady Richards held up a piece of paper with a *fleur-de-lis* pattern.

"We use blue because it's less expensive."

"Really?"

"Indigo is one of the few crops the King does not tax. As a matter of fact, he pays the planters a bonus for growing the crop. Which is just another issue that, if handled differently, could have precluded this awful war."

"You have a point. Things were handled very badly indeed, and the consequences have been most dire," said Mrs. Cheek.

Surprised at such a reasonable outlook from a loyalist, Lilyan stared at her. "Please, come and have a seat," she said, and then handed china cups to the ladies when they were settled.

"But Sara, how can you fault the king for this conflict?" asked Lady Richards.

"At the risk of sounding treasonous, I blame not only the king, but his cronies as well. I do not think one of them considered the consequences—the future—when they goaded these people beyond all endurance. The colonists are our very own. Our brothers and sisters. If they win this war, England must learn somehow to deal with them as a sovereign nation. If we are victorious, we will have to find a way to mend the terrible rift in our relationship."

She paused and took a sip of cider. "You need only look at the way we have treated the wounded prisoners. Yes, there are some people, like my dear husband, who do their best to behave in a civilized manner. All you have to do is visit his hospital and you

45

will see that the wounded colonists receive the very best care he has to offer."

"The same cannot be said of the prison ships," Lilyan interjected, remembering the last time she held Andrew and the feel of his bony shoulder blades.

"No. Unfortunately it cannot. Although James has requested three times to be allowed to board the ships and tend to the men, the Admiralty has refused him every time on the senseless grounds that, although he is a doctor, he is not a ship's doctor and has never had any naval experience."

Lady Richards sighed. "I must say, in the midst of all this seriousness, I feel rather frivolous to be selecting something to decorate my home."

"Please, rest yourself on that account," said Lilyan. "I held similar thoughts about my wallpaper business, but came to the conclusion that everyone has her part in this war, and it falls on some of us to keep things going—to keep life on some sort of even keel."

"I could not agree more," said Mrs. Cheek. "A sense of normalcy is a valuable commodity in times when hot tempers prevail."

"So." Lilyan picked up one of the samples. "Let us talk about the kind of mural you are interested in, Lady Richards."

During the next hour, Lilyan explained the process of creating a mural, and then the three of them came to an agreement on a design. The ladies had not been gone but a few minutes when Gerald rushed in, his face red with exertion, and his eyes bright from his sprint across town.

"They're moving them, Mistress Cameron. They're moving them," he blurted out between breaths.

The panic in Gerald's eyes made Lilyan heart trip. "What are you saying?"

"The prisoners. They're loading them into boats. Down at Blake's Wharf."

To General Greene
Prison Ship Torbay

Charleston Harbour
… we have only to regret that our blood cannot be disposed of more
to the Advancement of the Glorious Cause to which we have adhered.
A separate Roll of our names attends this letter.
With greatest respect, we are, sir,
Your most obedient and humble servants,
Stephen Moore,
Lieutenant Colonel North Carolina Militia
John Barnwell,
Major South Carolina Militia, for Ourselves and 130 Prisoners

Chapter Six

WHEN LILYAN FINALLY REALIZED what Gerald meant, she threw on her cape and headed out the door.

"Bring the telescope," she shouted over her shoulder.

They ran the several blocks to the wharf and joined a small crowd gathered along the railing.

"God bless you, Thaddeus Taylor," one woman shouted, frantically waving a handkerchief.

"Take care, Kevin Sanders," another called out.

Lilyan grabbed the telescope from Gerald, slid it open, and trained it on the two boats making their way away from shore. Rain was already pelting the occupants, making it difficult for her to spot Andrew. She slid the lens forward as far as it would go, bringing the craft into such focus she felt she could reach out and touch the helmsman.

"I see him. Larboard side. All the way toward the bow," she exclaimed and swallowed the lump in her throat as she watched the rain soak into the shoulders of Andrew's wool coat. Fear, black and heavy as a lump of coal, settled in the pit of her stomach.

"And Herald? Do you see him?" asked Gerald.

Lilyan watched as the person sitting next to Andrew clasped his collar up around his neck and turned to speak to him. "Yes. He's there too."

She glanced at Gerald, whose somber eyes now seemed too large for his pale face. She knew she should give him the telescope, but she could not let go of this one desperate contact with her brother. When she looked through the lens again, she realized that the vessel to the right of the one that held Andrew had veered away from the three prison ships.

"What's happening?" a man in the crowd yelled.

Lilyan felt someone step close and heard the *click* of a telescope. "They're being taken to the other ship—the one farthest out to the right," he said.

Lilyan recognized the man's voice—Captain Xanthakos. She turned to him, only to find that although his voice was familiar, his appearance was not. Dressed in a long black coat and white collar, a black cocked hat and white wig, he seemed the epitome of a schoolmaster. But the round wire-rimmed glasses could not disguise his extraordinary eyes.

"Captain!"

He winked and touched a finger to his lips.

She felt Gerald tugging on her arm.

"Please, Mistress Cameron. May I have the spyglass?" he pleaded before taking it from her. "Wait. They're not taking Herald and Andrew to the *Torbay*. Or the *Success-Increase*. But to the *Brixham*, the smallest ship of them all."

"What can we do?" she asked the captain so softly he had to stoop closer.

"We will think of something. I promise," he whispered.

Although Lilyan hardly knew the man, standing so close beside him that the warmth of his breath stirred the tendrils of hair at her temple, she felt an inexplicable sense of security; a disconcerting yet welcome feeling.

A man on the other side of the captain jabbed him in his arm. "Can't make out that flag yonder. White with a blue square in the middle. Ain't familiar to me."

The captain focused on the vessel. "That is Cornwallis' ship. The flag is a signal that there will be no leave for the men on board— they won't be anchored long enough."

"Why are they taking some of the prisoners to Cornwallis'

ship?" the man asked.

Captain Xanthakos lowered the telescope and glanced at Lilyan. "They have been pressed into His Majesty's service."

A woman standing nearby pulled her apron up to her face and began to sob.

Sadness crept across Lilyan's heart, and she grasped the captain's sleeve. "Can they do that?"

The man behind her stepped closer. "Cor, yes. Government's got every right to impress any Englishman it wants to."

"You mean *poor* Englishman," commented another man. "Them what's got shillings in their pockets or important family ain't bothered."

When a few drops of rain landed around them, the captain drew Lilyan's hood up over her head. "Storm's making its way here. Come, Gerald," he said, draping Lilyan's arm through his, "let us go to the shop."

Desolate, Lilyan looked back at the ships now indistinguishable behind a gray wall of rain.

Will I ever see my dear brother again? The thought rammed through her heart like a lance.

The captain covered her trembling hand with his. "Try not to worry so much, Miss Cameron. We will deal with things as they are. Problems don't seem so overwhelming when tackled bit by bit."

Deep in thought, no one spoke on the way, and when they arrived, the squall had played itself out. Inside, the captain slapped his hat against his leg and hung it on the wig stand beside the door.

Lilyan trudged through to the back, depositing a trail of water behind her. "Gerald, stoke up the fire, would you? I think we could all use a cup of coffee."

She shook out her cape and draped it over a hook on the back door. Looking in a small mirror hanging on the wall, she tucked several loose curls under her cap and pressed her hands against her damp cheeks.

The captain appeared in the mirror behind her.

"You look lovely," he said and then, meeting Lilyan's eyes in the mirror, he gave her a smile that sent an unfamiliar tingle up her spine.

She turned around to find him so close she could feel the warmth emanating from his body. She tilted her head, and an unexplainable urge prompted her to slide the round wire spectacles from his face. The discovery of the tiny brown flecks circling his irises wiped away the memory of what she had been about to say. They stood toe to toe, drawing in each other's breath. Lilyan could not have felt closer to him if he had wrapped his arms around her.

"Coffee's ready," Gerald yelled, breaking through the cocoon of intimacy that had spun around them.

The captain stepped aside. Flustered, Lilyan led the way to the front room, where they pulled chairs close to the stove.

"So, do you have a plan?" Lilyan asked.

"Not yet." The captain rested his chin on his thumb and tapped a finger on his bottom lip. "It will take a great deal of intelligence gathering, planning, and time."

"But how much time do we have? I've heard so many rumors about when the ships will leave and where they will go that my head swims."

"I am fairly certain the ships will leave soon after Christmas."

"But that is only five weeks away." Her hands shook, sloshing her coffee.

He set his cup on the floor and took Lilyan's hand. "I know how much Andrew means to you, but you have to realize that on board those ships are some people, including Lt. Colonel Stephen Moore and Major John Barnwell of the South Carolina militia, who have kept this war alive in the South."

He stroked the tips of her fingers. "Rest assured. There is, at this moment, a group of people right here in Charlestown sorting through information, trying with all their might to come up with a way to save the prisoners."

Encouraged by this glimmer of hope, Lilyan leaned forward. "How do I become one of them?"

He glanced at Gerald, who nodded.

"Are you sure?" He scooted forward in his chair, touching his knees to hers. "This is not a game, you know. It is a deadly business. Once you are committed, you cannot turn back. Other people's lives are at stake here. You must be prepared to do anything."

"I will do anything."

"Lie, cheat, steal?"

"Yes."

"Kill?" He interjected. "Be killed?"

Lilyan stared straight into his eyes. "Yes," she answered without hesitation. "Just tell me what to do."

"For now, keep your eyes and ears open. Pay attention. Here in your shop, wherever you go. You might be surprised at the bits of information you can pick up."

"But what if I do hear something? What am I to do to with it?"

As if on cue, Gerald walked to the display window and picked up the stamp he had designed. He handed it to the captain and sat back down.

"Do you see this?" The captain pointed to the flower carved into the block of wood.

"A chamomile?"

He smiled. "You nearly knocked young Gerald for a loop when you made mention that it is the same design on his mother's pies."

"It's the same design that is on Gerald's shoulder-pouch. And I've seen it somewhere else too—I know. Mrs. Blanchard makes a soap in that shape." Lilyan paused. "It's a signal."

"Well, I'll be," Gerald exclaimed.

The captain's eyes twinkled. "I knew you were smart."

Lilyan pressed her fingers to the base of her throat, where the small pulse raced. "Just observant. I *am* an artist."

"You are a wonderful artist, Lilyan," he said, pronouncing his words with a heavy Greek accent.

"Thank you, Nicholas." Lilyan smiled. Their mutual exchange of given names seemed natural, comfortable, pleasing.

They sat quietly, Lilyan's skin tingling from the pressure of his knees, her thoughts occupied by the contrast between his soot black eyebrows and his white wig.

"Ah, hum." Gerald cleared his throat, breaking the silence.

Nicholas blinked as if he too had been caught up in the moment. He stood and handed the stencil block to Gerald. "Whenever you hear something you think is of value, tell Gerald, and he will pass it along."

"To whom?"

"That is something you do not need to know."

"But—"

"Truly. There are only a handful of people who know the

identities of our sources. It's not a matter of trust, but of safety. If someone is caught, the fewer particulars he knows the better for everyone."

Or the fewer particulars she *knows.* Lilyan shivered. "What if Gerald isn't here?"

"Then place the stamp in the display window facing out where someone passing by could see it."

"I will paint a chamomile too. You know, as a sample. We could use that as well."

"Good thinking." He dropped a hand onto her shoulder. "Now, finish your coffee and try to keep warm."

His silky voice drifted like a shawl around Lilyan's shoulders. He retrieved his hat from the stand, and Lilyan followed him to the door.

"Remember, Nicholas, if there is a plan, you must include me," she said anxiously.

Standing in the open doorway, he tipped up Lilyan's face and traced his thumb across her mouth. "What a pleasure it is to hear my name on your lips."

Lilyan's heart skipped in her chest as unfamiliar yearnings played havoc with her emotions.

"And, most assuredly, Lilyanista, you will be included in much more than you know."

With that tantalizing declaration, he swept out of the door, leaving Lilyan feeling as if a glorious windstorm had blown into her life and sucked the air from her body.

Dear Sissy,

Will tell you straight away I am well. Although I Fear I cannot say the same for many aboard. It is my want to offer you Encouragement, but I ain't going to lie. The situation here is much Worse than we had been told.

Chapter Seven

A WEEK CRAWLED BY, and no word about the prisoners. One morning Lilyan skipped breakfast and hurried to the widow's walk atop her house. With the wind whipping her cloak about her, she peered through her spyglass, training it on the *Brixham*. The ship bobbed in the water still choppy from a storm that had passed over the city at dawn.

It wasn't as if she would be able to see her brother; the vessel had anchored too far away. Somehow though, simply capturing it in her telescope brought her comfort.

"Lilyan, come quickly," Elizabeth shouted from inside.

Lilyan shut the spyglass and slipped it into her pocket. She scurried into the house, a blast of air slamming the door behind her.

Elizabeth met her halfway up the stairs frantically waving a letter. "It's from Andrew."

Lilyan took it from her, plopped on the step, and started to break the seal with her fingernail before she realized someone had already broken it. "The British must be censoring the letters."

"Oh, no," she murmured after scanning the first few sentences.

Elizabeth sat on the stair below. "Please, what does he say?"

"He says the ship's hold is so crowded, as many as six prisoners must lie abed on their sides in a space only several feet wide. The rations are terrible and the drinking water is worse. Some of the men suffer from scurvy and dysentery, and each day more and more are succumbing to other diseases. He thinks some have measles. He says, at least he won't get the pox, since we had it as children."

She ran her finger across the letter, and with her breath now coming in painful gulps, she read aloud. "The very air is poison and sickens even the healthiest among us, but no help is on the way, no medicines, and no fresh supplies."

Lilyan pressed her hand to her cheek. "But what is this? Can he be ill after all?"

"What do you mean?"

"He asks after our mother."

"Let me see," said Elizabeth, craning her neck. "His words have the look of being hastily scribbled. And see there, at the bottom." She pointed to Andrew's signature. "He made a very large *F* for his middle initial."

"But his middle name is James."

"I believe he's trying to tell us something."

Lilyan stared at the paper until she felt her eyes might bore holes in it. "We must get this letter to someone who would know."

They hurried to the parlor just as someone knocked on the door. Elizabeth opened the door and greeted Gerald, while Lilyan slipped the letter into her underskirt pocket.

"Here to walk the mistress to work." Gerald doffed his hat to Elizabeth.

Lilyan joined him on the stoop. "We received a letter from Andrew—"

"I say, that's right good news."

"Yes. But there's something peculiar about it. Elizabeth and I think it may hold a hidden message. You must hurry to the tavern. Have your mother let it be known that I have news. I'll put my chamomile in the shop window. Between us we should get a response soon."

"Yes, miss." Gerald made to go, but turned around. "Did Andrew give news of Herald?"

"Yes. He is well."

He grinned. "Mother will be happy to hear it."

Cold wind coiled through the entrance. Lilyan secured her

hood and clasped Elizabeth's arms. "It may take a while for our message to make its way to our allies, but I promise I will let you know something as soon as possible."

Elizabeth nodded. "Take care, dear one. This is dangerous business."

LATER AT THE SHOP, Gerald returned from his mission and stationed himself at the counter to work on his woodblock carvings. Lilyan spent most of the day sketching, an undertaking that required deep concentration and kept her mind from ricocheting from one dire scenario to another. By late afternoon, though, she could no longer hold her anxiety in check. Sitting at the table in the back room, she unfolded Andrew's letter and examined it for what seemed the hundredth time. Nothing in his words stood out except the bit about their mother and the odd signature. She held it at arm's length to get a different perspective. The space between the lines did seem uncommonly wide.

She studied the writing so intently that when the shop bell tinkled she snapped up her head so fast she pulled a muscle. Rubbing her neck, she headed to the front of the store and ran headlong into Nicholas.

He clasped her forearms. "Whoa," he said with a chuckle in his voice.

"Hello," she murmured, keeping her eyes trained on the crisscross ties at the top of his shirt and mentally sorting through the intriguing aromas wafting from his buckskins. Pine. Smoke. Lime soap. Something indefinably male.

He tipped up her chin and captured her eyes with his. The knowing expression she saw there made her cheeks burn.

"Hello." After a moment, he released her arms. "'Tis pleasant to see you again, Lilyan. You have a message?"

Gerald hopped around behind Nicholas. "Show him. Show him the letter."

"I will, Gerald. But lock the door, please."

Nicholas motioned for her to lead the way to the back room. He sat beside her at the table while Gerald craned his body over Lilyan's shoulder as she smoothed out the folds in the pages. Nicholas picked up the first page and studied it, then did the same with the second. He brushed his finger across the sentences and then looked at Lilyan, his brow furrowed.

"Are you searching for something in particular?" Lilyan asked.

He nodded. "For a cipher."

Lilyan raised her eyebrow.

"Letters, symbols or numbers used in the place of real words," Nicholas explained. "But with a cipher, the receiver has to share a common key with the sender."

"A key?" asked Gerald.

"Yes. Some of us have made up our own, others use books like Entick's spelling dictionary." He caught his bottom lip in his teeth. "I see no cipher here, nor a code."

Lilyan had had no idea her brother was involved in such secretive maneuvers. "What sort of code?"

"In a coded letter each secret word is represented by a series of three numbers—the page number, the line number, and the number of the word on a line counting from the left."

"I understand."

"But I don't detect a code either."

Lilyan showed him the second page. "He asks about our mother. But she died when he was very young. Could that be some sort of clue?" Lilyan pointed to the signature. "Also see here. He writes his middle initial as *F*, but his middle name is James."

Nicholas sat up straight. "Bring me a lighted candle, Gerald."

"As you say, sir." Gerald ran to the front of the store and hurried back with a candle.

Nicholas placed it in front of him. He held the paper close to the flame, but when it started to turn brown Lilyan gasped.

"What are you doing? It will catch fire."

"Look closely," said Nicholas.

To Lilyan's amazement, words began to appear in the spaces between Andrew's sentences.

"Magic!" Gerald exclaimed.

Nicholas chuckled. "No. Science. It's invisible ink."

"I've never heard of such a thing." Lilyan peered at words that now seemed burned into the paper.

"Ferrous sulfate," said Gerald. "The ink, I mean, ferrous sulfate and water."

"But how would Andrew find such chemicals?"

"From Herald," said Gerald. "He's a courier, so he keeps things like that with him--onions, lemons, ferrous sulfate crystals..."

Nicholas pressed out the creases in the paper. "Words written with the chemical mix are invisible. But by applying heat or acid, we can see them. By writing the letter F so prominently, Andrew let us know to use fire."

"So he would have written an A if he had wanted us to use acid?" asked Gerald.

"Rightly so," said Nicholas.

"What's the secret message?" Lilyan asked.

Nicholas angled the paper. "It says, '*Brixham* to leave for St. Augustine December 28. Recruiters for King's navy have come three times. Impressed fifty able-bodied among us. Caned, kicked, severely beat others. Forced them into boats. Herald and I pricked our skin with reeds to look like measles. Both look like skeletons. Fooled them for now. Pray for us.'"

Lilyan shivered. "Horrible. It's too much to bear."

Nicholas took her hand. "Courage, Lilyanista. We cannot falter now."

Lilyan glanced at Gerald. His shoulders slumped and he groaned. "I felt his hunger," he murmured, his eyes now swimming with unshed tears.

Lilyan surveyed his gaunt features and his rail-thin body. She had noticed his pronounced weight loss since his brother's capture. Mrs. Snead often remarked on it and had visited the shop on several occasions with cheese and freshly baked bread to tempt him, but went away each time with a worried, anxious expression. Lilyan had heard stories about twins and wondered at being so close to another human being that you felt what he felt, no matter the distance between you. She understood now that his loss of appetite was a reflection of his brother's suffering.

She folded Gerald into her arms and rubbed his back. "Take heart. We will find a way to rescue them." She stared at Nicholas. "Won't we?" she mouthed.

"Yes, my sweet. I promise." He stood and clapped Gerald's back. "I must go. We have a definite date now, so we must hasten our plans."

"Thank you, Captain. My family will be forever in your debt." Gerald bowed and left the room.

"Walk with me?" Nicholas took Lilyan by the hand.

They stepped out onto the dock behind the building, and he turned his back to the sea, sheltering her from the blustery weather.

"Our mission has become most urgent," he said solemnly.

"Yes." She clasped his jacket lapels. "The thought of Andrew and Herald being beaten and enslaved on a warship …" She gulped. "Will I ever be able to sleep again?"

"We will make it our mission to keep the press gangs away while we make our plans."

Words dried in her mouth.

He caressed her bottom lip with his thumb. "You and Gerald go home. Rest. We will need both of you."

Lilyan sighed. "You need me?"

"More than I can say."

As good a test of flour as can be had at sight, is to take up a hand-
ful and squeeze it tight; if good, when the hand is unclasped, the lines
on the palm of the hand will be plainly defined on the ball of flour.
Throw a little lump of dried flour against a smooth surface, if it falls
like powder, it is bad.

Chapter Eight

VERY LATE IN THE EVENING, Lilyan stood kneading dough at the marble-topped work table in the outside kitchen, taking out her frustrations with every fold. The day after receiving Andrew's letter, she had fired up the ovens, which had been ablaze now for three days warming the air in the cozy room filled with the scent of freshly baked cinnamon-and-raisin bread.

She sprinkled flour across the dough and slammed her fists into the springy mixture, stretching it right and left, then folding it again and again to trap the air that would make the bread soft on the inside, crunchy on the outside.

Lilyan was the first to admit that she was not a good cook. But she was an excellent baker, often drawing neighbors to her back-yard with tantalizing aromas that wafted through the air.

She rubbed the back of her hand across the bridge of her nose. She plopped the dough into a wooden bowl and covered it with cheesecloth. With instinct born of years of experience, she sensed that the latest batch of bread was ready. She grabbed a cloth, opened the oven door, and pushed the long wooden paddle inside, retriev-ing a pan, which she slid onto a nearby rack.

"Must be what heaven smells like." Nicholas' voice came from behind her.

She whirled around, toppling the flour tin with the paddle, and billowing a white cloud in the air.

"I didn't mean to startle you." He leaned against the brick wall and crossed one ankle over the other.

She sneezed twice, knocking her mobcap askew. She grimaced at her flour encrusted dress and shoes.

I must look a sight.

"Please." The hint of mirth in his eyes undermined his serious tone. "Don't let me interrupt. I'll be content to watch."

With her heart hammering, she straightened her cap and brushed as much of the flour from her apron top as she could. "Won't you have a seat?"

She dragged a chair away from the table and motioned for him to sit.

"Are you here about Andrew?" She sat in the chair next to him.

"No."

"Oh? Well …"

"Just wanted to talk. Spend some time with you." He picked up a towel, leaned forward, and wiped her nose and cheeks. And then he smiled, a crooked, sultry smile that reached his eyes and made them dance. "Much better."

She felt the pulse fluttering in her neck. "Thank you. I'm not usually so messy."

"You look very fetching."

And you are the most wonderfully made man I have ever met. That thought held such strength she wondered for a moment if she had spoken the words. Feeling quite lightheaded, she searched for something, anything, that would ground her, get her back in control of her racing emotions.

She cocked her head to the side. "Who are you, Nicholas?"

He moved closer, resting his arm on the table. "What would you have me tell you?"

With her face only inches away from his, Lilyan found it difficult to form thoughts, much less give voice to them. What did she want to know?

"Anything … everything."

He leaned back in his chair, and Lilyan was glad of the breathing room.

"I grew up on my parents' farm in Macedonia. My father passed away four years ago. My mother not too long after."

What a sad thing for us to have in common.

"I am so sorry about your parents."

"I'm sorry they are not here to meet you. They would have loved you."

"What made you come here?"

"My older brother inherited what little my parents had, so, about three years ago, I decided to try my luck in the colonies."

"Where do you call home now?"

"A place called Eden Land in the Blue Ridge Mountains."

"I've been there. With my da when I was ten."

"And how long ago was that?"

"Nine—nine years. I'm nineteen," Lilyan faltered, certain she sounded like an idiot.

"Nineteen," he exclaimed. "I am twenty-five. It is a good difference. Yes?"

"Oh, yes," she whispered.

Steady, she warned herself. "You've been in the colonies three years. What happened to your plans for a homestead?"

"When I arrived in Charlestown I needed money, so I started working for a trading company. Then when the war reached South Carolina, I joined the town garrison. Now I'm with the militia."

"What made you side with the Patriots?"

"The idea of independence, of rebellion against tyranny. It's very Greek, don't you think?"

His crooked grin was charming, and the light in his eyes made Lilyan smile. "You have been fighting for years. It must be difficult."

He glanced away.

Lilyan hurried to change the subject. "You mentioned a brother? Do you have other brothers? Sisters?"

"Only the one. Alexis. He is two years older than I."

"And where did you say he is?"

"He stayed in Greece to work the farm. He married two years ago and has twin boys."

"You're an uncle. How nice."

Andrew would make a good uncle. Her shoulders slumped.

"Why this sadness?"

61

"I was thinking of my brother."

"Do not fret so. All will be well."

He curled his hand around hers, and she admired his long, tapered fingers and clean nails.

How brown his skin is compared to mine.

"Would you like a piece of cinnamon bread?" she asked.

"I thought you would never ask. I must confess I have a sweet tooth."

She reached across the table and pulled a towel from one of the loaves still warm from the oven and cut off a thick slab. "It's much better with butter …"

He took a bite of the bread, closed his eyes, and dropped his head back. He chewed and then swallowed. "U-m-m. Wonderful. Nectar of the gods."

"An appropriate description. These raisins alone cost a king's ransom." She picked up a small clay pot half full of the golden fruit and held it toward him.

He picked up one of the raisins and studied it in the candle-light. "I suppose because they are all imported."

"Yes. And very, very heavily taxed."

He plopped the raisin into his mouth. "Well, when I start my vineyard that will change."

"Grapes will grow in North Carolina?"

"Most assuredly. The valley where I plan to build my home is almost the same latitude as my birthplace."

An image of Nicholas standing on a rise, fists on his hips, surveying gentle green slopes covered with grapevines, made her catch her breath. "Your valley? Is it very beautiful?"

"So much so, it almost hurts my eyes. Much as the sight of you baking bread in your kitchen." He paused, his expression intent.

Unsure of a response, she glanced at the oven. "Excuse me. I must put the last batch in."

She stood and walked to the sideboard where she removed the cloth from the pan and punched her hand into the middle of the dough. She turned the sticky mixture out onto the floured surface, cut it in half, and dropped the pieces into pans she had already lined with oil. Using the wooden paddle she pushed the loaf pans into the blistering hot chamber and closed the door. She wiped her hand on a towel and when she turned around, discovered that

Nicholas was standing beside his chair staring at her.

"Lilyan—" he began, but stopped when he saw Elizabeth ease across the threshold.

"Captain Xanthakos," she greeted him in a subdued tone. "I must warn you. Captain McKenzie has returned. It would not be a good thing for Lilyan to be seen talking to you."

Nicholas craned his neck to check out the courtyard behind her. "You are right. I should go."

"Wait," Lilyan exclaimed. "Please."

There were so many things she wanted to say, but hesitation overwhelmed the desire for declarations, and she suddenly felt flustered.

"Here. Take some of this with you." She grabbed a cinnamon loaf and wrapped it in brown paper. "For your sweet tooth."

He took it from her, smiled, and winked. He nodded to Elizabeth and walked to the entrance, looked to the left, then to the right, and hurried away.

"That man is smitten with you," Elizabeth said. "His eyes burn with it."

"Burn," Lilyan echoed, staring at the doorway in a daze, and then she sniffed. "Burn. Oh, my. The bread!"

Like a chamomile bed -
The more it is trodden
The more it will spread
unknown

Chapter Nine

DAWN BROUGHT WITH IT a new kind of awakening for Lilyan. She opened her eyes to an overwhelming urge to know what it would feel like to press kisses on Nicholas' firm jaw from his ear to the dimple in his chin. Would the dark stubble on his face tickle or scratch? Wrapped in his arms with her face cuddled against his chest, could she hear his heartbeat? What kind of expression would those glorious golden eyes hold when he woke in the morning, his head nestled on the pillow next to hers? The extraordinary images created a sensation that tingled from the tip of her toes to the top of her head.

So, this is desire, she marveled. That realization led to an even more astounding discovery. *I love Nicholas.* And even more incredible, something inside assured her that he felt the same.

Would it be an enduring love? The kind her parents had shared?

As a young girl Lilyan had enjoyed watching their marriage dance. The subtle steps—holding hands, adjusting a collar, lifting a curl from the nape of a neck. The more intricate, dramatic movements—hungry, sad tears when her father went away on trading missions; the tears of joy when he returned; their muffled, laughter-filled conversations that lasted long into the night; the times they made Lilyan go to bed early so they could be together.

Lilyan closed her eyes, evoking memories of her mother's obvious delight when her husband would approach behind her, clasp his arms around her, and lift her off her feet—even when she was pregnant with Andrew. More than once Lilyan witnessed her father bury his face into her mother's neck and breathe her in, like a parched traveler gulping a drink of water.

Will our love stay the course and grow in intensity through the hard times and good times? Oh yes. Most assuredly, as Nicholas was prone to saying.

Overwhelmed, Lilyan felt she could weep from pure joy. Part of her wanted to bound downstairs and share her revelations with Elizabeth, part of her longed to remain in bed and savor her new-found sensations a while longer, and still another part determined to store her discovery in the treasure chest of her heart.

Downstairs she greeted Elizabeth with a smile. Elizabeth commented on her sparkling eyes, even checking her forehead and asking if she felt feverish. On the trek to work she experienced a profound sense of well-being. It was a grand morning; one of those peculiar breaks from the winter cold—so warm that many people walked about with no jackets and their sleeves pushed up. Backwoods settlers often feared this time, when Indians would take advantage of the weather to raid their homes and steal their winter supplies. But for Lilyan the air breathed sweeter. She stepped more lively over leaves that had spilled onto the ground in circles of vibrant ocher, crimson, and persimmon like one of her mother's crocheted coverlets. It was not until she reached the docks and sighted the prison ships that her euphoria plummeted.

Andrew, how are you faring? Are you getting enough to eat? Do you have adequate shelter?

How is it possible to feel so ecstatic and sad at the same time, she wondered as she fought back the guilt.

She opened the shop, more determined than ever to devise a way to save Andrew. Before closing the door, she spotted Gerald rounding the corner, pushing a wheelbarrow laden with buckets of chalk and lead white pigment, brushes, cloths, various tools, and the rabbit-skin glue he had prepared.

"Headed for Mrs. Coatsbury's," he said as he drew near. "She wanted her fireplace done in time to decorate for Christmas. Figured this would be a good day to apply gesso."

"Good thinking, Gerald. If it stays this warm, I should be able to begin painting in a couple of days."

"I'll see you later, miss," he called out as he turned away.

Gerald was a fine lad. Dependable, stalwart, amiable. She wondered how he was really taking Herald's imprisonment.

However he feels, he hides it well. Something I am going to have to master if I want to be of help to anyone.

Suddenly excited about her newly acquired identity as a rebel spy, Lilyan quickly gathered the supplies she needed and set about painting a chamomile. To her relief, no one patronized the shop that morning, leaving her to concentrate on her task. Her heart pounding with a passion she had not felt in a long time, she swept her brush across the canvas, forming long, gray-green stalks with feathery thread-like leaves. Blossoms, so heavy that they drooped from the end of the stalks, shone with brilliant white ray florets surrounding centers in the rich yellow hues of egg yolks. Within an hour she stepped back to peruse her work. Nibbling on the tip of her brush handle, she was amazed at her progress. Chamomiles looked a great deal like daisies, except their centers were conical compared to the flatter centers of daisies, so she was pleased with her ability to illustrate the difference. A few more strokes completed the painting, except for her signature. She dipped a fine horsehair brush into a dollop of gamboge yellow, but on impulse instead of her signature she wrote *The Chamomile* in flourished letters.

As she set the canvas on her desk to dry, she glanced out the window, shocked to see the *Closed* sign swaying on the door of the book store across the street.

Was it already eleven o'clock?

Lilyan hung a placard on her door, obeying British orders restricting marketing hours to sunrise till eleven in the morning. Normally she resented this intrusion on her right to keep whatever business hours she chose, but today she relished the time to work on the plan that was slowly coming together, piece by piece.

Later that afternoon as she leaned on the rail of the deck behind the store, Lilyan mulled over what Elizabeth told her when she had brought dinner; Captain McKenzie was to remain in town for several weeks. That news catapulted her thoughts toward a scheme in which he would serve a pivotal part.

She hurried to the display window and placed the chamomile painting in the center.

It is therefore recommended to the several states to set a part Thursday, the 7th day of December next, to be observed as a day of public thanksgiving and prayer; that all the people may assemble on that day to celebrate the praises of our Divine Benefactor; to confess our unworthiness of the least of his favors, and to offer our fervent supplications to the God of all grace....

Done in Congress, this 18th day of October, 1780, and in the fifth year of the independence of the United States of America.

Chapter Ten

WAITING WAS NOT ONE of Lilyan's strong points, and the next two hours frayed her nerves. She wanted to check on Gerald's progress at Mrs. Coatsbury's, but she feared missing her contact.

What makes me think someone will come today, anyway? Will it be Nicholas? Goose bumps tickled her arms from that delightful thought.

Go or stay? Go or stay?

If Lilyan detested waiting, she hated indecision even more. When she'd had enough, she chucked several small crocks of pigments and a handful of brushes into a basket that she slipped over her arm, and then she scribbled a note explaining that she would return in an hour. Outside, she locked the door and pushed the note onto a nail she kept there for that purpose.

At Mrs. Coatsbury's house she found Gerald wiping the layer of cloth he had glued to the wooden paneling.

"Good work, Gerald," Lilyan said, resting her hand on his shoulder. "And very tidy. There is hardly any cleaning up to do."

"Thank you." He studied her hand and quickly glanced away. "I'll do the first coat of gesso tomorrow and the second coat the next day. Should be ready for you to start painting after that."

He spied the jars of pigment in Lilyan's basket. "Tempera?"

"Yes. I am looking for an effect that is soft and gentle—"

"Just like yourself," came a voice from the foyer.

Lilyan turned to find the officer who had been so offensive to Elizabeth at British headquarters. When he stepped closer and reached out his hand, she swung her basket from one arm to the other, blocking his attempt to kiss her hand.

Bradenton tapped his lips with his handkerchief. "Soft and sweet is very agreeable, but I prefer a little spirit. Which reminds me. Where is my little Indian maiden?"

He leered at her.

She is not *your* anything, Lilyan wanted to shout. Instead, she smiled, though it made her mouth hurt.

"She is at home."

Gerald stepped closer to Lilyan. "Beggin' your pardon—"

"Never interrupt me, boy." Bradenton cut Gerald off with an edge in his voice as sharp as the rapier buckled at his waist. His lids narrowed to slits.

The captain draped a hand over the hilt of his sword and stared at Gerald with glassy eyes. The younger man blanched. Lilyan's intuition told her that, despite his foppish ways, the vile man knew how to use the weapon. And that thought frightened her.

Bradenton dismissed Gerald with a glance and slid his gaze in Lilyan's direction. "I'll have my man bring around my card."

"We are not in a position to receive guests," said Lilyan.

"But my dear, we have so much to discuss."

Lilyan felt queasy. "What would we have to talk about?"

Bradenton tapped his hands together, studied his fingernails, and then stared into Lilyan's eyes. "Your brother, for one. Andrew is his name, I believe?"

Dread filled the base of her throat. "What about him?"

"I might could help you there." He tugged a tendril of Lilyan's hair that had escaped her mobcap. "That is, I could be tempted to help."

Lilyan cringed, barely resisting the urge to slap his hand.

"Miss Cameron," Mrs. Cheek called out and hurried across the room. "I come here to see my dear friend and find you visiting as well. What a pleasant surprise."

Thank heavens you did.

Bradenton stepped away from Lilyan and bowed to Mrs. Cheek. "My dear lady, how good to see you again. You know my little friend here?"

Mrs. Cheek curtsied. "Indeed. Miss Cameron is a very talented artist."

"An artist, you say? I hear they can be wonderfully passionate creatures," said Bradenton.

Mrs. Cheek's eyes widened, and she looked at the man as if his wig had suddenly spun around on his head. "What an incredibly odd thing to say."

Bradenton jerked his head back and twirled his handkerchief in the air.

Lilyan giggled nervously, but Bradenton's steely glare stopped her short.

He bowed so low his handkerchief swept the floor. "Do beg your pardon, madame."

"Apology accepted," said Mrs. Cheek, a pleasant expression restored to her face. "The gentlemen are gathering in the parlor before tea. I should think they would enjoy an opportunity to hear news of court? And I should like to become better acquainted with Mistress Cameron."

Thinking she had never heard such a gracious dismissal, Lilyan watched several emotions flicker across Bradenton's face—irritation, then resignation, followed by a vile smirk of recognition that the lady insisted upon his presence elsewhere.

"Excellent suggestion. Ladies …" He snapped his heels together, bowed his head, turned, and strode from the room.

"Odious man," Mrs. Cheek muttered. Then she sighed. "Now, Miss Cameron, I would so love to see what your plans are for this wall."

"I would like nothing better, but first"—Lilyan hesitated—"there is something very important I must ask you."

"Of course." Mrs. Cheek glanced outside. "Perhaps in the garden?"

Lilyan followed her onto a patio that spanned the back of the house.

"No need to wait for me, Gerald." Lilyan closed the glass doors behind them.

Mrs. Cheek pointed to a teakwood bench screened from the

house by a camellia bush. "There is a good prospect."

When they had seated themselves, Lilyan remained quiet, gathering her thoughts, wondering how to phrase her request. She looked into Mrs. Cheek's sherry brown eyes and was encouraged by the concern she saw in them. "I do not know if you are aware that my brother, Andrew, is a prisoner on board the *Brixham*."

Mrs. Cheek clasped Lilyan's hands. "No I was not. I am so very sorry."

"He has been there—" Lilyan's voice cracked, and tears welled in her eyes. "Oh, dear. I was not expecting ... that is ..." She clamped her teeth on her bottom lip. "I did not want to cry."

"But of course you are upset. I would be too." Mrs. Cheek patted Lilyan's hand. "Is there anything I can do?"

Lilyan struggled against the tide of sadness that threatened to surge over her. But a vision of Andrew—skinny, hungry, hunkered down with others trying to stay warm in the dark underbelly of a ship—forged despair into resolve.

What a ninnyhammer I am. My crying will not help Andrew.

"Do you remember the conversation we had in my shop? About your husband's efforts to visit the prison ships?"

Mrs. Cheek nodded.

"Is there a possibility your husband could try ... one more time? I thought if we could appeal to their Christian charity ... maybe ask for the visit to occur on Christmas Eve?"

"I think my James would be very open to such a suggestion. And the timing could not be better."

Lilyan furrowed her brow.

"You see, Lilyan, many ladies of my acquaintance are horrified by the atrocities we have heard about. A group of us, every denomination, dissenter and Anglican. Whig and Tory, I might add. Have signed a petition demanding more humane treatment of the prisoners. Before, my James appealed to Mr. Rosette, the British commissary of prisoners. That is who refused him. But this time, we are taking our petition straight to Lieutenant Colonel Nisbet Balfour—"

"The city commandant? But he's ... his reputation—"

"Is quite reprehensible, I know. But he has the ear of Sir William Howe and other leaders of the king's troops. He is Lord of Charlestown now, and therefore has much power. But I do not think even he could ignore some of the names on our list. Those same ladies are, as we speak, gathering all manner of clothing, blankets, food, medicines, and tobacco."

Lilyan clasped the locket that rested against her chest. "That is wonderful news. What are your plans?"

"As we discovered from some of our ladies, in October your Continental Congress recommended that the colonies set aside December seventh as a day of thanksgiving. A day of prayer to thank God and ask for His grace to comfort and relieve people who are afflicted or distressed. We determined that that day would be ideal for disbursing the supplies. In such a holy purpose, we felt that Lord Balfour could not possibly refuse our request. That is, not without irreparably damaging his reputation among the more genteel of our society."

Mrs. Cheek drew her fingers through the lace on her sleeve. "Unfortunately, it is taking us longer to procure the supplies than we intended, so our original deadline will not suit. Therefore, it might be better for us to wait until Christmas Eve, as you suggest."

"This is so much more than I had hoped for." Lilyan paused, wanting to phrase her words carefully. "Do you think it would be possible for me to go along with the supplies?"

Mrs. Cheek frowned. "I do not think it wise. The conditions … the things you would see … would not be appropriate for a young lady."

"Oh, please." Lilyan jumped up and paced back and forth, dragging the locket across the chain around her neck.

She sat and searched the woman's face. "You must understand. Andrew is all I have in this world. I simply must have this chance to see him again." She fumbled with her locket. "Would you like to see what he looks like?"

She opened the locket. "I painted it myself. From memory, mostly. Andrew was too impatient to sit for me."

Mrs. Cheek leaned forward. "He looks very much like you. The same beautiful red hair."

Lilyan closed the locket and pressed it against her heart. "I was not very kind to him the last time we spoke. I would bear anything, do anything, to have a chance to make amends."

Mrs. Cheek looked at Lilyan with eyes soft and moist from

71

emotion. "I can see how strongly you feel about this. So, if Lord Balfour grants us permission to distribute the supplies, I will see that you are allowed to accompany the boarding party."

"Might I be invited? I do so love a good party," said Bradenton, who sidled around the camellia bush and stood before them.

And we know that all things work together for good to them that love God. To them Who are the called according to his purpose.
Romans 8:28

Chapter Eleven

How MUCH HAD BRADENTON heard? Had he really accepted Mrs. Cheek's explanation?

Those questions still tormented Lilyan hours after she'd said good-bye to Mrs. Cheek. In an effort to overcome the tide of anxiety that ebbed and flowed through her body, she had ripped the plaster from the sample wall in her shop and replaced it with a gleaming white layer of fresh stucco. Mentally and physically exhausted, she wilted onto a chair.

Lilyan's intuition told her that underneath Bradenton's facade of courtliness dwelt a complex man who was not only capable of inflicting harm, but who also would take great pleasure in doing so.

What if he did hear us talking about the supplies? What would make him jump to any conclusion other than that of a group of women trying to do some good?

Someone tapped on the door, and Lilyan jerked so hard she dropped the trowel.

"Who is it?" her voice hoarse with tension.

She retrieved the tool and, holding it in front of her like a weapon, she advanced toward the door.

"It's Mr. Lewis, Miss Cameron."

Lilyan pressed a hand to her heart, laid down the trowel, and opened the door.

Mr. Lewis removed his beaver skin hat and limped inside. "Good evening. I hope I didn't startle you."

Only out of five years of my life. "No." She clasped the folds in the side of her skirt. "What can I do for you?"

He glanced around the room. "You are alone?"

"Quite."

"I've come about the chamomile."

"The chamomile?"

Mr. Lewis cleared his throat.

Lilyan blinked, and then realization flooded through her.

"Oh, the chamomile. Do forgive me. I'm so very new at all of this. Please." She motioned to the chairs in front of the stucco wall.

He preceded her, his irregular gait more pronounced than usual. A short, wiry man, Mr. Lewis had a reputation as one of the best painters in Charlestown. A year ago, he and Lilyan had worked together on one of the residences on Meeting Street. She remembered it in particular for it was on that job she watched in horror as he fell from the scaffolding and broke his leg. Lilyan could not forget how brave he was as he showed her how to brace his leg until someone could fetch the doctor. The injury had not mended well and had left him lame, though his resolve to carry on his business seemed stronger than ever.

Lilyan took a seat and examined her hands. Plaster had caked under the tips of her fingernails, turning them into alabaster quarter moons. Embarrassed, she slipped them underneath the folds of her skirt.

At a loss for the protocol for passing along information to a fellow spy, she said the first thing that came to mind. "Would you like a cup of coffee?"

Mr. Lewis's lip twitched. "I think not. We should get on with it. What is the nature of your communication?"

After several awkward starts, her words spilled out as if a dam had burst inside her brain. Mr. Lewis listened intently as she told him about her plan and her conversation with Mrs. Cheek.

"As soon I can, I want to talk to Captain McKenzie," she said. "Try and persuade him to use his influence as well to get us on board. Then, I imagine, it is up to someone else to come up with a way to get the prisoners off the ship." She paused to gauge Mr. Lewis's reaction, but his expression revealed nothing. "What do you think?"

Mr. Lewis scowled. "Bold, but risky. Very risky."

"Can we do this?"

"Are we capable? Yes. Definitely. Should we? I don't know. I don't make those decisions."

"Does Captain Xanthakos?" Speaking Nicholas' name filled her with a yearning that shook her insides.

"Among others." He stood stiffly, rubbing his leg.

"Is that who you will be sharing my information with? Will you be seeing him soon?"

"It's safer not to ask such questions, Miss Cameron."

When Lilyan handed him his hat, he smiled and added, "Cultivate patience, Miss Cameron. In this business, it will become your best friend."

Later that evening, pacing her parlor waiting for Captain McKenzie, Lilyan wondered how one cultivated patience. You either have it or you do not, she determined. Finally, after exhausting what little patience she possessed, she heard the captain trudge up the steps and open the front door. She dashed toward a chair, ran her fingers through the creases of her skirt, crossed one ankle over the other, and tried not to look like a duck ready to pounce on a bug.

She watched the captain shrug off his mantle and hang it on a hook, then he removed his hat and laid it on the wig stand.

When he turned to walk up the stairs, Lilyan called out, "Good evening, Captain."

He turned with a start and bowed. "Mistress Cameron."

"Do you have a moment?" Lilyan swept her arm, inviting him toward a chair.

"At your service." He crossed the room and sat beside her.

For someone so tall and burly, he walked with grace. She had known this man only three months, but during that time had come to regard him as one of the most amiable people of her acquaintance. His was not a handsome face. In fact, if considered one at the time, his features could be described as very unattractive: bushy eyebrows, bleached almost yellow from the sun; a bulbous nose; a ruddy complexion; and a chiseled, square jaw. But to a discerning eye, taken as a whole his face exuded a fineness of character, confidence, and straightforwardness. His eyes—his best feature, hazel with light brown flecks—studied her now with a quizzical expression.

Lilyan smiled at him. "We have not seen you in a while. We were becoming concerned."

"Not to worry about me, lass. You've enough on your plate with your brother and all."

"You know already?"

"Yes. I heard it when I returned this morning. I couldna believe it. So I looked up Andrew's name on the list of prisoners."

"Captain—"

He held up his hand. "I have to tell ye up front, I canna help ye get your brother off the ship. He made a choice. He took action. Something I can admire. But every man knows, or should know, what you sow you reap. This is war—although a cursed, misbegotten one. Life and death. Serious business. And Andrew's got to bear the consequences of his choices."

"But—"

"I'm fond of the lad. I truly am. He reminds me of my Davie, but to help him would mean goin' against my own. And I canna, I willna do that."

"No, no. I would never ask something like that of you. You've been kind to us. I consider you a friend and I would never impose on our friendship … put you in jeopardy." She leaned toward him. "I assume you've heard about the way the colonists are being treated? How over and over again they were promised supplies? How the supplies that did finally arrive were disbursed among your soldiers, right before the prisoners' eyes?"

"Aye. To our everlasting shame."

"There is a group of women—caring, honorable and influential women—who are going to petition Lord Balfour for more humane treatment. They've gathered food, blankets, and clothing, which they want to deliver to the prisoners on Christmas Eve. All I ask of you is to use whatever influence you have to help this happen."

The captain slapped his knee. "Now that, I can do."

He stood, and as Lilyan rose to meet him, he took her hand. "I pledge my word, my bond. I will do what I can. And don't you worry about your brother. Remember what St. Paul told us in his book of Romans, 'God works for the good of those who love him.' I guarantee ye, something good will come out of all this."

The magnitude of what Lilyan had set in motion stunned her. *How will this all end?*

76

proto mas fili, our first kiss

Chapter Twelve

A BRILLIANT SUNSET SPREAD an apricot blush across the magnolia leaves in the wreath Lilyan attached to her shop door. Pleased with the decoration, she rubbed the chill from her hands and stepped back inside. Christmas was a week away and, as she lit two candles in her display window, she contemplated the challenges it presented. The joy of celebrating the birth of Christ, the merriment of parties, and the excitement on the children's faces only magnified her heartache. Despair hung in the air like a scrim.

She glanced at the chamomile painting she had placed in the window for the second time a week ago; no one had responded to her signal. Gerald had passed along news that Lord Balfour had given permission for the supplies to be delivered to the *Brixham* on Christmas Eve. Although promising, the information did not satisfy her. She needed more particulars. How would the guards be overcome? How would the prisoners be transported? Where would they go once they escaped? Would she be protected, or should she take a pistol?

A gust of wind whirled around her, pressing the candle flames to the side. Alarmed, she crept toward the storeroom and hovered in the shadows. She summoned enough courage to peep at the back entrance, and her heart leapt.

"Nicholas!" she exclaimed, centering herself in the doorway.

He looks . . . wonderful. From his buckskin leggings and fringed jacket to the black feather on the side of his leather hat. The collar of his coarse linen shirt lay open, exposing his chest and neck. He needed a shave and he seemed tired, until his lips curled into a smile that lit his golden eyes—eyes that were drinking her in as well. He pulled his hat from his head and clutched it at his side.

Of all the ways Lilyan had envisioned this meeting, not one of them involved her standing like a statute; nor had any of them come close to the feelings shooting up from her toes and playing havoc within her ribcage.

The silence should have felt awkward compared to the conversations she had imagined. But it seemed so natural, so right, especially when he opened his arms, beckoning. Without another thought, she rushed into his embrace, slipped her arms around him and reveled in the touch, the smell of him.

He released her but continued to study her face. "Lilyanista," he whispered, and then captured her lips with his.

The kiss lifted her senses like the gentle swell of an ocean wave— she felt buoyant, floating up and over the crest. Nicholas took her face in his hands and pressed his lips to her forehead, underneath her eyes, her chin, and then back to her mouth. With each caress the ebb and flow of her responses magnified until she wondered if she might drown in the current that swirled around her.

Held in the circle of his arms, Lilyan marveled at how perfectly they fit together. As if she had been a puzzle, lacking the very center piece, and this man—precisely the right size, the right shape— dropped into the middle of her life, completing the picture.

"You feel it, don't you?" he whispered. "This sweet ache of homecoming. As if you have been on a long, long journey and finally arrived."

Lilyan nodded and then, suddenly feeling very shy, she stepped back.

"*Aga'pi mou*," he murmured. "I had hoped. I had dreamed ..."

Lilyan laughed softly at the incredulous joy she read in his face. "I know. It's strange and ... wonderful ... how you have become such a part of me in so short a time."

She lifted the drawstring that dangled from his collar and

twirled it around her finger. "What does *aga'pi mou* mean?"

He smiled. "It means *my love*."

"You love me." Stunned, she paused to savor the thought. "And I love you."

He clasped her face. "Wonderful words from such beautiful lips," he murmured.

She searched his glorious eyes, enjoying her discovery of the amber specks circling his irises. "Quite wondrous. And ... and unnerving."

He raised an eyebrow.

She backed away. "I am a single woman, alone with a beautiful man"—his eyes lit with obvious delight, bringing heat to her cheeks—"throwing all propriety out the window."

How the gossips would chew on this morsel. If women of Mrs. Melborne and Mrs. Stafford's ilk held her lifestyle as a tradesperson in contempt, what would they think about her behavior now?

She could imagine them prattling, "Women ought to be sensible, polite, and delicate."

In a way, her brashness appalled even her. Yes, she had intentionally turned away from society's laws of female propriety in order to pursue her art. But one thing she was not was a hypocrite. She enjoyed the feel of this man's arms around her, the caress of his hands, and the touch of his lips. Mayhap too much at this moment.

"What is propriety compared to this?" he asked and then swept her into his embrace.

She could have swooned from the storm of feelings that surged through her body. She cupped his face in her hands and, nearly drowning in the passion she saw in his eyes, she searched for the right words to rein in the passion so easily sparked between them.

"I admit, dearest. Being held in your arms is quite wonderful. But I am not sure how to proceed. The suddenness of it all ... I have never been so tempted. ... I am a bit frightened."

"You must never be frightened of me, beloved." He took a step back. "And you are correct. We will move more slowly. Hmm?"

His tone was warm, soothing and utterly charming, sending shivers over Lilyan's arms.

"Why don't we sit?" She slipped past him and took a seat.

He sat in the chair beside her. "This is more comfortable for you? Yes?"

She adopted a demure look that made him chuckle.

Suddenly a thought struck her. "Are you here in response to my signal?"

He nodded.

She scooted forward until their knees touched. "How are you going to get Andrew and the others off the ship? Tell me everything."

Nicholas frowned. "I cannot tell you everything."

"Tell me what you can, then."

"As you know, we have permission to board the *Brixham* on Christmas Eve. We plan to start late in the day, so that it will be dark by the time we have finished loading the supplies. My men will crew two longboats; six of us to a boat—"

"So few? Can they take over such a large ship?"

"Normally not." Nicholas grinned. "One of the fair ladies of the city has planned a ball that evening and has invited the companies from all of the prison ships to attend. We figure there will be ten men left on board at most. Once we have overcome them, we will signal to two other boats waiting on shore."

Lilyan took a deep breath. "How many can each boat carry?"

"Twenty at the most."

"But, there are almost two hundred prisoners."

Nicholas clasped her hands. "We cannot rescue them all. Only the able-bodied ones."

Lilyan chewed on her lip. "But you will make sure Andrew is one of them, right?"

"I cannot make that promise, my darling. I don't know your brother's condition."

"But—" She vaulted from her chair to pace the room.

She had never considered that Andrew might be too ill to manage the rescue. She stood behind her chair and grasped the spindles until her knuckles turned white.

Nicholas, who had observed her every move, remained silent.

She sighed. "You're right. I cannot ask you to play favorites. And I would not want to put the others in jeopardy by insisting that you take Andrew if he's too ill to travel. It's just that—"

"What a fine woman you are, Lilyan Cameron. I thought I loved you before. Your lovely face expresses your every emotion."

Lilyan's stomach tumbled. She could feel her cheeks glowing, and she clasped the back of the chair.

His expression grew earnest. "Every moment I spend with you convinces me that I have found a treasure. A talented, sensitive woman of courage and devotion and generosity. I don't think I could ever be as proud of you as I am now."

His words, fine and soft as silk, spun into a cord that seemed to bond their hearts and minds together. A sense of intimacy, of oneness, enveloped her. She studied him a few moments, overwhelmed by an urge to loosen his hair from the rawhide cord, comb her fingers through the curls, and splay them across his shoulders. *Will they feel wiry or more like ebony satin? What does his hair smell like? Salty like the ocean? Woodsy like an inland stream? Or fresh like water from a rain barrel?*

His eyes danced as if he were reading her mind. Her heartbeat thrummed in her ears, and she pressed her hand to her breast. The sound intensified until she realized the pounding was coming from the door.

Nicholas spun out of the chair and pushed her behind him. Step by step, as he entered the front room, she followed closely until he stopped and stood arms akimbo behind the counter. Curious, Lilyan peeked through the crook of his arm to spot Callum peering in the window.

"Lilyan. Are you in there?" Callum yelled.

"Just a moment." She unlocked the door and stood back as Callum swooped in and stared first at her and then Nicholas.

"Ye well, lassie?"

"Why, yes. I'm fine."

Callum clasped her shoulders and sucked in a deep breath, an ominous sound that put Lilyan on her guard.

"Then can you tell me, why in the name of—St. Andrew—are you not at home?"

"You see ... Nicholas—"

"Nicholas." Callum pivoted on his heel and stared at him as if wondering how long Nicholas and Lilyan had been alone in the store. "Evening, Captain."

"Evening, Callum." Nicholas sounded mildly amused.

"And just what were you doing?" Callum demanded.

"Talking." Lilyan held out her arms, beseeching him to believe her.

Callum stared at her and then slid his glance to Nicholas. Lilyan blushed, and even Nicholas looked a bit sheepish.

"Humph. Well, lassie, I say there's been enough *talking* for one night. I'll get your cape."

As soon as Callum stomped out of the room, Nicholas clasped Lilyan to him and kissed her soundly.

"Should … should we tell him?" she asked breathlessly and pressed her hands to her flaming cheeks.

Callum's grumbling grew louder.

"Now is not a good time." Nicholas winked. "I cannot afford to be pummeled to death by your protector." He strode toward the back room and then turned to face her once more. "Take heart, my sweet, our time will come."

Those beautiful words, so full of promise, sustained her through the barrage of reproaches Callum grumbled at her the entire way home.

Am I a soldier of the Cross,
A follower of the Lamb?
And shall I fear to own His cause,
Or blush to speak His name?

Since I must fight if I would reign,
Increase my courage, Lord!
I'll bear the toil, endure the pain,
Supported by Thy Word.

Chapter Thirteen

"I CANNOT LET YOU GO without me." Lying in bed, Elizabeth coughed and pressed her fingers to the base of her throat. She rolled up onto her elbow and started to throw off the covers.

Lilyan pushed her back and tucked the quilt under her chin. "As much as I would like you with me, you are too sick. Besides, Dr. Cheek will accompany me."

Elizabeth's dark eyes, moist from her cold, entreated. "Promise me." She swallowed and winced. "Promise you won't do anything rash."

"Try not to worry. Everything will go as planned."

Lilyan grabbed the long handle of the bed warmer and pulled it from the roaring cedar logs that filled the bedroom with a sweet aroma. Smoke rose from the pan's perforated top and she could see the fiery coals inside. She wrapped the pan in a woolen blanket and slipped it under the covers next to Elizabeth's feet.

"There, now. All toasty." She lifted the knitted cover from the pot on the night table. "Shall I pour you a cup before I go?"

"No, thank you. I will just lie here and close my eyes for a while."

"Fine, then." Lilyan opened the door and started to leave.

"Lilyan?"

"Yes."

"Give Andrew my love."

Lilyan nodded.

"And I will be praying for you."

"We could use it." Lilyan shut the door behind her.

Downstairs she paced from one room to the next. The mantel-piece clock's loud ticking marked the crawling pace of the minutes. Details of the escape plan roiled around in her mind like a cork in a rolling current. She longed to see Andrew, but abhorred the thoughts of what conditions she might witness him enduring. Her courage and confidence waxed and waned. Anxiety for Nicholas conjured up scenarios she could not block.

She found herself humming a hymn. *Am I a soldier of the cross?* She mentally stumbled over the next two stanzas, remembering only a word here or there, and then rallied toward the end. *Increase my courage, Lord! I'll bear the toil, endure the pain, supported by Thy Word.*

She drew comfort from the song and, when the long-awaited knock came at the door, she greeted Dr. Cheek with confidence. "I'm ready."

The doctor, a tall, lean man with kind eyes, helped her drape her pelisse across her shoulders. "I see that you are, Mistress Cameron. But I feel it my duty to caution you once again about the conditions you will be subjected to." He waited on the stoop for Lilyan to close the door behind them. "I worry, too, about the diseases you will be exposed to."

Lilyan led the way into the street. "I appreciate your concern. I do. Perhaps there is something I can tell you that will ease your mind."

He nodded and gauged his steps to hers.

"When I was five, my father made a trading visit to the Cherokee Indians, but left them earlier than planned to get away from an outbreak of smallpox. Unfortunately, my brother and I—Andrew was one at the time—came down with the illness. It hit my brother particularly hard. We almost lost him."

Dr. Cheek frowned. "That terrible plague decimated the Indians. That you and your brother survived is nothing short of a miracle."

"Yes. But for me, getting smallpox turned out to be a blessing. Years later when I accompanied my father on an expedition, we came to a village where so many were sick with smallpox; there was hardly anyone to take care of them. And because we had already had the disease, my father and I were able to nurse many of them through."

Nine years had passed since that time, but Lilyan could close her eyes and recall every detail—the moaning, the oozing sores, the wailing, the stench of death. She remembered especially Golden Fawn, a girl almost her own age, whose face had been so ravaged she was almost unrecognizable. And the two babies—she shook her head to free her mind from that memory.

"To have seen so much that young—" the doctor spoke softly.

"Mistress Cameron. Wait," a voice called out, the rolling *r*'s identifying the speaker at once.

They turned to find Captain McKenzie hurrying toward them. When he drew near, he bowed and signaled for them to continue.

"What brings you out this evening, Captain?" Dr. Cheek asked as they turned south toward the wharf.

"I'm coming with you."

"But ..." Lilyan searched for something to say. "There's really no need."

The captain raised an eyebrow. "Nevertheless, I will accompany you."

Heavens above. How had he known she was going? She had not known herself until hours earlier when she received a message from Mrs. Cheek. There had been no way to notify Nicholas and his men. And how would Captain McKenzie react once they boarded the ship? Would he be attacked? Suddenly, she realized how naïve she had been. She had thought only of rescuing Andrew. People were bound to be injured ... killed.

But men would be freed from a horrible, tortured imprisonment. Would not the end justify the means? She knew now, this was what Nicholas had meant when he warned her that war was not a game.

She gripped her reticule in her chilled fingers. *Courage and wisdom, Lord. Please, grant me courage and wisdom.*

When they reached the dock, Lilyan's heart hammered so it drowned out the rush of the breaking waves. Hoping to spot

Nicholas, she scanned the two boats berthed at the mooring plank, but she could not find him among the men as they tossed barrels and crates into thick rope nets.

"Ready to cast off," someone shouted. "Got room for one more here."

Dr. Cheek turned to Captain McKenzie. "I'll go ahead in this one. You'll watch after Miss Cameron?"

"Aye."

The doctor boarded the craft and took a seat in the stern, and the crew locked the oars. When they were away, he turned and waved. Out of the corner of her eye, Lilyan noticed a man jump from the other boat onto the dock. The hem of his black greatcoat almost swept the ground as he sauntered close and stood toe to toe with Captain McKenzie, turning his back to Lilyan. A blue bandana, tied at the back of his neck, swathed his head. Over that he wore a sealskin hat, pulled low on his forehead. Lilyan considered his thick ebony beard and the gold loop dangling from his ear. He looked like a tall, lean pirate—and a very dangerous one.

"You got business here?" he asked gruffly.

The captain stiffened. "Miss Cameron has Lord Balfour's permission to board the *Brixham*"—he jabbed his finger toward the ship out in the bay— "and I'm here to accompany her."

The man snorted. "Not bloody likely."

Lilyan sprang next to Captain McKenzie and faced the man. The moment he slid his glance her way she knew—Nicholas. But instead of the warm, inviting glow she expected, his tawny eyes glared at her with barely concealed anger.

Captain McKenzie's presence has caught him by surprise. He's furious. Considering other options, she came to a more troubling conclusion. *Oh, my. He was not expecting* me *either. This cannot bode well.*

"Ach! Away with all this swagger," barked Captain McKenzie. "You have no authority here. Stand aside, unless you want me to summon my troops."

Lilyan stared as the two men squared off; determined hazel eyes locked with defiant amber ones. Captain McKenzie meant what he said, and if Nicholas continued this tack, he could endanger their mission. She sensed the moment Nicholas came to that same conclusion. Without a word, he turned on his heel and stomped back into the boat.

Thank goodness we got past that hurdle. Lilyan rubbed her neck where the muscle had knotted.

Captain McKenzie followed Nicholas, stepped into the boat, and then helped Lilyan aboard and set her gently onto the seat beside him. Several of the oarsmen glanced over their shoulders to stare in disapproval.

Nicholas glowered at her once more, then turned his back and ordered the men to cast off. They obeyed, efficiently propelling the craft across the bay. From her vantage, she watched the crew unload the preceding boat and hoist the doctor aboard in a bosun's chair. By the time her boat came alongside the *Brixham*, the setting sun had cast a pale golden tint across the calm waters—painting a serene scene in direct contrast to the anxiety that clamored in Lilyan's mind.

I am committing treason. The thought struck her like a lightning bolt. *If we fail. If we are caught, will we also wind up in a prison ship headed for St. Augustine? If the mission succeeds, will people believe that I had nothing to do with it? That the Patriots took advantage of my efforts to bring some Christian comfort to the prisoners?* That story was beginning to sound flimsy.

She remained seated waiting for the sailors to transfer the supplies, one net full at the time. On Nicholas' orders, after his men attached the last load to the pulley, they scrambled up the ship's ladders.

"Move up here, miss," Nicholas instructed.

"The sling!" His shout jangled Lilyan's nerves.

The plank dangled above her, descending inch by inch. A breeze shot across her skirt and slapped the chair against the side of the ship. She startled, biting her lip as she peered at the frigid water below.

"You'll be fine," he mumbled.

Nicholas motioned to Captain McKenzie. "I'll see to the lady. You ride up with this last load."

Captain McKenzie raised a brow and looked at Lilyan, who nodded her consent. "See you on board then, Miss Cameron." He planted his feet into the net and slipped his arms through the ropes.

Lilyan watched him being lifted up and over the side, until Nicholas clasped her by her waist and dumped her onto the narrow board of the sling, bringing her to his eye level.

"What are you doing here?" He ground out the words through clenched teeth.

"The ladies asked me to represent them…to help the doctor see to the men."

"The ladies asked you?" He strapped the harness around her and, raising his hand to either side of her head, grasped the ropes that suspended the seat. "Or did you volunteer?"

"I asked—"

"Well, no one asked me!" His words exploded in a barely controlled whisper.

"Nicholas, please do not be angry. This might be my last opportunity to see Andrew for a long, long time."

"You don't have any idea what is up there do you?" He jerked his head toward the ship.

"I told you I was ready to face anything. And I am."

"What are we waiting for?" someone yelled from overhead.

Nicholas yanked on the cables. "Haul away the sling."

"Brace yourself," he whispered.

She rubbed her cheek against his hand and focused on his face as she was hauled up in a surprisingly swift and gentle motion. She smelled the prisoners before she saw them and realized that Nicholas' warning to brace herself had nothing to do with the ride up in the bosun's chair. The stench of unwashed bodies, sickness, and human misery tugged with the contents of her stomach. For a few moments as she dangled above the deck, she could only stare at the nightmarish scene below, and then the sailors swung the pulley and deposited her into what seemed a hell on earth. Her nerves jangled as two British marines shouted orders and prodded a group of men into rows.

The prisoners, emaciated and clothed in filthy rags, stood with their eyes downcast. Some, as if pushed beyond endurance, leaned on the men standing next to them. Still others lay wherever they had fallen, unable to move as if struck like ninepins in a tragic bowling game. One of them, a young man with a bloodstained rag tied across one eye, stared at her with such overwhelming need, she suddenly felt bereft … inept. It took every ounce of courage she possessed to keep from crying and to smile at him with reassurance.

Captain McKenzie helped her out of the harness and offered

his arm. Scarcely able to contain her feelings, she scoured the gaunt faces looking for Andrew.

The captain whispered, "He's standing on the end of the second row."

Lilyan had already spotted him. He stood shoulder to shoulder with his fellow soldiers, his rail thin body at attention, his eyes sunken deep into their sockets, staring straight ahead. Her little brother was gone, and in his place stood a seasoned soldier … a man … who had weathered the storms of hell. She had always loved him, without question. But the intense tide of emotion that welled up in her breast comprised so much more pride, admiration. Everything within her yearned to rush to him and sweep him into her arms. Instead, she dug her fingers into the captain's arm.

"That's the way, lass. Steady on." The captain led her to one of the marines. "Who's in charge here?" he demanded.

The man snapped to attention. "That'd be me, sir."

"No officers on board?"

"No, sir. All gone off to the celebration."

"How many are you?"

"There's ten of us, sir."

"So few?"

"The officers figured we can handle things. Most of these fellows ain't in any kind of shape to make trouble." He snorted. "Kinda like they lost their stomach for fightin'. If you know what I mean?"

Captain McKenzie grimaced. "You know why we're here?"

"Yes, sir. We was told to expect ye."

"Then I suggest you put these men at ease and let's set about getting some food in their bellies." A frown dug deep furrows in his brow. "Don't like the look of things here. No, don't like it at all."

He released Lilyan's arm. "Where is Dr. Cheek?"

"The doctor's below with them that's real bad."

"For God's sake, man, let's see some order. Clear up this rubbish. Make some room." He jabbed his finger toward the prisoners. "Put the sick here, sicker next to them, and sickest next to them."

"Don't have enough men, sir—"

"I don't want to hear it. Just do as you're told," the captain barked. "Set some tables up here. Let the prisoners stand down. They can help. And the dockworkers over there." He gestured toward Nicholas and his men, who were busy pulling the cargo from the nets.

Lilyan pulled a sheet of paper from her pocket and walked toward Nicholas. "Sir?" she said as she reached his side.

"Miss." He tapped two fingers against the brim of his hat.

"I have here a list of the supplies. Each piece has been marked with a number that corresponds with this list." She paused, trying to read the expression in his eyes. "If you would, please, ask your men to put the food on the tables being set up. The blankets and clothing should be distributed right away. As for the medical supplies, some should stay up here and the rest below."

He held a corner of the paper and dipped his head as if studying it. "The guard will change in two hours," he whispered. "Eight bells. That's the signal. Pass the word as you can and stay close to Andrew." And then in a loud voice, he said, "I'll see to it, miss." He strode away, clutching her list in his hand.

Lilyan felt a tap on her shoulder and turned to find Andrew.

"Sissy? It's really you?" His face looked even more haggard up close.

Unable to speak, Lilyan held out her arms. But Andrew stood and stared at her.

"Go ahead. Give her a hug," Captain McKenzie prompted. "There's not a man here would think any less of you."

Without another word, Andrew stepped into Lilyan's embrace. She wound her arms tightly around him and rested her cheek against his chest. Neither of them spoke as he dropped his chin onto her head. As she clung to him, she realized not only his importance as her beloved brother, but as a link to her past, her memories of family and home and a way of life that would never be the same again—sad thoughts that brought tears to her eyes. This time she could not keep them from rolling down her face.

"I am so very proud of you," she managed to whisper through her trembling lips. "Elizabeth sends her love." Her voice cracked and she gulped.

Andrew stood back and brushed her wet cheeks. "Don't cry. Please. Don't cry."

Lilyan gave him a tremulous smile. "I'm sorry. I'm just so happy to see you."

"And what about me?" Herald jostled his way from behind her.

He had lost weight too and, if possible, was even skinnier than

Andrew. His hair, usually the light blond color of sea oats, was caked with dirt, sweat and oil. But Lilyan found his crystal blue eyes as full of devilment as ever.

"Of course. You too," she said, wrapping him in her arms. "And here's a hug from your mother."

Herald stood back. "What about Mother? And Father? How are they?"

"Worried about you, of course. But they are fine." Lilyan cocked her head to the side. "You did not ask after Gerald."

Herald's eyes danced. "Don't have to ask. I'd know it the moment something ever happened to him. The same goes for him. Been that way since we were born."

The prisoners had already lined up in front of the makeshift tables, filling their plates.

She slipped her arm around Andrew. "Come, let us get you fed."

They made their way to the tables and picked up tin plates. Volunteers, mostly other prisoners and a couple of Nicholas' men, filled their plates with ham, beans, potatoes and corncakes.

"Not too much. Not too fast," one of the servers warned. "You'll be sick."

When they reached the end of the table laden with desserts, Herald stopped short. "Look there. One of mother's pies."

Lilyan wondered how he could tell and then smiled when she spied the chamomile carved into the crust.

"I'll have an extra helping," he demanded.

Andrew grinned. "Me too."

For only a moment their animated faces gave Lilyan a glimpse of the young boys they used to be.

"You're not eating?" Andrew asked her.

"No, I've already had something." She hadn't, but she did not want him to know that, in her present state, swallowing food would prove impossible.

I feel so suspicious. And guilty. She fidgeted with the ties on her pelisse. *I have to keep control and act innocent, even if I am not.* She cast furtive glances at the guards and worried that they might sense her turmoil.

Andrew found an empty barrel, rolled it next to the mainmast away from the others, and motioned for Lilyan to take a seat. He and Herald leaned back against the barrel on either side of her legs and put their plates and tins of water in front of them on the deck.

"Would you say grace?" Lilyan asked Andrew, recognizing him as head of their household.

He nodded, sending her a look of gratitude. They bowed their heads and, Andrew, in a low and steady timbre, asked for blessings upon the food and upon those assembled. At the end of the prayer Lilyan noticed many of the other prisoners offering thanks as well.

The two boys tucked into their meal with gusto, barely pausing between bites to wash it down. Lilyan took pleasure in watching them, but her nerves were worn ragged as she waited for the moment when she could tell them about the escape without being overheard. When she bent over to convey the news to Andrew, the *bing-bing* of six bells startled her so, she almost fell off the barrel.

Andrew poked Herald with his elbow. "Say," he mumbled, "isn't that Captain Xanthakos?"

Herald set his cup on the deck and stared at Nicholas and his men. "It sure as heck is. And look, there's Jim Shepherd with him. And some of the men we met at the James Island camp. What's goin' on?"

Lilyan placed her hands on their shoulders and leaned in close. "They're going to get you out of here," she whispered.

They stared up at her wide-eyed, looked at each other, and then back at her.

"When?" Herald asked.

"Tonight."

Andrew quickly glanced at his plate, but not before Lilyan saw tears pooling in his eyes.

Good heavens. He has been through so much.

She kneaded Andrew's shoulder blade. "Things will begin at the changing of the watch. In about an hour. The signal will be the end of the eight bells."

Andrew looked around the deck. "What are we to do?"

"Nothing. As soon as Nicholas—Captain Xanthakos—and his men have overtaken the guards and secured the ship, they will signal to two more boats waiting offshore. Then they will start helping the prisoners board the ships."

92

Andrew and Herald stared at each other. "Wilson," they said at the same time.

"Wilson?" Lilyan asked.

Herald started to rise. "A good friend. He's down in the hold."

"Wait." Lilyan pressed on his arm. "I thought only the really sick men were below decks."

"So?" asked Andrew.

"Well." She paused. "The boats can only hold twenty men each. Not everyone can go. Only those who can walk without assistance."

"Bloody hell!" Herald's words rang out across the ship, and one of the guards shot a glance their way.

Lilyan froze until the man turned away.

Herald slumped back down and grumbled, "Bloody hell."

Andrew pushed away his plate. "So, we wait, then."

Herald folded his arms in front of him.

They looked so dejected, Lilyan searched for something to say. "It must hurt terribly to have to leave your friend behind. But the decision has been made for the good of all. And he will not think less of you. If the situation were reversed, you would understand, would you not?"

Lord, You promised to sustain us and never leave us. We need You now more than ever. Please comfort us all as only You can.

Neither man spoke, but continued staring straight ahead.

Let us, like these good shepherds, then employ
Our grateful voices to proclaim the joy
Trace we the Babe, who hath retrieved our loss
From His poor manger to His bitter cross
Treading His steps, assisted by His grace
Till man's first heavenly state again takes place.

Then may we hope, the angelic thrones among
To sing, redeemed, a glad triumphal song
He that was born upon this joyful day
Around us all His glory shall display
Saved by His love, incessant we shall sing
Of angels and of angel-men the King

Chapter Fourteen

MEN HUDDLED HERE AND there trying to draw cheer from the soft glow of lanterns that accentuated the lines etched in their grim faces. One of them pulled a fife from his pocket, blew a series of scales, and began playing *God Rest Ye Merry, Gentlemen*. Caught up in the carol, the prisoners hummed and sang along. Lilyan found herself tapping her toe to the lively tune and smiling at faces that reflected their raised spirits.

The music shifted to *Hark the Herald Angels Sing*, and Lilyan noticed a pleasant baritone softly resonating from behind her. She looked back over her shoulder and, to her surprise, discovered that the sound was coming from a young British marine.

When the fifer lowered the pitch and began playing *Christians Awake, Salute the Happy Morn*, his audience grew quiet, suddenly subdued by the hauntingly sweet notes.

The song came to an end, and Lilyan wondered at how strange, how dreamlike this interlude seemed. To be singing carols when in a few minutes the entire ship would be turned upside down made her feel as if she were acting in a play.

But what a comfort to know that despite the outcome of this terrible war, believers could hold fast to the promise of an eternal triumph. Lilyan's heart swelled, and as she scanned the men's faces, she wondered how many of them felt the same. Her eyes came to rest on Nicholas, who was rolling up a length of rope and talking to one of his men. Suddenly he jerked his head and studied her with an intensity that made her heart trip.

Are you still angry with me, dearest? Her eyes pleaded with him.

A smile breached his mask of gravity and then disappeared as quickly as it had come. Lilyan's spirits lifted and she held her breath in wonder at how a subtle shift in his expression could awaken such acute emotions. One of his men approached him and he turned away, leaving her yearning for his attention once more.

"Give me your plates," she said to Andrew and Herald. "I'll take them back."

She scooped up the dishes, carried them to the wash barrel beside the food tables, and dropped them into the water. She started toward Nicholas, but turned around to find Captain McKenzie in her path.

"There will be a star in your crown for what you've done this evening, Miss Cameron." He swept his arm toward the prisoners, now satiated, properly dressed, and with coats and blankets to ward off the cold.

"Me? Oh, no. I cannot take any credit—" Her response died in her throat with the sounding of eight bells.

In what seemed only moments, scuffles broke out in several places on the upper deck. Fearful yet fascinated, she watched the prisoners wrestle the marines to the planks.

Beside her, Captain McKenzie yelled, "What the—"

Lilyan heard a loud *thwack* and shuddered in horror when the captain's body slumped against her and slid to her feet, streaking a trail of blood across the hem of her dress. Somehow, in the midst of the pandemonium that followed, Andrew and Herald rushed over and stood on either side. With her brother's arm wrapped around her, she covered her eyes and buried her face into the crook of his neck.

"Quiet!" Nicholas' command broke through the chaos.

Lilyan peered through her fingers at Nicholas, standing arms akimbo atop a crate. The men stopped and turned to him.

Nicholas pointed to the marines. "Tie them up and take them below. Jake, you signal the boats. The rest of you, gather whatever provisions you can and make ready to climb overboard."

Steeling herself, Lilyan peeked down at the captain. Blood oozed from a gash in the back of his head, but he was still breathing. Her stomach threatened to turn.

Andrew grabbed her shoulders and shook her. "Herald and I must help the others. Can you manage, Sissy?"

She nodded. While the men scurried to follow Nicholas' orders, she dropped to her knees, ripped a strip of muslin from her petticoat, and wrapped it around the captain's head. For several excruciating minutes, she cradled his ashen face, a stark contrast to his auburn hair. Guilt weighed heavy in her breast. Before tonight, that men's lives were at risk had seemed a distant possibility, but now that Captain McKenzie lay injured in her arms, the gravity of the situation struck her. Finally, his eyelids fluttered, and a rush of relief flowed through her. He groaned and then, clasping his head in his hands, tried to rise up on his elbow.

A man walking nearby, his tattered clothes hanging on his emaciated body like wash on the line, stopped and sneered. "Back with us again? Supposed to be dead, ain't you?"

He whipped a knife from his waistband, "I'll make sure this time." Clinching the dagger in his fist, he lifted it over his head and plunged it down.

Lilyan threw her body across the captain, raising her arm to thwart the deadly blow.

"No!" she cried out and then watched in horror as the blade sliced through her pelisse and ripped into her skin. She screamed as pain seared up her arm like a bolt of lightning.

"No! *Diavolo!*" Nicholas bounded through the sea of men gathered around Lilyan. He knelt before her, grabbed her arm, and shoved her sleeve up to her elbow.

Stunned, Lilyan looked up at him, and though she wanted to say something brave, to encourage him to look out for the others, with tears pooling her eyes, all she could manage was, "It hurts."

Nicholas' expression turned thunderous. He jerked his head toward the man holding the knife and pinned him down with his eyes. "Get him away from me. Now!"

"He's a damned Brit—"

Several of the men dragged him away before he could finish.

Two men rolled the captain away from Lilyan's lap, clearing the way for Nicholas to sweep her into his arms. Dazed and shaking, Lilyan dropped her cheek against his chest.

"Andrew," his voice rumbled against her ear, "fetch the doctor. We'll be in the captain's quarters."

"I have you now, my love," Nicholas murmured.

"Nicholas. Please. Captain McKenzie. Don't let anyone—"

"No harm will come to him. I promise." He carried her through the subdued crowd of men who cleared a path as he neared them.

Someone ahead of them threw open the door to a cabin, and, with her eyes squeezed tightly from the ache in her arm, Lilyan felt herself being gently deposited onto a mattress. She groaned not only from the pain but her removal from the cradle of Nicholas' arms.

"Shepherd," Nicholas said to a man standing beside him, "see to the men. I'll be there soon."

"Sir," the man responded and hurried away, leaving them alone in the room.

Nicholas pulled a knife from his boot, slit the edge of the sheet, and ripped a strip of cloth away. He opened her pelisse, sliced the sleeve from her dress and wrapped the bandage around her fore-arm, all the while murmuring phrases in Greek. Though she could not understand his words, the tenderness in his eyes and the gentleness in his voice communicated everything she needed to hear.

She raised her other arm and cupped his face in her hand. "I'm so sorry."

Nicholas kissed her palm fervently, then took her hand in his and pressed it to her side. "It is I who am sorry—"

"As well you should be, you ruffian," Dr. Cheek shouted from the doorway. "Move aside," he ordered, and then took a seat on the bed beside Lilyan.

"Let me take a look," he said, unwinding the bandage.

A twinge streaked from her wrist to her elbow, and Lilyan clench her jaw so hard it throbbed.

"Hmm," was the doctor's only comment. He took a bottle from his bag and poured its contents into a cup. "Take this, Miss Cameron and you will soon feel better." He slipped his arm up under Lilyan's neck and pressed a cup to her lips.

Lilyan swallowed. The bitter liquid brought tears to her eyes and made her choke. Within minutes the laudanum filtered its way through her body. Her arms and legs sank into the mattress, while her mind seemed to float overhead. She stared up at Dr. Cheek with eyes fast losing the ability to focus.

"She will be well, yes?" Nicholas' voice cut through her fog.

"No thanks to you, sir," came Dr. Cheek's gruff reply. "Now if everyone would leave, I have some stitching to do."

Oh, dear. Is he making clothes? Lilyan chuckled at the silly thought and closed her heavy lids.

So Joseph also went up from the town of Nazareth in Galilee to Judea, to Bethlehem the town of David, because he belonged to the house and line of David. He went there to register with Mary, who was pledged to be married to him and was expecting a child. While they were there, the time came for the baby to be born, and she gave birth to her firstborn, a son.

Chapter Fifteen

LILYAN WOKE TO A JARRING twinge in her arm and a sharp ache in her head. Blinking away the fog in her brain, she focused on a pair of somehow familiar, warm sherry brown eyes. It took a moment for her to recognize the owner of those eyes, now full of concern and watching her closely.

"Mrs. Cheek?" Lilyan glanced around the room, surprised to find herself in her own bed. "What ... what are you—? What time is it? How long have I slept?"

"Now, there. It is ten in the morning, and you have slept the night away."

Lilyan started to rise, but Mrs. Cheek pressed her shoulders back onto the pillow.

"Truly. You must stay as still as possible. Doctor's orders." She smiled. "Plenty of rest for Charlestown's newest heroine."

Lilyan blinked. "What do you mean?"

Mrs. Cheek fussed with the covers, drawing them up under Lilyan's chin and tucking them around her sides. "Why, everyone is talking about how you risked your life. How you suffered a terrible knife wound in order to save our dear Captain McKenzie." She knit her brows. "Mind you, our ladies were upset at first. Worried

99

that we had made a disastrous error in judgment, allowing you to go there in the first place. But we have decided that you represented us magnificently. We are all so very proud."

Confusion reigned and then gave itself over to astonishment. *Not only are they not going to throw me into prison, they may quite possibly throw a party for me.*

Lilyan heard a deep-throated grumble and knew exactly who it belonged to.

"Oh, dear." Mrs. Cheek lowered her voice. "There is a very … how shall I say it without sounding impolite? Irascible … old man who planted himself in a chair outside your door last night. He refuses to move and demands to know the moment you awake." She slid a glance toward the open door. "Shall I allow him to come in?"

"Yes, please."

"Very well." Mrs. Cheek grabbed another pillow, leaned Lilyan forward, and fluffed it up behind her shoulders. "But only for a moment."

She walked to the door. "You may come in now, sir." She turned back to Lilyan. "Do you feel like eating something? There is some potato soup that a Mrs. Snead brought by this morning."

Lilyan, who could still taste the acrid medicine on her tongue, nodded. "It sounds wonderful."

"Good. I will bring some for Elizabeth as well."

"How is she?"

"Do not worry yourself. Her fever broke this morning. She will be fine."

"But where is she?"

"Down the hall. Captain McKenzie, gentleman that he is, moved out and gave her his room."

"He is well, then?"

"He has a mighty lump on his head, and his face will be swollen for a time. But all things taken into account, he is a fortunate man."

Such good news.

Lilyan looked up to find Callum standing in the doorway with a thunderous look on his face. Not one to waste time on patience or decorum, he marched past Mrs. Cheek and strode to the bed.

Mrs. Cheek hesitated in the doorway. "You'll be all right?"

"Quite all right. Callum is a dear friend."

"I'll get the soup, then." Mrs. Cheek frowned at Callum. "I'll leave the door open a bit," she said before heading downstairs.

Callum scowled, and Lilyan braced herself for an onslaught of recriminations. But instead he knelt, took her hand and rubbed it against his cheek. For the first time in her life since she had known this gruff, plain speaking man, he seemed unable to say a word. Nothing he could have said would have affected her more deeply than the mixture of pain and relief she read in his hound-dog eyes.

Lilyan caressed him underneath his chin. "Callum? Did everyone get away?"

"Aye. They got away. And with such headway, no one will be able to catch up with them. The Brits be stewing in their own juices."

She slumped back, grimacing from the ache in her arm. "Thank God."

"Thank God is right."

"Do you know where they have gone?"

He rose from his knee and sat in the chair beside her. "I suspect to fight with Marion."

"With Marion. In the swamps. In the cold." Lilyan groaned. "Would they have been better off on the ships?"

"Never!" The word exploded from his lips. "This way they got a choice. A say in the way they live or die. The other was a living hell."

She sighed. "I know. But I worry about what they are up against."

"Don't ever underestimate Marion. He knows how to lead men. How to march them seventy miles in a day without eating for twenty-four hours. Just look at how he outfoxed Tarleton, who set out after him with twice the men. Ran Tarleton around the swamps until he gave up and headed back to the upcountry to try his luck finding General Sumter.

Marching seventy miles a day without food. Lilyan appreciated Callum's efforts to reassure her, but she didn't have the heart to tell him he was having the opposite effect.

"Callum?"

"Yes."

"Are you angry with me?"

"I was. At first. But I'm here to tell ye that once I knew you were fine, I couldn't stay angry anymore."

He leaned closer. "But be prepared, lassie. I'll not be leaving your side again. And that's a fact." He puffed up his chest as if ready for an argument.

"Good."

He blinked several times, and his body sagged. "You must be feelin' mighty poorly to agree to such a thing. Maybe you need some more rest. I hear Mrs. Cheek coming back upstairs, so I'll leave you for a wee bit. I've moved my gear into Andrew's room upstairs. Just call out, and I'll come a runnin'."

Lilyan nodded, fighting back tears. *What a dear soul. A treasure of a friend.*

She pushed herself up against the pillows and immediately regretted it, gritting her teeth against the pain that shot up her forearm. She frowned at the thick bandage, suddenly reminded of the sight of Captain McKenzie lying at her feet in a pool of blood.

Mrs. Cheek, bright and cheerful, swept into the room carrying a tray. "There was no tea to be had in this house, so I sent for my special blend. It's a lovely flavor. I think you will enjoy it."

Lilyan did not have the heart to tell her that tea was contraband in the Cameron household. When the first sip of the aromatic brew slid down her throat, she felt only a small twinge of regret at this betrayal. After all, it was her first cup of tea in a year. And it was *heavenly*, she thought as her toes curled into the mattress.

After breakfast, as soon as Mrs. Cheek busied herself downstairs, Lilyan sat up on the side of the mattress and then had to wait for the wave of wooziness to subside. She gingerly slipped from her bed and, trying not to jostle her arm, she headed in search of Elizabeth. Down the hall, she cracked open the door and peeked inside to find her sitting up in bed, shoulders sagging, eyes downcast, her fingers plucking an imaginary string from the coverlet.

Elizabeth glanced up. "Lilyan." She held out her arms, and a broad smile chased the gloom from her face.

Lilyan hurried across the room, and they clung together, silently drawing comfort from each other.

When they pulled away, Elizabeth grimaced at the bandage covering most of Lilyan's arm. "Does it hurt much?"

"It does, rather. But it will get better in time." Lilyan perused the dark circles under her friend's eyes and the pallor of her cheeks.

"And you? How are you feeling?"

"Much better." Elizabeth patted the bed. "Come. Tell me all about it."

Lilyan propped herself up beside Elizabeth and, trying to ignore the throbbing in her arm, she began a moment-by-moment account of her adventure, spurred on by Elizabeth's breathless comments and incessant questions. After talking for what seemed like hours, Lilyan stifled a yawn and glanced over at Elizabeth, who was struggling to keep her eyes open. She nestled under the covers, but before they nodded off, Elizabeth clasped her fingers and whispered, "Merry Christmas."

And what a strange Christmas Lilyan discovered it to be. When she and Elizabeth awoke from their nap, they dressed and went downstairs to join Callum in the parlor. During the day, they greeted several people who stopped by to wish them merry and to deliver mince meat pies, tea cakes, and gingerbread cookies. Callum, who sat in the corner puffing on a clay pipe, in his own direct way made sure the guests did not tarry. Mrs. Snead and Gerald brought a tureen of ragout and stayed long enough to satisfy her concerns about her son. How did he look? What did he say? How did he behave? Had he been mistreated?

Captain McKenzie, dashing in his dress uniform and with a bandage tied around his head, came to offer his gratitude. When Lilyan studied his somber hazel eyes, dramatically ringed by black and blue circles, she wondered if he suspected her part in the conspiracy. If he did, he departed after a brief visit without giving her any indication of his suppositions.

Finally in the late evening after laying out a supper, Mrs. Cheek left Lilyan, Elizabeth, and Callum to enjoy the blessed, comforting silence that enveloped the house. Their conversations during dinner were subdued, and after they finished the meal, they returned to the parlor. When Callum opened the Bible and began reading aloud Luke's account of the birth of Christ, Lilyan realized that it was the first time in her life she had not attended church on Christmas Day.

Not that they would have been able to attend services anyway. Her beloved Presbyterian church had closed its doors when the British government threatened to replace the pastor with one of its own. She wondered where the members of the Lutheran church on

Archdale Street and the Congregationalist church next door were meeting. The British had turned both of those churches into stables for their horses. And the pristine Meeting House was now a store-house for army supplies.

With her arm encased in a sling, Lilyan stood and leaned against the window casing, scanning the stars that had punched their way through the black velvet sky. She studied the houses lining the street, many with candles or lanterns glowing cheerfully in every window, a familiar signal of good news.

"To think. Families like ours are meeting in their homes all over the city tonight. Holding their own services. Praising God for the wonderful gift of His Son." Lilyan's throat closed with emotion.

Elizabeth came and stood beside her and draped her arm around her waist. "What a joy to be a part of it. To share in this beautiful kindred spirit of praise."

Lilyan contemplated the sky again. *Nicholas, are you somewhere in the swamps? Cold? Hungry? I pray not. I pray that you are warm and safe, looking up at the same stars, sharing the same spirit of praise. Merry Christmas, my darling.*

January 8, 1781
My Dear Mistress Cameron,

It is my particular Pleasure to offer you an Invitation for a Commission to paint a Countryside Mural in my dining room at Violet Plantation. I ask that you give all Pos'ble attention to this Request. I shall endeavor to await patiently for your response.

With Sentiments of Esteem,
Felicity Melborne

Chapter Sixteen

LILYAN SPENT THE NEXT three weeks in her house avoiding well-wishers and curiosity seekers. Dr. Cheek came often to check the progress of her wound, which was healing well, although the sling he insisted she wear chafed her neck.

The authorities held a perfunctory inquisition into the escape from the *Brixham*. According to the Police Board's official report, "The conspirators took scurrilous advantage of a Christian act of mercy by the generous Loyalist ladies of Charlestown to conduct a treasonous act against the King." They never called on Lilyan as a witness. To be spared from answering direct questions about the escape was a great relief, one she knew she owed to Mrs. Cheek and her friends and to Captain McKenzie.

When she finally ventured to her shop, she discovered a pile of calling cards and letters from people wanting to commission her. She found it difficult to talk about "her adventure," as some patrons insisted on calling it, and relied on Callum to cut their visits short.

One afternoon, Callum, who had trudged out to purchase tobacco, came running back and threw open the door, almost dislodging the bell that clattered overhead.

He planted himself in the entrance and yelled, "Tarleton's been beat! We gave him a thrashing."

Lilyan jumped up from the table where she had been sketching, knocking over the cup that held her brushes and scattering them across the floor. Gerald ran around from behind the counter.

"How? When?" Lilyan clasped the locket at her throat.

Callum slammed the door and flopped into a chair by the stove. "A couple a days ago. In the backcountry near the mountains. At the cow pens, the grazing place near the Broad River."

He threw his tobacco pouch on the table. "Tarleton had over eleven hundred men. Crack troops they were. Dragoons. Fusiliers. Highlanders. Our General Morgan had a thousand troops. Continentals, militia—"

"Militia?" Panic shot through Lilyan's body.

Callum studied her a moment. "None of Marion's men, lass."

Lilyan blew out the breath she had been holding in.

"But there were some Overmountain Men. Same ones who gave the Brits hell at Kings Mountain." He puffed up with pride.

Callum rubbed his hands together in glee. "*Butcher* Tarleton thought he had Morgan trapped with his back against the Broad River, but after a battle that lasted an hour, he had to run crying back to Cornwallis with less than a third of his men left. Could be the turning point for us."

Lilyan returned to the table and raked her locket back and forth across its chain. "Does this means there is an end in sight?"

Callum shook his head. "It's the best news we've had in a coon's age, lassie, but I wouldna gut the fish till ye hook them."

The bell jingled once again as Mrs. Snead entered and closed the door behind her.

"Brrr. It's miserable out there." She headed for the stove, pulled off her gloves, and spread her fingers toward the fire.

Gerald stood beside his mother. "Ma? What are you doing here?"

Mrs. Snead pinched her son's cheeks. "Can't a mama come see her boy?"

"Sure. But—"

"Well, in truth, I came to see Mistress Cameron." Her eyes darted from Callum to Lilyan. "About a chamomile."

Lilyan shot up from the chair. "I see. Would you like to join me in the back?"

"Hold on." Callum leaned forward. "I may be getting old, but I ain't a *gleòman*. Something's afoot here."

Of course, he is right on both counts—he is far from stupid, and something is definitely afoot.

Mrs. Snead sighed, crossed her arms, and rested them on her stomach. "I've come to ask Mistress Cameron's help. But we ought to go out back as you said." She nodded toward the front door. "Gerald, it's best you stay out here. Give us a warning if someone comes."

Gerald plopped back into the chair. "Yes, ma'am," he mumbled.

In the storeroom, Lilyan and Mrs. Snead sat on chairs beside the gesso wall, while Callum leaned back against the doorjamb.

"I'll get right to it," said Mrs. Snead. "Even though this news about Tarleton was good to hear, we need much more information than we're getting. About the British plans and especially about Cornwallis."

"How can I help?" Excitement curled in Lilyan's chest.

Callum harrumphed. "I think you've helped enough, lass."

"Compared to some, I've done very little, Callum." She paused. "I promised Nicholas when I agreed to work for the Patriots that I was prepared to do anything. I have not changed my mind."

"Stubborn. Like your da. Just so long as you know that 'whither thou goest.'" He slouched back against the wall and crossed one arm over the other.

"We may have need of you for this mission, anyway, you old curmudgeon." Mrs. Snead's smile softened the edge of her words. "Now, let me get on with it."

Nose in the air, she returned her attention to Lilyan. "According to an informant, there's a woman, Mrs. Felicity Melborne—her husband's a captain serving under Cornwallis—who wants to commission you to paint a mural. We want you to accept."

Lilyan groaned. "We've met, and I don't think she would want me."

"How so?" asked Mrs. Snead.

"I was rude to her when she came to my shop a couple of months ago."

"Well, I have it on very good authority that she is chomping at the bit to have the 'Heroine of the *Brixham*' come to her plantation.

107

She may have already sent you an invitation."

"There *was* a pile of letters waiting for me." Lilyan thought a moment.

"Gerald," she called out, "bring me the letters on my desk. If you would, please."

A moment later, Gerald hurried through the doorway and handed her a sheaf of papers. "These the ones you mean, miss?"

Lilyan placed the bundle in her lap. "Exactly. Thank you."

When Gerald left, Lilyan sorted through the stack. "Here it is."

She ran her finger under the wax seal, opened the folds of the paper, and scanned the embellished handwriting, as flamboyant as its author.

"You're right. She has asked me to come to her plantation."

Mrs. Snead nodded. "She's sprucing up the place—new furniture, draperies, paint. All in preparation for a grand ball. We think Cornwallis himself is invited. But not only that, it seems that Mrs. Melborne is quite the hostess. Her weekend parties have become the talk of society. High-ranking British officers come and go. So you see, we need your eyes and ears there."

Lilyan gripped the letter in her fist. "I can do that. Yes, I absolutely can. I will respond to Mrs. Melborne right away."

By MID-FEBRUARY, after she received Mrs. Melborne's effervescent response to the acceptance of her commission, the items on Lilyan's list multiplied until they filled a covered freight wagon— barrels of chalk, marble dust, rabbit-skin glue and white pigment to make the gesso, jars of pigment, yards of thin muslin sheeting, boxes of brushes, kegs of linseed oil, as well as personal items and clothing for several weeks for Lilyan, Elizabeth, Callum, and Gerald.

Early on, Callum had petitioned for and received a license for the wagon and a permit to leave the city. Finding horses to draw the wagon proved more difficult and costly. As it turned out, he had to settle for four horses instead of eight.

Finally, on a cold, dreary February morning, they set out on their journey. Lilyan and Elizabeth sat on the wagon seat next to Callum, with a quilt spread across their laps. Gerald saddled and mounted the horse on the left closest to the wagon, prepared to take over the reins when necessary.

According to the rough map Callum had drawn for them, they would voyage twelve miles up the east coast of the city to a ferry that would take them across the Cooper River at its narrowest point. From there, they would travel another twelve miles south to Violet Plantation, situated on Haddrell's Point, an inlet on the northeast side of Charlestown Harbor.

They moved slowly at first, maneuvering their way against the flow of travelers and merchants headed toward the market in the center of the city. They were obliged to stop at several guard stations and show their papers, so it took an hour to cover three miles. Ordinarily, Callum would have stopped to rest the horses, but they had arrived at the seedy part of town and he wanted to hurry her past it. Lilyan smiled at the memory of how she had teased Callum about the women "selling their wares."

As they journeyed north, towering magnolias and majestic oaks gave way to the wetlands, covered in wavering peninsulas of dense bulrushes and cattails that had exploded their spikes into feathery gray fronds. Slate blue herons and snow-white egrets stalked their prey amidst the thick magenta salt-marsh grasses. Fat brown pelicans swooped from their rookeries, plunged into the brackish water, and flew away with fish flapping inside their rubbery, drooping gullets. Not many people ventured into the tidal marshes, but Lilyan did spot several slaves wading knee-deep in the coal black water filling their tightly woven grass baskets with clams and oysters, while others stood watch for alligators.

Farther north, the road took them away from the water into thick patches of palmettos, live oaks, and wax myrtles and then dumped them onto the sand- and clay-covered banks of the river. There they lined up behind other wagons and horsemen waiting to cross to the other side.

Lilyan had never been on a ferry before, and when Callum guided the horses and wagon onto the flatboat, her senses burst alive with anticipation. Like an unquenchable sponge, she soaked in the sights, sounds, and smells. She stared, fascinated by green-black eddies that spun in the roiling water and swirled against slimy moss-covered boulders lined along the riverbanks.

As the raft ventured into the deepest part of the water, straining against the current, pulling taut the ropes that stretched from shore to shore, Lilyan looked at Elizabeth's brown eyes, bright with exhilaration, and grinned. When they finally rumbled off the flatboat and up the embankment, she felt a tinge of disappointment that the excursion had ended so soon.

They traveled about two more miles when Callum looked up at the sky and reined in the horses.

"Time for a break. I'm hungry enough to eat a pound of raw haggis," he bellowed.

As soon as Lilyan's feet touched the ground, her muscles and joints let her know how rugged the journey had been. She kneaded the small of her back and jogged back and forth to work out the kinks in her spine. Callum and Gerald watered and fed the horses while she and Elizabeth spread a blanket underneath a palmetto tree and laid out their dinner of ham, cornbread, cheese, and cider.

When they finished eating, Lilyan leaned back against a tree, studied the bleak pewter-colored sky, and wondered about what lay ahead. In the weeks spent preparing for this journey, she had spoken several times to Mrs. Snead and her husband about how she would pass along any intelligence she came across. They had decided she would tell Gerald, and he would ride to a nearby farm owned by the DeKruif family. They had a daughter named Lisa, and a fabricated relationship with her would serve as Gerald's cover for frequent visits to their home. Regarding the information Lilyan gathered, she was warned not to consider anything as too insignificant. Even the smallest tidbit could prove vital.

"You are very quiet," said Elizabeth, who had stretched out beside her.

"Just woolgathering."

"Are you worried?"

"Honestly? Yes. But not for myself. What if I pass along false information that gets someone killed? What if I miss something that could save someone's life?"

"It is up to all of us—all of us—to do this thing. And as Mrs. Snead said, there are many, many others working together. Gathering information, sorting through it, and acting upon it." She patted Lilyan's hand. "We will do our best. No one can ask any more than that."

"I suspect you're right." Lilyan took an envelope from her pelisse pocket, opened it, and withdrew several sheets of paper.

"What is that?" asked Elizabeth.

"It's a letter I'm writing to Nicholas. I started working on it two weeks ago."

"But how will you mail it? You have no idea where he is."

Lilyan brushed her fingertips across Nicholas' name. "I know. But writing it comforts me. Telling him about the things that have happened. Letting him know how much I miss him. It makes me feel close to him."

"Time to stop this *draoluin*, ladies," Callum yelled as he stepped up into the wagon. "Let's be on our way. We've got four more hours of traveling ahead of us."

Elizabeth gathered the cups and napkins and packed them into a sack. Lilyan stuffed her letter back in her pocket and shook the sand from the blanket. They both folded it, and then Lilyan draped it over her arm. "Callum is loving this, you know. Finding our way. Ordering everyone about."

Elizabeth winked. "Especially ordering everyone about."

They giggled like two schoolgirls as they settled themselves on the seat next to Callum, who mumbled under his breath and slapped the reins against the horses.

About an hour later, Lilyan looked at the trail and spotted a Negro boy curled into a ball next to one of two tall, blue granite pillars that served as the entrance to a plantation. As the wagon drew closer to him, the boy leaped to his feet and brushed the sand from his blue satin trousers and matching waistcoat. He approached them and presented them with a formal bow. Callum slowed but did not stop, and the boy hopped alongside, the queue of his white wig bouncing with each step.

"Good day to you fine ladies and gentlemens." He paused. "Weary travelers. The Commodore Robert and Lady Lynne Westra humbly … ah … most humbly offers you the honor of their hospitalities." He looked up at the sky, deep in thought, and then touched his fingers as if ticking off a list. "If you care to break your journey." His eyes lit and he grinned, showing a mouthful of teeth.

Lilyan reached under the seat and pulled out a brown paper parcel. "Please tell Commodore and Lady Westra that we thank them for their gracious invitation, but we are close to our destination and do not have time to stop today." She unwrapped the paper, removed a couple of pralines, and stretched her arm out as far as she could. "Here, these are for you."

111

He jumped up and took them from her hand. When he realized what they were, he let out a loud whoop. "Thank you most kindly, ma'am."

Lilyan laughed and waved and then licked her fingers, savoring the sweet smoky taste of molasses and pecans.

By the time they reached the entrance of Violet Plantation, the sun had set, and their relief was palpable. Lilyan felt bone weary, Callum would not stop grumbling, and even the ever-pleasant Elizabeth seemed wilted. The gate boy greeted them with a lantern and a bow and then ran ahead to announce their arrival to his mistress. Along the way he lit pole lamps, illuminating the corridor of live oaks leading to the plantation house. The trees intertwined their branches forming a canopy overhead. Low-hanging swaths of moss swayed in the breeze like rows of ghostly shawls on a wash line.

Callum stopped the wagon at the bottom of the dozen or more steps leading up to the entrance of the mansion, where the mistress of the house stood flanked by four slaves. The three women wore dresses of fine gray linen with white frilly lace kerchiefs. The male, who regarded her with lively, intelligent eyes, stood tall in a black silk justaucorps.

Had they interrupted a party? Or did their hostess greet all her guests with such pretention?

Lilyan and Elizabeth climbed from the wagon and approached Mrs. Melborne. Even in the lamplight Lilyan could tell that their hostess was wearing one of the most costly dresses she had ever seen. Morning glories embroidered in crewel decorated the side panels of her skirt, which were pulled back to reveal a thick, quilted petticoat embroidered to match the overskirt. Venetian lace adorned the neckline of her chemise and cascaded from the ends of her sleeves down her forearms.

"Welcome to Violet Plantation." Mrs. Melborne presented a curtsy.

The courtesy of a bow from the lady of the house to the lowly artisan. What playacting is this?

"We are happy to be here." Lilyan bowed stiffly in return.

"Poseidon," Mrs. Melborne addressed the tall Negro beside her, "show Mistress Cameron's man and her help the way to the outbuildings and see they get some supper before they retire."

"Yes'm." The gangly man took the reins of the lead horse.

The autocratic woman's dismissal of Lilyan's dear friends as *her man* and *her help* stirred a hornet's nest of emotions. *I have not been here two minutes and I already want to choke the woman.*

Spies should have more self-control, she warned herself.

She looked at Callum and then Gerald. "Good night, gentlemen. God bless you both. I hope you sleep well."

Gerald, his eyes dull from fatigue, nodded.

"Good night, lassie," said Callum gruffly before allowing Poseidon to guide them around to the back of the house.

"Hannah," Mrs. Melborne addressed one of the girls, "go with Poseidon and then bring back the ladies' bags."

She took Lilyan's arm. "I cannot wait to hear of your exciting adventure. It is quite the coup for me, you realize, to be the first to invite the 'heroine of Charlestown' to my home," she whispered like a fellow conspirator as they climbed the steps and entered the foyer. "And how I would love to hear the latest tidbits of news from town. But we have guests coming tomorrow, so I will just have to make myself wait to hear everything." She giggled and snorted. "Like making oneself wait to eat the last bonbon in the box."

As they ascended the stairs, Lilyan glanced over her shoulder at Elizabeth, who had clamped her lips together. It took every ounce of her willpower not to roll her eyes.

With the two servant girls' lanterns lighting their way, Mrs. Melborne led them toward the end of the west wing of the house.

"You and your companion will sleep here." She opened a door to a chamber dwarfed by a wardrobe and a bed that left just enough floor space between it and the walls for the occupants to edge onto the mattress. The spread and curtains were decorated with clusters of purple violets, and two chairs flanked a cheerful, though tiny, fireplace at the foot of the bed. The modest accommodations reminded Lilyan that, even though her hostess touted her as the Heroine of *Brixham*, she wanted to affirm her guest's place as a hired merchant.

"Cook has prepared a light supper for you. Someone will bring it to your room shortly." Mrs. Melborne took a lantern from one of the girls, placed it on the nightstand, and then pointed to a brass bell. "Ring this if you require assistance. I bid you adieu until tomorrow."

When the door closed, Lilyan threw her pelisse onto a chair and spread her fingers close to the fire. "Well, I am sorry, Elizabeth, but it seems you have been relegated to companion to the merchant girl."

Elizabeth hung their coats on a hook by the door. "I do not mind at all. Especially if it means that I take my meals with Callum and Gerald and not with that insufferable woman."

"She *is* quite the snob." Lilyan frowned. "This may prove more difficult than I imagined."

Later, after a meal of cold sliced meat and scones, they threw logs on the fire, donned their nightdresses, and climbed into bed.

Lilyan stretched her arms overhead and yawned. "I'm so exhausted I'll probably fall asleep before my head touches the pillow."

That announcement proved wrong as two hours later Lilyan rolled over for what seemed the hundredth time as question after question surfaced in her mind, each snatching her from the brink of slumber.

Who are the guests coming tomorrow? Will I recognize useful information when I hear it? For all her seemingly shallow character, Mrs. Melborne is no one's fool. Is she as clever as she is vicious?

What a cat and mouse game this will be.

Lilyan rose up on her elbow as she recalled the old saying, "A cat in gloves catches no mice."

I must sharpen my wits. But who will be the cat, and who will be the mouse?

Frustrated, she sat up and looked at Elizabeth, envying her restful sleep. She stepped from the bed, took a dress from the wardrobe, and pulled it over her gown. She slid on her shoes, lit the lantern with a punk stick, and slipped out of the room.

The floor creaked on her way down the staircase, and she hunched her shoulders, praying she would not be discovered.

Indigo—the color of kings ... the devil's dye

Chapter Seventeen

LILYAN CREPT THROUGH THE darkened hallways of Violet Plantation. Though eagerness to begin the mural might be a reasonable excuse for roaming the house in the dead of night, she suspected Mrs. Melborne would not approve of her nocturnal explorations. Once downstairs, she peeked into several doorways before she found the dining room, which held an imposing mahogany table and sixteen chairs. Pine paneling covered two walls, and a fireplace dominated the center of another.

She tiptoed to the windows that spanned the length of the remaining wall. A full moon illumined an entrancing prospect of manicured gardens with a series of steps and plateaus stretching to the river. Moonlight draped a gossamer veil over statues of Greek gods and goddesses that seemed poised on the brink of life.

She visualized Nicholas and herself strolling hand in hand along the manicured rows of tea olives. The breeze would sweep up from the riverbank, and they would pause for Nicholas to push a stray tendril of hair from her neck and kiss the skin where the curl had rested. That delicious thought sent a quiver through her body.

Will there be moonlight walks for us?

Turning away from those thoughts, she spun around and studied the wall she assumed would hold the mural. She tapped her knuckles lightly along the paneling and deemed it sturdy enough to support the thick layer of gesso that would be her canvas. She was about to pass the fireplace when a shadow caught her eye. She stepped closer to the wall and lifted the lantern. To the right of the mantle, a small square of pine jutted out so slightly from the other slats of wood that most people would not even notice. Lilyan did because she had seen that exact configuration long ago.

During her *wonder time*, she and her father had visited a plantation on the Ashley River side of Charlestown. The lady of that house had told Lilyan how, having lost her family in the French and Indian War, she had grown up hearing the horror stories of families trapped inside their homes and burned alive by marauding Indians. The woman swore she would never allow that to happen to her and her family and made her husband design an escape route into the building plans—accessed by a panel beside the fireplace. Lilyan vividly recalled every detail of her first entry into the passageway, as well as the fear and excitement that shook her young body from head to toe.

With a similar quiver of excitement, she pressed the piece of wood in and to the right. After several clicking sounds and a scraping noise so loud she feared it would wake the household, the panel slid open. Her heart hammered as she stepped forward and found herself on a platform large enough for one person. She held out the lantern, exposing a handful of steps that sloped and then made a hard right turn. A punched tin lantern, a flint box, a pair of gloves, and an oil can, all covered in thick cobwebs, hung from hooks in the brick wall. The air smelled stale, forcing Lilyan to take shallow, guarded breaths.

Ugh. No one has been here in a while. Probably not since the British took over the plantation.

Grimacing, she quickly swiped the dust and spider webs from the can and dribbled some of the oil on the exposed pulley system. She waited a few moments before moving the lever and closing the panel, which made considerably less noise than before. Eager to explore, she cautiously made her way down the steps and into a tunnel wide enough for one person and tall enough for her to walk without stooping. She had crept along about fifty feet through a thick layer of powdery dust when the walls widened and changed from brick to stone. The air grew distinctly cooler, and Lilyan felt a breeze play against her skin. After another thirty feet, she found herself in a cave with crates and barrels stacked up against a wall. Her skirt brushed against a wooden box, and a mouse hopped past. She squealed, then pressed a hand against her mouth so she wouldn't shriek again. The lantern light revealed another narrow passageway on the opposite side of the cave and she hurried to explore. The temperature dropped a few more degrees, and gusts of cold air lifted the hem of her dress. She thought she heard running water and stopped to listen. Spotting a dim light ahead, she drew the wick down on the lantern, and set it on the ground. She inched up a set of steps to find herself on the bank of the river with currents so swift, they danced in the moonlight. A thick hammock of live oaks and a thicket of thorny vines engulfed the area; a perfect camouflage for the hidden passage.

Muffled voices echoed across the water, and like a thief on the run, Lilyan fled back inside, grabbed the lantern, and sprinted back through the passage. She did not stop until she reached the platform. There she pressed her cheek against the door and strained to listen over her pulse that thundered in her ears. She kicked her shoes together to loosen the dust and brushed the cobwebs from her skirt before pulling the lever. This time the panel made a swishing sound as it slid to the side to let her out, and again when she closed it after her. She arched her back against the sensation of the hairs tingling across the nape of her neck.

Someone else was in the room.

Thou shalt not kill. Exodus 20:13

Chapter Eighteen

𝒜 TALL FIGURE SLID OUT from the shadows a few feet away. It was Poseidon, the slave she had seen when they arrived. Feeling like a trapped animal, she danced from one foot to the other, trying to decide whether to run or stand her ground.

Poseidon lifted his hand. "Not to worry, missy. I won't tell nobody where you been." He spoke the words slowly, calmly.

Relieved, Lilyan drooped her shoulders.

"I done heard your friends—the old man and the boy—talkin'. From what I can figure, you all is here to help make it so these people what took everything is gonna have to leave and let my mistress come back home."

"I do hope that will happen someday, Poseidon. We're going to try."

"The way I see it, you gonna needs your rest. So, it's best you go on back to bed now." He stepped close, took a rag from his pocket, and wiped the floor behind Lilyan. "Better give me your shoes, ma'am. Looks like they got mighty dirty down there. I'll have them ready for you fore you get up tomorrah. Leave your frock by the door, and I'll gets Hannah to come by. She'll wash it up as clean as new. And she won't tell nobody either. She's a good girl."

Lilyan scrutinized her dress. Water had soaked into the hem, and the skirt was spattered with mud and streaked with cobwebs. She sat in a chair, pulled off her shoes, and handed them to the soft-spoken man whose sable brown eyes revealed a gentle spirit. "God bless you, Poseidon. I will hold you in my prayers." She patted the gnarled, scarred knuckles of his leathery brown hand.

His face lit. "Thank you, miss. Knew you was a Christian the first time I laid eyes on you. Just got that way about you. It's an honor to serve you, ma'am." He bowed and left the room as quietly as he came.

Lilyan crept back upstairs, shrugged out of her dress, draped it over the door handle, and then crawled into bed.

What other discoveries await me tomorrow?

LILYAN WOKE BEFORE SUNRISE. Trying not to wake Elizabeth, she slid from the bed, tiptoed around the room gathering her clothes, and dressed as quickly as possible. On her way out, she realized that someone had removed her soiled dress and had set her cleaned shoes just inside the door. She grabbed them, stepped into the hallway, and pressed one hand against the door as she closed it without making a sound. She donned the shoes and hurried downstairs to the breakfast room, where Hannah informed her that she would dine alone, as the mistress of the house rarely rose before noon.

Well, no information gathering this morning.

After breakfast, Lilyan strolled outside and met Gerald at the wagon behind the main house. He had suspended an iron pot over a low-burning fire and was warming a mixture of rabbit-skin glue and water. Nearby, a large bucket held chalk, marble dust, and white pigment. Once the glue reached the right temperature, he poured it slowly into the dry ingredients and stirred it into a smooth paste.

Lilyan dipped a wooden spatula into the gesso. "Perfect," she announced. "No bubbles. Excellent consistency and color. And just the right amount. A master plasterer could not have done better."

Gerald blushed at such high praise. "I nailed the first layer of muslin to the paneling this morning, so I'll carry this over and get started."

He grabbed the bucket handle, but Poseidon hurried toward him and took it away. "I'll do that, young massah. You jess tells me

119

where you wants it."

"Well, thank you kindly. I'm happy for the help. Let me get my tools."

Poseidon waited patiently while Gerald gathered the equipment he needed, and they left for the house.

Lilyan climbed into the wagon and rambled through boxes until she found her brushes, a jar of brown pigment, and large sheets of sketching paper. Once she and Mrs. Melborne decided on the final details of the design, she would sketch it on the panels of paper while waiting for the gesso to dry. That would take about three days; valuable days she could make use of trying to engage her hostess in conversation.

Once the gesso dried, she and Gerald would attach the templates to the wall and punch tiny holes along the lines of the drawing. Then they would wash sinopia paint across the holes, creating a faint outline that would serve as a guide to assure the correct perspective for the mural.

Lilyan returned to the house, and in the dining room, while Gerald spread a thin layer of gesso across the wall, she made notes as Mrs. Melborne selected the predominant colors she preferred.

"This is going to be splendid, I can tell. I cannot wait for you to begin," Mrs. Melborne gushed as she stood to leave.

When she reached the doorway, she wheeled around. "Oh. Miss Cameron, it would please me if you would join us for supper tonight. I am expecting two naval officers, so there will be four of us. Since it is such a small party, and you have begun work in here, we will dine in the breakfast room."

"I would be delighted." Lilyan rose and curtsied, plastering a gracious smile on her face.

"See you at seven, then." Mrs. Melborne nodded regally before withdrawing.

"That should give me plenty of time to practice smiling," Lilyan muttered.

Gerald snorted.

"Laugh if you will, sir. But I do not think this is going to be an easy task."

Gerald stopped working. "I would help you in any way I can, miss."

"I know I can count on you." She approached him and regarded his earnest expression. "There is one thing I ask."

"Ma'am?"

"Pray for me? For wisdom and discernment." She smiled. "And most of all, for patience."

"That I will do. And gladly."

Later that afternoon, Lilyan and Elizabeth sat by the fire in their bedroom taking tea and whispering about ways to pry information from Mrs. Melborne. Lilyan took particular delight in using the word pry, envisioning a dentist pulling a tooth from the woman's mouth. She shared that thought with Elizabeth, and they were laughing when a furtive knocking at the door disturbed them.

"Come in," Elizabeth said, raising a quizzical brow at Lilyan.

The servant girl, Hannah, dashed in and made a hasty curtsy. "Mrs. Melborne sent me to invite Miss Elizabeth to dine tonight." She sucked in several breaths. "A very important visitor has just arrived, and the missus can't have an uneven number at table."

Elizabeth nodded. "Thank you, Hannah. Tell Mrs. Melborne I accept her gracious invitation."

When the girl left, Elizabeth shot a look at Lilyan. "I don't think we were intended to hear the last of that message. Seems I am needed to avoid a gooseberry."

Lilyan twisted the locket at her neck. "Although I am thrilled you'll be there tonight, I cannot imagine Mrs. Melborne standing on such ceremony. I wonder what she is about."

They entered the breakfast room that evening to find Captain Bradenton leaning against the mantel.

Barely quashing her keen dismay, Lilyan glanced at Elizabeth, who had hesitated on the threshold. She looped her arm through her friend's, drumming up her courage as they stepped forward.

The moment Bradenton spotted them, he sidled toward them and made a bow so low, his lace handkerchief almost swept the floor.

He took Elizabeth's arm in his. "Imagine my delight when I discovered that you—the two of you—were here at Violet Plantation. Happily, our hostess needed no persuasion to invite you to join us. Especially when I made her aware that we are old acquaintances." He led Elizabeth to the table, seated her, and then slinked into the chair beside her.

Elizabeth kept her eyes lowered, but the set look on her face and the pulse beating rapidly at the base of her neck told Lilyan of her acute discomfort.

The way he lurks over her. And nobleman or not, the man is a boor, seating himself before his hostess. Lilyan's blood simmered at his high-handed breech of etiquette.

To her credit, Mrs. Melborne maintained a pleasant expression as she made the formal introductions. The two other gentlemen, Ensign Miller and Ensign Huntington, both handsome in their crisp, tailored uniforms, made their bows.

When Huntington stepped forward and offered his arm to Lilyan, she recognized him as one of the officers she and Elizabeth had spoken to at British Headquarters in Charlestown.

"John Richard Huntington at your service, ma'am. But I believe we have already met," Huntington greeted pleasantly.

He winked and gave Lilyan such a devilish grin, she could not resist smiling up at him over her shoulder as he helped her into her chair. *Will the presence of such a fine gentleman shame Bradenton into behaving less boorishly?* Somehow Lilyan thought not.

They sat at a round table with Miller to Lilyan's right, and Huntington on her left. On Miller's right, Elizabeth, whose face remained unreadable, sat so rigidly Lilyan feared her back would snap.

During the first course, Mrs. Melborne pressed Lilyan to describe the incident aboard the *Brixham*. Lilyan obliged, offering as few details as possible.

"So, my dear," Bradenton said, carefully placing his knife and fork across the top of his plate. He propped his elbow on the table and rested his chin on his fist. "Are we to believe that your being on board the ship and the escape of the prisoners—one of whom was your brother, I might add—was simply a coincidence?"

Lilyan looked him square in the eye. "That was the official finding of the Board of Police inquiry."

"It does make one wonder, though. Here"—he paused, turning his palm upward—"we have the flowers of British society, coming together to feed and clothe sworn enemies of the Crown—despite the fact that those very men had murdered soldiers of the King's army. And as the representative of those noble ladies, you just happen to be caught up in a vile rebel mission to free the prisoners."

"And here,"—he lifted his other palm upward, imitating a

scale—"we have a rebel sympathizer who takes part in a plan that provides my enemies access to the ship."

He leaned forward and peered at Lilyan. "So the question is, Mistress Cameron, are you a loyal subject of the King who was innocently taking part in an act of mercy, or are you in league with the colonials?"

Lilyan's mouth went dry. Trying to remain nonchalant, she reached for her water glass, took a sip, and licked her bottom lip.

Mrs. Melborne tittered nervously. "But my dear captain. Miss Cameron risked her life to save one of our officers."

"Yes, I do believe I heard such an account." He raised a quizzical brow. "May we see this famous wound?"

"I say," Ensign Huntington protested.

Lilyan smiled at the young officer. "Do not trouble yourself. It is of no consequence, I assure you."

She pulled up the lace on her sleeve and rolled up the cuff, exposing the five-inch scar that was still puckered and red around the edges. The others, except for Elizabeth, leaned forward and stared. Ensign Huntington looked at Lilyan and then glanced away. Mrs. Melborne grabbed her fan and fluttered it in front of her face.

"Tsk, tsk." Bradenton's eyes glittered. "What a pity to mar such a lovely bit of flesh."

Out of the corner of her eye, Lilyan caught Elizabeth staring at Bradenton's hand and saw her hesitate before she placed her hand on his, immediately drawing his attention.

"May we speak of something else?" Elizabeth pleaded.

Bradenton slumped back in his chair, took Elizabeth's hand, and pressed a lingering kiss on it. "Whatever you say, my lovely. Myself, I would like to know more about *you*. You are Cherokee, are you not?"

Elizabeth pulled her hand away and, when she slid her hand into her lap, Lilyan wondered if she was scrubbing it with her napkin.

Elizabeth glanced around the table. "But there are so many more interesting things to talk about."

But no matter what the topic, Bradenton managed to steer their conversation toward the Cherokee, and what a handsome people they were; toward Elizabeth and her upbringing and her appearance.

"Mrs. Melborne, your husband fights with Cornwallis, does

he not?" Lilyan asked, trying to change the tack of the conversation. "You must be anxious, not knowing where he is or how he is faring."

Mrs. Melborne smirked. "Quite the contrary. My dear husband remains in constant communication with me. His legions are traveling, as we speak, to join with General Gates in North Carolina. The last letter I received, they were at a place called Cowan's Ford."

Lilyan tucked away this piece of information, which she would pass along as soon as possible in case it proved valuable. She quelled her excitement and, in an effort to seem more casual than she felt, she traced her finger along the stem of her wine glass before taking a sip.

As the evening progressed, Bradenton inched his chair closer to Elizabeth and further and further away from his hostess, straining even her forbearance. His constant leering and his insipid comments made Lilyan yearn for a poleax with which to silence him. His behavior seemed to wear on even Huntington's congenial personality.

With extreme difficulty, Lilyan held her tongue, but only for the sake of the mission. If she expressed her disgust, she and her companions might find themselves tossed out on their ears. She assumed the same realization must be holding Elizabeth in check. As for the two officers, she could only surmise that they feared Bradenton's wrath more than they desired to come to the aid of his female victim. In Lilyan's eyes, it was left up to their hostess, but even that haughty woman seemed to have qualms about reproaching this particular guest.

Who is this man that he can pin us down like so many bugs on a slab of specimen wax? He is disgusting. Is his family so powerful that he can behave any way he chooses?

Finally at the end of the meal, Elizabeth scraped back her chair and pleaded a headache. Lilyan yammered something about having a pleasant evening and wanting to see to Elizabeth, and then shadowed her out the door. Neither spoke as they ascended the stairs, but the slamming of their bedroom door behind them let loose a floodgate of words Lilyan had never heard her friend speak before.

Elizabeth paced the room, intermittently muttering epithets and stamping her feet. "Insufferable. I should have stabbed him with my fork. How dare he treat me in such a fashion?"

She grabbed her cape from the foot of the bed and threw it over her shoulders. "Air. I need some air," she announced and yanked open the door.

At first, Lilyan decided she should allow her friend time to herself. Within minutes, she decided to go after her. She threw on her pelisse, but by the time she reached the top of the stairs, Elizabeth was already out of sight.

Lilyan ran into Gerald at the bottom of the steps as he loped from the dining room. His sleeves were rolled up, and flakes of gesso speckled across his arms, face, and hair.

"What's wrong with Elizabeth? Why'd she fly out of here like the house was on fire?" he asked.

"Someone was rude to her at dinner."

Gerald brandished the trowel. "Who would do such a thing?"

"Calm down. We can handle this."

"But—"

"I promise. We will call you if we need you." Lilyan mustered a reassuring smile, and then, remembering the message about Cornwallis, she motioned for him to step back inside the dining room. "Come. Let me see the progress you have made."

He looked at her with a puzzled expression, but obeyed her instructions.

Standing in front of the gesso wall, Lilyan leaned close to him and in a lowered voice told him the information she had gleaned about Cornwallis and his troops.

Gerald started to untie his apron. "Should I go right away?"

Lilyan chewed on her bottom lip. "No. It's late. And besides, you'll have an easier time finding the DeKruifs' if you go first thing in the morning."

"Whatever you say, miss," he said as she left the room.

Outside, Lilyan found a soldier stationed at the bottom of the stairs. She detected the scent of tobacco smoke as she searched the wooded lawn sporadically lit by sheet lightning that danced across the sky.

"Excuse me, sir," she addressed the soldier, who upon her approach fastened the top button of his coat.

He slapped his rifle against his shoulder and stood at attention. "Ma'am?"

"The woman who just left. Did you see the direction she took?"

"That way." He pointed to a path that meandered through the woods and to the river.

"Thank you." She hurried away, but when she reached the start of the stone walkway, thunder rumbled overhead, and she flinched.

"Not a good time to be out, miss," the soldier yelled. "You and your friend need to get back here fast. Storm's coming."

"I don't think she has gone far," she called back.

She strode the manicured lane until the beams from the lanterns on the gravel driveway grew dim. Using the lightning, she picked her way across the stones and through a patch of shoulder-high tea olives.

She heard a muffled cry. Then a scream.

"Elizabeth?" Dread slammed against her ribcage.

Another scream tore through the darkness, and she whirled around searching frantically until she caught a flicker of light in the distance. She raced across the lawn and in seconds neared a gazebo eerily illuminated by a lantern someone had placed on the seat. Still running, she watched in horror as Bradenton lunged spread-eagled on top of Elizabeth, who sprawled facedown on the floor. With one arm Bradenton had captured her hands behind her. With the other, he pushed her skirts up around her hips. Elizabeth kicked him with the heel of her shoe, and he shoved her arms toward her shoulder blades. She gasped in pain.

God help us! God help us! Lilyan's heart screamed.

She seized Bradenton's arm, but he twisted loose and shoved her away like so much refuse. She tumbled down the stairs and landed with a painful thud at the base of a small stone statue.

Elizabeth sobbed, and anger like white-hot lava shot through Lilyan's veins. She grabbed the statue, heaved it up over her head, ran headlong up the steps, and smashed Bradenton's head. She heard a loud *crack*, and a spray of thick, sticky blood spattered across her arms and face.

Bradenton slumped, and with strength Lilyan had not known she possessed, she grabbed his legs, twisted him off Elizabeth, and pushed him aside. She gathered her friend into her arms and rocked her as she would a child.

"Dear one," she choked, tears soaking her face. "Please. Please be unharmed."

Elizabeth's body shook. "I-I-I—" was all she could manage.

Rain pounded the tin roof of the gazebo, and thunder rumbled all around them.

Lilyan looked at Bradenton's still form and grimaced. A vision of him jumping back up and attacking them made the hairs stand up on her arms. "We must get out of here. Right away, before he awakes. Do you think you can walk?"

"Yes, I think so. But … my arm. I cannot move it."

They struggled to stand, and with Elizabeth leaning heavily against her, Lilyan reached over to pull her skirts down from her hips and spotted a gaping tear in her chemise.

Had he … ? Lilyan could not bring herself to think the words.

She pulled Elizabeth's cape close around her, lifted the hood onto her head, and helped her traverse the first step, and the next, trying not to jostle her injured arm.

Elizabeth moaned. "Oh, it hurts. I feel lightheaded."

"I know. I know. We'll fix it soon. I promise." Lilyan glanced around, not sure where to go.

She wrapped her arm around Elizabeth's waist, and they stepped onto the grass. Just as she began to doubt if they could make it, a figure materialized in front of them. Her heart slammed hard inside her chest, and she lost her breath.

"Don't be scared, missy. It's just me. Poseidon." He peered at the floor of the gazebo and back to the women. "Dear Lord almighty! What done happened here?" He stared at Bradenton again. "Never you mind. I think I know."

Poseidon loped up the steps and bent low. He remained silent for long moments, and then he let out a troubled sigh and shook his head.

Lilyan couldn't make herself look back at him. "Is he?" Her mouth went dry.

"Yessum. Gone to his just rewards, I suspect."

I killed someone. I killed someone. God help me, I killed someone. The words bludgeoned her conscience. Bile pushed up into the back of her throat, and panic threatened to overtake her. To avoid throwing up, she sucked in several deep breaths. Through lashes soaked with rain, she looked up at the sky, which had begun to clear as the moon peeped at them from behind a cloud.

"We have got to go. Now," she said, desperate for a way out. "But where?"

Poseidon sprinted the steps and swept Elizabeth into his arms. "I know. Follow me."

With a now gentle rain misting on her shoulders, Lilyan trudged along behind Poseidon as he headed toward the river in the steady gait of a man who knew the way well. She kept her eyes on the backs of his legs, not looking right or left, concentrating on the path, shoving back the memory of the horrible sin she had committed. They stopped once for him to shift Elizabeth in his arms. Soon they reached a boathouse, where they took a sharp turn upriver and into a dense patch of palmetto and live oak trees. They picked their way through a thicket with thorns that clawed at their clothes. Lilyan's evening shoes, soaked and tattered, provided no protection against the harsh terrain.

"Won't be much longer now," said Poseidon, panting.

They reached a clearing, and suddenly Lilyan knew where she was; the mouth of the escape tunnel. Poseidon carefully placed Elizabeth on the ground and leaned her against a boulder.

"You wait here. I'll be right back."

Lilyan eased onto the ground beside Elizabeth and clutched her hand.

"We are going to be safe. I know where we are now."

"Thank God," Elizabeth whispered.

"Yes, thank God," Lilyan echoed.

But will He forgive me, she wondered.

... Tyranny, like hell, is not easily conquered; yet we have this consolation with us, that the harder the conflict, the more glorious the triumph. What we obtain too cheap, we esteem too lightly: it is dearness only that gives everything its value.

Thomas Paine

Chapter Nineteen

POSEIDON RETURNED WITHIN MINUTES. He handed Lilyan a lantern and, despite Elizabeth's protests, he picked her up, and told Lilyan to lead the way. The holes of the pierced tin lantern cast just enough light to keep them from stumbling over rocks and debris as they descended the steps and wended through the tunnel and into the cave. When Poseidon laid Elizabeth on the ground, she flinched and drew her cape around her body.

"She's freezing, and I think her shoulder needs to be pushed back into place," said Lilyan. "What can we do?"

"Sorry, missy. Her shoulder's gonna have to wait." Poseidon pointed toward a stack of crates. "There's blankets in them boxes, and there's firewood just over there. You know how to keep a fire going?"

Lilyan nodded.

"Good. Cause I gots to hurry and go fetch Massah Gerald and the old man. Won't be long 'fore somebody goes looking for that man, and when they finds him, your friends oughtn't to be no-where in sight."

Lilyan turned away her face.

Poseidon clucked his tongue. "Don't you go beatin' yourself

up about that evil man. You done what you had to do to save this sweet lady here."

Poseidon pulled a lantern from one of the crates along with a handful of roughly hewn tallow candles and set them down beside Lilyan. He swung open the door of the tin lantern, lit one of the candles, and handed it to her. "You go on ahead now and make a fire. I'll be back as soon as I can."

Lilyan scooted toward logs someone had already arranged in the shape of a tepee and touched the glowing wick to the tinder at the base. Leaning down, she blew on the struggling flame, coaxing it to life. "Last time I saw Gerald, he was working in the dining room. Callum is probably asleep already."

Poseidon nodded, took his lantern, and soon disappeared through the tunnel.

She and Elizabeth huddled together shivering as much from the shock as the cold rain. She watched impatiently as flames licked their way up the logs, wishing with all her heart that they could be sitting at home in front of their fire, sewing or reading, or talking about ordinary events of the day. But life would never again be ordinary, would it? She wrestled with those disturbing thoughts until the fire eventually grew hot enough to make steam rise from their wet clothes.

"Elizabeth, dear—" Lilyan began, hesitant to start the conversation.

Elizabeth stared into the flames. "He did not shame me."

Relief flooded through Lilyan's body. "Do you wish to talk about it?"

"No."

They remained silent until Elizabeth turned her face toward Lilyan. "Do *you* wish to talk about it?"

"No."

"Good." She threaded her fingers through Lilyan's. "We need never speak of it again."

Though they may never talk about it, Lilyan's sadness went bone deep, and she knew the memory of the attack on her friend would haunt her for the rest of her life. How naïve she had been, how incredibly unaware of what she was saying, when she told Nicholas she was prepared to do anything. Kill or be killed. What a brash promise.

They both heard footsteps at the same time. Lilyan vaulted up and grabbed a stick, planting her feet in front of Elizabeth.

"Don't panic," Gerald called out from the passageway. "It's only me."

Elizabeth slumped forward, grimacing with pain. "Thank goodness you are safe."

"I might be safe, but I tell you I just got scared out of my wits. One minute I'm leveling out the gesso and the next an arm reaches out from a hole in the wall and jerks me to who knows where. I couldn't even yell. That scared I was."

He stared at Elizabeth. "What happened, miss? Why are we here?"

Lilyan sat next to Elizabeth, and Gerald joined them by the fire. She helped Elizabeth sit up, distressed to see the color drain from her face.

"I will tell all soon, but right now we have to help Elizabeth." She looked toward the passage to the house. "Where is Poseidon?"

"Said he was going to get some of your things and some food. If he could. And then he was going to fetch Callum."

"Gerald, have you ever helped set a shoulder socket back into place?"

"Lord, no, miss. Why do you ask?"

Lilyan gingerly untied Elizabeth's cloak and pushed it off her shoulders.

"Well, you're going to help me do it now." She pointed to Elizabeth's collarbone. "I will push with all my weight here. You press your foot against that stone underneath her arm, take her by the wrist and elbow, and pull with all your strength."

She knew she sounded confident, but was not about to tell either of them that she based that confidence on a nine-year-old memory of watching her father do the procedure.

"Uh-h-h," he stuttered.

"Come. She will be in great pain until we do this."

"As you say, ma'am."

Elizabeth's scream at the moment her arm snapped back into place made sweat pop up on Lilyan's brow, but she could tell right away that they had succeeded. Gerald flopped onto the ground and held his head in his hands.

Elizabeth pulled a deep breath through her nose. "Thank you."

"Gerald, see if you can find a way to open those crates. Poseidon said there would be blankets in them." She ripped a strip of cloth from her petticoat and fashioned a sling around Elizabeth's arm.

Gerald took his first good look around. "Right jolly place. You think pirates or smugglers made it?"

"Nothing so adventurous. Many families who lived through the Indian wars dug tunnels and caves like these to keep from being cornered in their houses."

About an hour later, Poseidon and Callum entered the cave by way of the river. Lilyan, never more thankful to see anyone in her life, ran headlong to her faithful protector. She felt safe clasped in his sinewy arms, with her face pressed against his buckskin jacket, breathing in the familiar smell of campfires and tobacco. Caressing her hair, he spoke in low gravelly tones that made his chest vibrate against her ear, telling her he knew what had happened and was sorry he had not been there.

Later, settled before the fire, they supped on cornbread, jam, and turkey that Poseidon had commandeered from the kitchens. When they finished eating, Callum motioned for Gerald to follow him. With sadness pulsing through her veins, Lilyan watched as, in barely suppressed whispers, Callum explained to her young apprentice about Bradenton. Callum returned to their circle and sat silently staring into the flames. Grimfaced, Gerald sought out a piece of wood and began to whittle. Poseidon handed Lilyan and Elizabeth their valises he had managed to sneak out of the house.

When Lilyan opened hers, she laughed with joy, for among the clothing she discovered the letters she had written to Nicholas. With all the horrible events of the past few hours, she had not given a thought to her personal possessions. What a relief to know that they were not lost to her. And even better, the vicious Mrs. Melborne would never have access to them. She dug deeper into the valise and found three other treasures: her mother's Bible, the Clan Cameron pin, and the moccasins Elizabeth had made for her. She pulled off her tattered shoes, slipped her chilled feet into the moccasins, and then attached the pin to her dress, vowing never to let it out of her sight again.

Gerald stopped whittling, rummaged around, and opened another barrel. "Look. Buffalo jerky. We could stay here for days."

Callum harrumphed. "Not meself. I'm fashing to get out of

here already." He paused. "Poseidon?"

"Yessuh."

"You know the DeKruif farm?"

Poseidon nodded.

"Could you make your way there? Tell DeKruif what's goin' on and bring him here?"

Lilyan looked up from her letters. "Would that not put Poseidon in great danger?"

"No, danger, miss. No one pays me much heed. I kinda comes and goes as I please." Poseidon smiled. "But thank you jest the same."

"When would you go?" asked Callum.

"Soon as I can. Jest have to pick the time." He turned to leave.

"Poseidon," said Lilyan. "When you see the DeKruifs, would you tell them something for me? Something very important?"

"I'd be pleased to, ma'am."

"Tell them I heard some information. About Lord Cornwallis."

Poseidon nodded. "Cornwallis."

"That he's headed for the North Carolina border and plans to cross the Catawba River at a place called Cowan's Ford."

"Cornwallis. Catawba River. Cowan's Ford. I got it." Poseidon grinned.

"You know, if you take up arms with us, you would get your freedom," said Callum.

Poseidon turned back. "Thank you jest the same, but I already gots my freedom papers. My lady give 'em to me long time ago by now."

"And you stayed?" Callum lifted his bushy brows.

"Someone had to take care o' my lady. I bout all the family she gots left. The massah, he done went to his jest rewards—goin' on two years ago at Port Royal." He nodded to Lilyan and Elizabeth. "Guess it's 'bout time for me to go."

Lilyan stood and took the man's gnarled hand in both of hers. "You saved our lives. And for that I will be forever grateful. You are now in my evening prayers and will remain in them for the rest of my life."

"I's honored, ma'am." He bowed with great dignity.

Not long after Poseidon left them, they all seemed to grow

heavy-eyed and hunkered in their blankets. Callum took watch and promised to keep the fire going.

For two days, Poseidon stole back to the tunnel as often as he could manage. On one trip he brought Gerald his much needed linsey-woolsey coat. In addition to food, he also supplied the little band of fugitives with snippets of information.

After sending word to her husband, Mrs. Melborne had taken to her bed, seemingly unable to bear the horrible crime that had been committed on her property. She vowed to return to Charlestown as soon as her husband arrived, which Poseidon declared was the best news he had heard in a while. Planning for such an occasion, little by little he had been taking valuables that belonged to his mistress and stashing them in the cave. He told them that a large contingent of dragoons, commissioned by Tarleton himself, was combing the woods and questioning the neighboring plantations and farmers.

Lilyan's spirits remained as gloomy as the craggy gray walls of their chamber. She no longer felt nauseated when she thought about what she had done, but still felt at times as if a giant veil had been lowered in front of her, separating her from the others. She yearned for Nicholas, picturing minute details of the times they had spent together. But often those images induced a soul-deep loneliness that frightened her so much, she would sit on the top step leading to the outside, seeking the warmth of the thin rays of sunshine.

The fourth day in the cave, Poseidon lifted their hopes when he told them he planned to bring DeKruif back with him that night, once the British soldiers pitched camp.

For Lilyan, the afternoon dragged on. She ached to write to Nicholas, but since she did not have the supplies, she composed the letter in her mind as she paced from one end of the cave to the other. She would pen it as soon as possible, but decided to leave off the information about Bradenton. Some things should never be committed to paper.

Finally, Poseidon and DeKruif arrived. The stocky, heavily bearded man removed his hat and bowed to the ladies. His kind expression immediately engendered confidence. Speaking in a thick Dutch accent, he said he thought it best that their party remain in the cave at least two more days, allowing him time to spread a false rumor about someone spotting them farther north of Charlestown, near Oyster Point. The British knew him as a loyalist and would believe any information he provided. According to his plan, in three days at sunset he would take two of them in his milk wagon to his farm. The following night, he would take the remaining two. Hidden in his cellar, they would wait until an escort guided them to safety.

While DeKruif talked, Lilyan, Elizabeth, Gerald, and Callum gravitated to each other as if drawn by a magnet. They had endured much, living together as virtual prisoners, comforting each other through fears and anxieties, reading aloud from the Bible, and writing their names with soot on the walls of the cave. A bond, sure and strong, enfolded them.

"Could we not all go together?" asked Lilyan.

DeKruif scratched his head. "I think maybe two at a time vill be safer." He paused, studying their faces. "But, maybe one trip safer after all. Yah? I pile some more hay up in the wagon and stash you underneath. Ve fool them, I think."

So they agreed, in three nights they would leave the cave. After DeKruif and Poseidon departed, the tiny band of rebels spent the rest of the evening compiling a list of things they should carry with them. Eager, yet anxious, Lilyan found it particularly difficult to fall asleep, but for the first time in days, she slept through the night without waking to nightmares of Bradenton.

ON THE APPOINTED NIGHT, they lugged their minimal belongings out of the cave and made the half-mile trek through the forest to the road. Every stumbled footfall, every snap of a twig, tightened the panic coiled in Lilyan's chest. A quarter moon cast shadows through the pine needles that fluttered overhead like ghostly fans.

At the edge of the woods, DeKruif stepped out onto the road and over to the wagon, while Lilyan and the others waited behind. DeKruif spoke softly to a young woman who perched on the edge of the seat, holding a lantern. She immediately drew down the wick, and DeKruif motioned for the group to join him.

In hushed tones, they bade a sad good-bye to Poseidon and slipped into the bed of the wagon.

"Trouble knocked on the door, but, hearing laughter, hurried away." Benjamin Franklin

Chapter Twenty

LYING UNDER THE THICK blanket of sweet, grassy hay, Lilyan's senses came so alive, she flinched at the smallest sound, and her nerves jangled every time the wagon wheels slammed into a hole in the road. Gerald sneezed twice so loud that Callum poked him in his ribs, and Lilyan could not stifle her nervous giggle.

When they finally rolled to a stop and climbed out, Lilyan's leg muscles were so knotted, she limped into the farmhouse where Mrs. DeKruif greeted them.

A short, round woman, Mrs. DeKruif could have been Mrs. Snead's sister in stature as well as temperament. She offered coffee and meat pies, which they devoured in no time. Afterward, Mr. DeKruif pushed the kitchen table to the side, lifted a braided rug, and opened a passage to the cellar.

Frowning, Mrs. DeKruif folded her arms underneath her breasts. "I hate you must stay in the cellar, but Papa say the British vill come. Dis is the only way you stay safe." She paused when Lisa entered the room and draped her arm across her shoulders. "Lisa—my daughter—you have met?"

"We were in such a hurry, we did not have that pleasure." Lilyan and Elizabeth made their curtsies. "I am Lilyan, and this is

Elizabeth, Callum, and Gerald."

Lisa bowed, and when her eyes met Gerald's, she blushed a pretty pink.

Mrs. DeKruif's speculative glance told Lilyan that she had not missed the exchange. "Lisa and I spread straw and quilts for you. We put extra candles too. So, you go down now and have a good respite."

Mr. DeKruif led the way down the ladder, followed by Callum, then Lilyan and Elizabeth and Gerald. The cellar was surprisingly cozy, with two straw beds on the floor and a table and chairs in the center. Shelves laden with jars of preserves and crocks of soup and vegetables stretched along an entire wall. Baskets of onions and potatoes lined another wall. Cheese rounds, some white, some a pale yellow, and others a saffron red shade, sat on shelves.

Lilyan and Elizabeth flopped onto one of the beds. Sighing with relief, Elizabeth removed her moccasins and wiggled her toes. Mr. DeKruif bade them good night, but halfway up the ladder he stopped to explain the signal his wife recommended—two sharp raps on the floor with a broom handle meant they could safely come upstairs to eat, exercise, and use the necessary. Three raps would signal danger. With that message, Mr. DeKruif closed the trap door above them. A stillness settled over them as they listened to the table scrape into place. The candles wavered, casting shadows on the deep crags of Callum's face as he and Gerald lay on the makeshift mattress and pulled the layers of quilts up to their chins.

"Oh, look." Elizabeth pointed to the table. "They left us a brush and mirror."

"I am not so certain I want to see what I look like," said Lilyan. "And as for the brush…" She pulled her long braid out from under her mobcap and draped it across her shoulder. "My hair is so filthy, I don't think I could draw the brush through it."

Elizabeth ran her fingers through the fringe of hair across her forehead. "Let us ask for a bucket of water tomorrow. I cannot bear another day like this."

"Is everyone settled?" Lilyan asked. "If so, I'll douse the candles. Unless someone wants to keep a light burning."

"Please, keep one burning," said Elizabeth before yawning.

Lilyan snuggled under the ample coverlets, pressed her back

against Elizabeth's, and rested her face on her hands. "The DeKruifs are dear people, are they not?"

"Very kind and generous," said Elizabeth.

"And brave," Callum added. "They're risking everything for us."

"Mrs. DeKruif reminds me of your mother, Gerald," said Lilyan.

"That she does." Gerald's voice held a touch of sadness.

He misses his family, thought Lilyan, suddenly reminded that he was a young man, plucked from his safe and secure life, and tossed into one filled with danger and uncertainty.

"And did you notice how Lisa's eyes and hair are the same color? Soft, rust brown. Like cattails," Gerald spoke softly.

His young heart has been pierced. We have something in common. Feeling melancholy, Lilyan closed her eyes and pictured Nicholas standing arms akimbo aboard the *Brixham.*

Silence wafted around them like thick fog as they each absorbed Gerald's comments. Elizabeth twisted around and peered up over Lilyan's back to look at him. Lilyan glanced back at her and they smiled.

Callum harrumphed. "Eyes like cattails. It's a wonder she'll let you close enough to see the color. Bad as you smell."

"You sayin' I stink?"

"Bad as some skunks I've crossed paths with. And quit liftin' the covers about. Only makes it worse."

"I guess you smell like a bed of roses?"

"Compared to you, I do." Callum proceeded to mumble under his breath.

Lilyan felt Elizabeth's body trembling. At first she worried that her friend might be ill, but she soon realized she was giggling. Laughter, sweet, bright and contagious, spiraled up from Lilyan's stomach. Callum and Gerald chimed in, and soon their merriment grew so loud, Lilyan wondered if the DeKruifs could hear them.

After another round of *good nights*, they settled back down. For the first time in what seemed a very long time, Lilyan fell asleep with a smile on her face.

THE NEXT AFTERNOON FOUND Lilyan and Elizabeth ensconced in rocking chairs in front of the fireplace in the DeKruif's bedroom. Wrapped in coverlets and sipping coffee, each was enveloped in one of their hostess' voluminous shifts while they waited for their clothes to dry. They had bathed and washed their hair and had feasted on a dinner of potato soup and freshly baked bread.

Bolly, the DeKruif's white long-haired cat, meandered into the room, brushed up against Elizabeth's legs, and hopped into her lap. He kneaded her stomach with his paws, sprawled out across her legs and lolled back his head, inviting her to stroke his fat belly.

Lilyan put down her cup and leaned toward the fire, raking her fingers through her damp auburn tresses that spilled across her back. "Someday I pray we can feel as content as Bolly looks."

She stood up, rolling her neck from side to side, and then touched a chemise that was draped over a quilt rod. "Almost dry."

She wrapped the quilt around her shoulders and padded across the polished wood floor, her feet and legs toasty in a pair of Lisa's crocheted wool socks. She gazed up at the dreary sky as gray as a mourning dove's wing, and watched a raindrop meander down the windowpane.

Suddenly a movement caught her eye, and her pulse raced as she watched Lisa sprint toward the house.

"Elizabeth," she rasped, her throat dry with panic. "Something is wrong."

Elizabeth jumped up, and they ran to the door and cracked it open.

"Mama," Lisa called out, catching her breath. "The men are here."

An officer, with a small party, preceded Lee a few days' march to find out Marion, who was known to vary his position in the swamps of the Pedee... With the greatest difficulty did this officer learn how to communicate with the brigadier; and that by the accident of hearing among our friends on the south side of the Pedee, of a small provision party of Marion's being on the same side of the river.

Lt. Colonel Lee

Chapter Twenty-One

LILYAN SEARCHED THE ROOM for a weapon. She seized the fireplace poker and hurried back to Elizabeth's side.

"What men, Lisa?" asked Mrs. DeKruif.

"Papa says to run ahead. Tell you they are the ones come to take our friends to safety."

"Thank God," Elizabeth whispered.

Lilyan's shoulders sagged with relief, she leaned the poker against the wall, and they both stepped out into the kitchen.

Mrs. DeKruif smiled at them. "It is good. Yah? You vill be safe soon. But not good, too. I have come to love all of you."

Gerald ran into the room, shadowed by Callum and then Mr. DeKruif.

"They've come to fetch us," Gerald exclaimed. "We're to ready ourselves as quick as possible." He pushed the table and rug to the side, opened the cellar door, and scurried down the ladder.

Lilyan stared at the swarthy man coming through the doorway. "Nicholas!" she shouted and dove into his arms.

He grasped the ends of the quilt that had slipped from her shoulders, pulled them around his sides, and wrapped his arms around Lilyan, enveloping them in a cocoon. He kissed the top of her head, then her forehead and her eyes. In between kisses he murmured wonderful, warm Greek phrases. He tipped up Lilyan's chin and locked his golden eyes with hers.

"Lilyanista. God is good." He pressed her check against his chest.

The embrace ignited a fire that warmed Lilyan's body from her toes to the top of her head. As Nicholas nuzzled his face in her hair, his caressing fingers kneaded away the loneliness and the anxious waiting she had endured the past weeks. She was not sure how long she stood listening to his heart thundering in her ear or how many times Callum cleared his throat before Nicholas pulled away and slipped her into the crook of his arm.

Lilyan glanced at Mrs. DeKruif, whose eyes sparkled. Lisa grinned, and Mr. DeKruif brushed an imaginary speck from the toe of his boot. Elizabeth glowered at the doorway behind them.

Wondering what put such a scowl on her friend's face, Lilyan looked over her shoulder to find Samuel leaning against the frame.

"As if we don't have troubles enough," hissed Elizabeth.

The volatility of Elizabeth's reaction to Samuel surprised Lilyan once again. It worried her too. Their journey would be perilous enough without constant sparks flying between the two of them.

"How happy I am to see you again, Samuel." Lilyan offered a warm welcome, determined to make up for her friend's cool reception.

He nodded and then stood near the fireplace.

"Someone take this," Gerald yelled from the ladder.

Lisa reached down and gathered up an armful of blankets from him. She placed them beside the table and reached for another load.

"Here, lass." Callum took Lisa's place at the ladder. "Let me do that."

Soon the men had hauled up all their belongings and piled them in the center of the kitchen.

Nicholas guided Lilyan away from the others. "We must be on our way soon."

"Where are we going?

"First to join up with General Marion, and then find somewhere safe for you and Elizabeth to stay."

"Will Andrew be there? With Marion?"

"He had not arrived before I left camp. But, yes, I believe he will be there."

The flicker of hope Lilyan kept stoked in her heart burst into a flame.

They stopped in the doorway, and Nicholas leaned in close. "Let me see your arm."

Lilyan pushed up her sleeve, exposing her forearm. Her breath caught in her throat as Nicholas pressed his lips to the scar, her body trembled from the molten tingle that ran up her arm, straight to her heart.

"I am at your feet," he murmured and then searched her face. "There is a terrible sadness in you, aga'pi mou. Callum gave me a brief recollection of what happened."

She glanced away, but he cupped her face, drawing her eyes to his again. "You are a brave, strong woman. Soon you will know what the rest of us know. You did what you had to do to save your Elizabeth and you rid the world of a terrible evil."

Lilyan's response caught in her throat. *Will there ever be a time I can think about that night without this horrible feeling of dread?*

"And now, you must dress quickly, my darling. We have a long journey ahead of us."

It dawned on her then that under the quilt she wore only an oversized shift, and her cheeks flushed hot with embarrassment.

As she rushed to prepare for travel, Nicholas chuckled, a deep, sultry sound. "You look lovely."

Lilyan tried to jolly Elizabeth out of her black mood as they dressed and packed. It was hard to see her friend so grim when she herself was so happy. They joined the others outside and watched Callum strap their meager belongings onto a mule already laden with coverlets, food, and sundries Mrs. DeKruif insisted on giving them. At Mr. DeKruif's bidding, they all formed a circle while he prayed for God's mercy and safe travel. His plea, plainspoken and sincere, did much to calm Lilyan's worried thoughts. After a round of embraces and kisses, the DeKruifs stood at their front door and bade the travelers Godspeed.

Nicholas checked the buckle of his horse's cinch. "There are only three horses. So, Lilyan, you ride with me. Elizabeth with Samuel. Gerald with Callum."

Lilyan caught Elizabeth's frown, and much as she hated to, she asked, "Could Elizabeth not ride with you, Nicholas?"

"Listen to me. All of you." Nicholas' expression grew stern. "We begin a perilous journey together, and I must have your word that you will follow my orders. No second thoughts. No questions."

Solemnly, they nodded their agreement.

"Good. Our lives depend upon it." Nicholas mounted his horse.

When he grasped Lilyan's arm, she hiked up her skirts, placed her foot in the stirrup, and allowed him to pull her up. She settled behind him, wrapping her arms around his body, enjoying the heat that emanated from his broad back.

He tucked her hands inside his buckskin jacket. "To keep you warm. Yes?"

Lilyan watched as Elizabeth sat behind Samuel and tied the strings of her cape tighter around her neck. Her expression remained stoic and her body rigid.

Callum, already mounted, scowled at Gerald and Lisa as she wrapped a crocheted muffler around the young man's neck.

Lisa took a step back and looked directly into Gerald's eyes. "I will wait."

The straightforward statement struck a chord in Lilyan's heart, and she leaned into Nicholas' back.

"Time to go." Callum looped the reins around his fist.

After Gerald vaulted up behind him, Callum studied Lisa. "He's worth the wait, lass. One of the finest young men I know." The gentleness of his tone brought a lump to Lilyan's throat.

Lisa blushed and hurried over to her parents.

When they reached the other side of the pasture, Lilyan glanced back to find the DeKruifs still waving good-bye.

Will we ever see them again?

SEEMINGLY ENDLESS RIDING LEFT Lilyan's thighs and calves so badly chafed that whenever they dismounted to rest the horses, she could hardly walk.

To avoid detection, the first two nights they had camped without a fire. Lying on damp, black earth that smelled like overcooked eggs, she and Elizabeth had huddled together, thankful for Mrs. DeKruif's coverlets. While they slept, Samuel would leave to scout ahead and return in the early morning hours. Lilyan wondered how he managed with so little rest.

One day they woke to frost on the ground, and Nicholas decided it safe enough to light a fire. Although Lilyan's moccasins kept her feet dry and snug, she knelt close to the flames, more for the cheery light than for its meager warmth.

Despite the hardships, Lilyan treasured this time with Nicholas. She enjoyed watching him, for he was a handsome, wonderfully made man—tall, lithe, and muscular. He had shaved the beard he wore during the rescue aboard the *Brixham*, but thick stubble darkened his jaw again. Once, when he lifted her from his horse and held her close, she traced her fingers over the outline of his chin and then cupped his roughened cheek with her hand. Later that evening he left the camp and returned clean shaven.

Lilyan delighted not only in his appearance, but found pleasure in his character, his personality, and spirit. He led with confidence and patience, keenly aware when he had stretched his little band of followers and their mounts to their limits. He spent time with Gerald, showing him how to navigate his way using the stars, the moss on the trees, and the almost invisible trails cut through the pine forests by migrating animals. Nicholas even showed his young protégé how to take a smoke bath; laying fir and cedar branches across the burning logs, opening his shirt, and allowing the fragrant vapor to penetrate his clothing. Lilyan tried the procedure herself and, although pleased with the freshened smell of her clothes, she still longed for a proper bath.

She found their journey a constant source of revelations. She thrilled to Nicholas' slightest touch, and her blood stirred from his dangerous smile. There was a yearning in the pit of her stomach, and she seemed to have lost all shame from the wanting of it. Feelings, confusing and frightening, washed through her body like waves of a spring tide. Is it proper for a lady, a Christian lady, to have such feelings, she wondered. She had no gauge to compare by except memories of her mother and father. They had seemed so in tune with one another—affectionate, constantly holding hands, touching, gazing. Even in public, they tended to gravitate toward each other. One of Lilyan's most vivid childhood memories was of her mother's hem brushing across the top of her father's shoe.

Her mother, a lady of the first order, had not hidden her desire for her husband, not even from her young daughter. And after all, did not the Lord create this desire, one for the other? Were not man and wife to cleave to one another and become one flesh? But God intended for that mysterious union to occur after marriage. So should the desire ensue after marriage also?

While pondering these questions, Lilyan made a surprising discovery about herself—she guarded her independence to the point of stubbornness and wondered if she really wanted to completely subject her will to a man, even Nicholas. From the outset of their journey, she had remained alert, anxiously searching the woods around them. Despite her fatigue, her vigilance made sleep almost impossible. Her eyes burned and her back ached from the constant tension. But little by little, she came to realize that they had entered Nicholas' domain, a place where his skills, knowledge, and authority reigned. The longer she rode behind him clinging to his waist, the more her confidence in him grew and the more she wanted to rely on him. Finally, late one evening after crossing a particularly treacherous stream, in her mind she surrendered her self-sufficiency to Nicholas. The moment she gave in, as if her bones had turned to liquid, her body melted into his—this was her man, her rock, her protector, her shelter from the storm.

On the afternoon of the fourth day of their journey, Samuel, who rode with Elizabeth ahead of the group, suddenly stopped his horse. At that moment Lilyan thought she heard a whistle in the distance. Samuel rose up in the saddle and imitated the sound that was so shrill; Lilyan clamped her hands over her ears.

Then suddenly, like ghosts floating up between the cypress knees in the brackish water, two men stepped forward.

"I thank you sir for your generous sympathy, but I die the death I always prayed for; the death of a soldier fighting for the rights of man."
Baron de Kalb

Chapter Twenty-Two

"COME TO TAKE YOU to Marion," one of the men announced.

Nicholas nodded, and they all watched in silence as the two men mounted their horses. Like a needle precisely threading its way through an intricate pattern, their guides led them into Wyboo Swamp, through foot-high brackish water, and between towering cypress trees laden with moss. Hours later the path dumped out into an encampment pitched on a knoll covered in golden brown sedge.

One of the guides stopped, leaned forward, and whistled the same piercing sound Samuel had made. Lilyan pressed her ear against Nicholas' shoulder.

Nicholas chuckled. "It is a signal General Marion taught his men. For us it is a welcome sound. You will get accustomed to it."

A score of people, mostly women, who had been moving among the tents and wagons, stopped their chores long enough to wave and shout greetings.

At the nearest cooking fire, Nicholas helped Lilyan dismount.

"You and Elizabeth stay here." He looked down at her from the saddle and nodded toward the camp. "The rest of us will ride on to join General Marion."

Lilyan placed her hand on his knee and looked up at him, trying to hide her fear. "How far is that?"

"Ten. Fifteen miles." He caressed her chin. "You will be well, yes?"

She nodded.

Elizabeth joined them and put her arm across Lilyan's shoulders. "We'll be fine."

Callum and Gerald approached on their horse. "I'm going to check things out," said Callum. "And then Gerald and I will be back here before you know it."

"Thank you, Callum. I know I can count on you." Lilyan paused. "Nicholas?"

"Yes?"

"If you hear news of Andrew and Herald, come and tell me. Straight away?"

"As fast as my horse can carry me, my sweet." He saluted and turned to leave.

Lilyan and Elizabeth waved good-bye and wearily turned to face four women who were looking them over. One of them stepped forward. She wore the pea jacket and petticoat breeches of a sailor, and had scrunched her curly red hair under a cocked hat. Although her attire was more suitable for a seaman aboard a navy schooner, she had a friendly, open countenance.

"Welcome to our camp, ladies. I'm Evelyn Stewart. This here is Karen Shipp and Linda Weed. The one stirring up the herbs in the kittle is Brenda Lyles."

"This is Elizabeth Archer and I am Lilyan Cameron." As the women greeted her in a chorus of *hellos* and *welcomes*, Lilyan curtsied.

"Just so you know, ain't no ceremony here. First names only." Evelyn motioned to the fire. "Come on over."

Evelyn sat on a piece of lumber balanced on two rocks and patted the place beside her. Elizabeth settled herself on the crude bench and moved over to make room for Lilyan.

"So, Lilyan. Are you Captain Xanthakos's intended?" Evelyn winked at the others. "I mean, the way he was looking at you, and all."

"Not formally, no. But if the words were spoken—"

"You wouldn't wait two seconds to say yes." Evelyn laughed.

"Neither would most the women in this camp. Even the married ones. He's a right fine man, he is." She slapped her knee and chuckled.

Lilyan joined in with the women's good-natured laughter.

"Let me fill you in on the lay of the land." Evelyn rested her hands on her thighs. "I don't know if you heard, but we ended up here 'cause weeks ago the British raided Snow's Island. Case you don't know, that was General Marion's headquarters. When we heard they was coming, our men destroyed what they could before we left. Then the British took care of the rest."

She pressed a thumb into her chest. "I'm here to take care of my son, Devon. The ladies asked me to take the helm. So I make sure everything is shipshape. I keep in touch with Marion's captain, who lets me know when it's time to haul anchor and cast off."

She shoved back her hat, and a frizzy red strand of hair plopped across the side of her face. "Though … sometimes we don't know till the last minute where we're going. The general's right protective of his plans. Most times, he don't even let his officers know where they're headed. But no finer gentlemen ever lived."

The other women nodded.

"Like I said. That there, stirring the kittle, is Brenda. She's here with her husband and brother-in-law. She's our nurse and midwife. The British shoot and maim our men, and she spends her time putting them back together again. She can make a fine stitch too. 'Cept not in material, if you get my meaning?"

Lilyan brushed her hand across her forearm. "I do."

"Karen is our seamstress. She can turn the rawest homespun into cloth as soft as a dove's wing. And she can make a button out of almost anything; seeds, pine bark, hickory nuts. She's here on account of her brother."

Karen, who sat on a tree stump, glanced up from her mending and looked over the top of her wire-rimmed glasses. She nodded and her smile reached her sparkling, slightly myopic brown eyes. Her hair, as raven black as Elizabeth's, was braided into a rope that draped over her shoulder.

Evelyn patted the arm of the willowy woman sitting on a stool next to her. "Linda's our cook."

Linda harrumphed and then plopped the potato she had been scrubbing back into the bucket she held between her legs. "Not that we have much of anything to cook around here." She blew a puff of air out of the side of her mouth, lifting the gray-blond fringe that stuck out from her coarse linen mobcap. "Sweet potatoes. Sweet potatoes. And more sweet potatoes," she mumbled.

"Lilyan? Where is the mule we brought with us?" Elizabeth asked.

Lilyan craned her neck around and scanned the place where Nicholas had dropped them off. "Callum must have taken it."

"Well, we have to get it back." Elizabeth smiled at the women. "The nicest woman, Mrs. DeKruif, who took us in for a while, packed all manner of foodstuffs for us. Cheese, strawberry preserves, flour, meal, jerky, dried apples, brown sugar—"

"Brown sugar and dried apples." Linda clapped her hands like a child. "Let's see. I have dried plums and walnuts. And wild oats." She ticked off the list on her fingers. "All the things I need for an apple crisp. Oh, my. I think I'm going to cry. Will they be back soon?"

"I hope so," said Lilyan, thinking more of Andrew than the food.

Evelyn pointed to Lilyan's feet. "Those are some mighty fine moccasins you have."

"Lovely beadwork." Karen snipped a piece of thread with her teeth.

Lilyan stuck her foot out from the hem of her dress. "Elizabeth made them for me."

"Tan the hides yourself?" asked Evelyn.

Elizabeth nodded. "I smoked the skin so they will dry soft after they get wet."

"You're Cherokee, ain't you?" asked Evelyn.

Elizabeth sat up straight. "Yes."

The lines at the sides of Evelyn's eyes crinkled with her smile. "You'll come in mighty handy round here."

Elizabeth relaxed, but everyone remained so quiet, Lilyan scanned their faces. They seemed to be regarding her with speculation.

Wonder what they're waiting for.

Elizabeth put her hand on Lilyan's shoulder. "Lilyan is an artist."

Oh, dear. They want to know what I can do. They're trying to figure out what an artist can contribute.

"She paints murals and she has done some of the most beautiful portraits I've ever seen," Elizabeth continued.

"Portraits?" Linda dried her hands on her apron. "Truly? Have you ever painted a miniature?"

"Yes, I have."

"Well, you see. My Ray has a watch. Takes it out of his pocket ten times a day." Linda paused. "You think you could paint a picture ... of me?" She blushed. "To fit inside the watch?"

"I would be honored."

Brenda tapped a long metal spoon against the kettle suspended over the fire and hooked it onto the iron spit. "Cup of coffee?"

With assured movements that spoke of long experience, Brenda took a rag and lifted a tin coffeepot from the coals, and poured the mud brown liquid into mugs. She handed them to Lilyan and Elizabeth, turned over a wooden bucket, and sat on it beside them. Lilyan wrapped her cold fingers around the cup, breathed in the pungent aroma, and waited for it to cool.

Elizabeth took a sip and sighed with pleasure. "This is so good. It's been days since we could relax long enough to enjoy a cup."

Karen dropped her sewing into her lap. "Why is that?"

Dreaded memories welled up inside Lilyan, and she trembled. She gave Elizabeth a sideways glance. *How much should we tell them?*

Evelyn leaned forward to study Lilyan's eyes, and, as if she had read her mind, she said, "You're not obliged to tell us anything you don't want to."

"I think they are, if they're bringing trouble our way," Karen countered.

Overwhelmed by an urge to lay her story at these women's feet, Lilyan put down her cup and squeezed Elizabeth's fingers. "It was never our intention to bring any of you trouble." She faltered. "But I realize that is most likely what we have done by coming here."

Karen pushed her spectacles up on her nose and stared. The other ladies remained still.

"You see, I did something ... quite horrible." Lilyan swallowed the lump in her throat. "I—I killed someone."

Karen, plying her needle, jabbed herself and winced. There was a collective gasp as the ladies leaned forward, waiting for Lilyan to continue.

Lilyan's words failed her, and she gazed at Elizabeth, silently entreating her help. She shivered, and her dear friend slid closer.

"She did it to save me. It was a British officer. He was attacking me."

"I'll be." Linda shook her head. "A British officer, you say?"

Karen sucked on her pricked finger. "What happened?"

Lilyan could feel the blood draining from her face. She simply did not want to reveal the ghastly details.

Evelyn clapped her hands and stood. "Ladies, looks like we have a genuine heroine among us. Well, huzzah and hurrah to you, missy."

Lilyan scooted forward on the bench. "But you don't understand. The British are searching for us."

Evelyn snorted. "Honey, they've been trying to run us down for months. I'm sure Captain Xanthakos will inform General Marion, and we might have to be a little more on guard. But it's not any worse than anything we've faced before. Welcome to our little band of fugitives."

Grateful for the woman's reassurance, Lilyan stood to give her a hug, but the sound of horses approaching caught everyone's attention. When she turned to see who it was, her heart leapt.

"Andrew!" She raced to her brother, who was now running toward her.

Their bodies slammed together in an embrace that had Lilyan alternately kissing his face and running her fingers over his arms, checking for wounds and broken bones. She stood back and searched his eyes. Something was different. Momentarily puzzled, Lilyan soon realized that his eyes had lost their luster. It was a subtle change in his face that only someone who knew him well would notice. She likened it to the almost imperceptible change in a lantern when she lowered the wick. A lump of concern curled in her stomach as she reached up and brushed a lock of hair from his forehead.

Maybe I'm making something out of nothing. My brother is here beside me. I can reach out and touch him. I should be rejoicing. It's what I've been praying for for weeks. Thank you, God. You are so good.

Andrew laughed, then picked her up and swung her around, and Lilyan felt giddy. Elizabeth joined them and the hugging began all over again. Callum stood off to the side, wiping his face on his shirt.

Herald and Gerald, their arms draped across each other's shoulders, grinned as their friend was smothered under Lilyan and Elizabeth's affection.

Out of the corner of her eye Lilyan spotted Nicholas, his arms crossed in front of him, smiling his warm, wonderful smile.

Later that evening she scanned the people sitting around the campfire, especially Andrew, Elizabeth, Callum, and Nicholas, who huddled so close, she could have reached out and touched them. She felt content. As content as she could be in the middle of a swamp, in the middle of a war.

These are my family, my clan. Father God, I'm asking you, here and now, please, do not allow us to be parted again.

Evelyn tossed her plate and spoon into a water bucket and sat on a blanket beside Linda on the other side of the fire from Lilyan. "Linda, you made yourself proud this night. I've never tasted apple crisp as good as that."

Everyone spoke in agreement. There was even a loud "Huzzah!"

"It was my pleasure," said Linda. "Herald, did you take a piece to General Marion like I asked?"

"Yes, ma'am, I did. But …"

"He gave it to someone else. Am I right?" Linda asked.

Herald nodded.

"Why would he do that?" asked Lilyan.

"Never have seen him eat much in the time I've known him," said Nicholas. "He's a temperate man too. Never seen him drink much wine or spirits."

Evelyn tossed the dregs of her coffee into the fire. "According to my son, Marion keeps that canteen of vinegar and water close by, though."

"Ugh." Lilyan drew up her nostrils.

Nicholas chuckled. "It does taste awful. But if it's good enough for General Marion, it's good enough for me. He grew up around here. Knows these swamps like the back of his hand, and if he thinks vinegar water keeps the swamp fever away, then I believe him."

Lilyan sensed the special relationship Marion had with his men. "You trust him, then?"

"With my life," Nicholas and Herald said together.

"I would follow him into perdition." Nicholas nodded to his

young friend. "Nobody ever had a finer commander."

"Except for General de Kalb." Andrew spoke softly. "I was there, you know … when he died. He was amazing even then."

All eyes riveted on the young man as he leaned back against Lilyan's legs. No one moved. Even the fire stopped popping.

Lilyan wanted to stop her brother from reliving something she intuitively knew would bring him pain, but she also knew it might help him to talk about it. She looked to Nicholas, and when he nodded, she patted Andrew's shoulder.

"I think we'd all like to hear more. If you're willing," she whispered.

Andrew drew in a breath and then he let the air out slowly. "You see, General de Kalb wasn't one of those officers that puts space between him and his men. He was one of us. Most times when we traveled, he didn't ride his horse, but marched along beside us. Came around each night and shared the food and fire. Slept on the ground with us. And stories? He could tell some of the best stories. Knew how to share silence too."

He picked up a stick and poked at a smoldering log. "At Camden, we were pretty much beaten. Six hundred of us to their two thousand. De Kalb sent his horse to the back of the lines early on, so he could fight side by side with us on foot. Time after time we charged, reformed, and charged again with the general leading the way." Andrew hesitated. "Someone laid his head open with a saber. He was shot. Bayoneted. Cut many times. But he still led one more charge. When the general finally fell, we closed ranks around him." He paused, staring at the fire. "Then Tarleton brought in his dragoons. We fought as long as we could, until most of us broke and ran.

"I was running for the woods with the rest of them, but I turned in time to see British soldiers headed toward the general to finish him off. They would have, too, but his aide, Chevalier de Buysson, threw his body on top of him and yelled, 'No! No! It's de Kalb. Brigadier General de Kalb.'" Andrew's voice cracked.

Lilyan felt hot, silky tears on her cheeks.

"About that time someone shot me in my shoulder and I fell to the ground. I woke up later and saw they had propped the general against a wagon wheel, but I was too far away to tell if he was breathing."

He shook his head. "We left him. We left him lying there and ran like rabbits." His voice broke, and he jabbed at the fire with a stick spraying sparks into the air.

"Steady on, soldier." Nicholas' calm voice, an octave deeper, washed over the camp. If Lilyan were a soldier, she would follow his voice anywhere; in some small way, she understood Andrew's devotion to de Kalb.

Lilyan did not trust herself to speak, but began to rub circles across her brother's shoulders. She looked across at Herald, who had lowered his head and pulled his hat to cover his face.

Andrew sucked in a breath. "Aboard the *Brixham*, someone told me that Cornwallis, once he knew who de Kalb was, ordered his own surgeons to try and save him. When the general died three days later, Cornwallis found out he was a Mason, same as himself. Had him buried with full military and Masonic honors."

Callum cleared his throat. "Guess there's some honor in the Brits after all."

"You're right," someone said from behind them.

Lilyan twisted around to find two men seated on horses only a few feet away. She wondered how they had gotten so close without being detected.

One of the men wore a black hat with a cockade and a blue uniform with an infantry sword strapped at his side. He was lean, swarthy and surprisingly short, though he sat his horse in such a way as to make her wonder where he ended and the horse began. But it was his face that captivated her, his aquiline nose and his black, piercing steady eyes. He had such a presence about him, an air of dignity and gravity. Lilyan knew it had to be Francis Marion himself.

The Negro mounted beside him tipped his hat and leaned forward, draping his arm across the saddle and dangling the horse's reins in his fingers. His alert expression belied his casual manner.

Lilyan had heard stories of a Negro who had distinguished himself so well that Marion had made him an officer among the other slaves who fought alongside the partisans.

Could this be him, she wondered?

The general doffed his hat to her and, when Nicholas and the others moved quickly to stand, he motioned for them to stay seated.

"And you're right about General de Kalb. He was a Patriot of the first order. I miss him sorely." Marion leaned forward and rested his arm on the saddle. "When I was informed of his last words, I vowed to share them with as many people as I could. So I'm asking you, remember. Tell your children and grandchildren that when a British officer spoke to the general about his misfortune, here's how the magnificent gentleman answered: 'I thank you, sir, for your generous sympathy, but I die the death I always prayed for; the death of a soldier fighting for the rights of man.'"

Lilyan studied the faces around her, assured that she was not the only person determined to commit the words to memory. Nicholas caught her eye. She watched the muscles in his cheek work as he fought against his emotions, and she knew they shared the same thought. *Our children will be told.*

Pantr'epsou me aga'pi mou. Marry me, my love.

Chapter Twenty-Three

During the following weeks Lilyan settled herself into a routine that almost lulled her into a sense of complacency. Almost. For deep inside she kept up her guard, knowing from experience how life could at any moment take an unexpected twist or turn.

Once the other camp followers and wagonners discovered Lilyan's willingness to paint portraits, they inundated her with requests. She tried to explain that she lacked the means to do so, but they insisted. They asked her for a list of supplies she would need and then set about procuring them. Their success stunned Lilyan. In a matter of days she had a stack of linen paper, compliments, one woman said, of a British officer who had abandoned his personal effects retreating from the militia back to Charlestown. Gerald whittled a set of brush handles and worked with Karen to fashion horse hair to the tips; resulting in the finest set of artist's brushes Lilyan had ever owned.

All manner of rocks, clay, weeds, seeds, and roots showed up at Lilyan's tent. Brenda volunteered to help grind them into powder using the mortar and pestle one of the ladies loaned her. The owner, a bright-eyed Mexican woman named Izell, called it a *mocajete*. The bowl, carved from volcanic rock, was decorated with a pig's head and rested on three short legs. Lilyan thought it peculiar looking, but it got the job done. Elizabeth, in between washing loads of clothes in a nearby stream, sewed string-pull pouches to contain the growing palette of pigment. When Linda heard Lilyan say she would need yolks to mix her paint, she promised eggs from the quail hens she kept in a cage in the back of her wagon.

Although Lilyan volunteered to help with cooking and cleaning, the women would not hear of it. Most of them came from families who could never afford a portrait, and they considered her paintings prized possessions. So it was with mixed feelings that Lilyan spent her mornings and afternoons creating miniatures for watches and lockets, and her favorites, the full-page portraits. Before turning over her artwork to her ecstatic patrons, she signed each piece with a line drawing of a chamomile encased in a *C.*

She enjoyed the time she spent getting acquainted with the ladies, but as the afternoons waned and the setting sun threw shards of pinks and vermilions across the skies, her attention would turn to the sandy path running through the cypress and gum trees. She scanned the thick patches of cane, holly, and gallbushes waiting for her men to appear.

Sometimes they stayed away for days. Those were the most difficult times for Lilyan, spurring her to abandon her painting, grab a pile of laundry, and scrub till her hands ached. Some evenings the men would arrive filthy and exhausted, their moods reflecting their success or defeat.

Most of Lilyan's news came to her from the Snead twins. When she learned that Lord Cornwallis had crossed into North Carolina and defeated General Greene at Guilford Courthouse, it reminded her of the message she had sent by Poseidon. The failure of her first real attempt at being a spy weighed heavily on her. Nicholas tried to console her, explaining that her message may have reached the militia in time, but they were outmanned. Besides, he said, it was her effort, her courage, that mattered to him.

Nicholas, Andrew, and Samuel never initiated conversations about their experiences as scouts. It was Herald and Gerald who, in identically excited voices, often finishing each other's sentences, informed her that General Marion considered his scouts his best men. They were the men Marion sent out in all directions at all hours of the night to seek out the enemy, to patrol, and to spy.

They had been known to sit in a tree half the night searching a British encampment, waiting for a chance to free a prisoner, steal a horse, or commandeer much-needed supplies.

Lilyan looked at her brother with new eyes. Her pride in him and in Nicholas and Samuel was matched only by her increasing fear for their safety.

Many nights Lilyan and Nicholas stole away from the others and huddled together on a makeshift bench at the edge of the encampment. Nicholas would pull her close and wrap his arm around her. He seemed to enjoy her stories about her days as a camp follower, so Lilyan deliberately exaggerated her descriptions and was delighted when they made him laugh.

Nicholas avoided talking about his days and spoke mostly about the future and his plans for a vineyard in the mountains of North Carolina. She loved the sound of his voice and the way he punctuated his conversations with his hands. When the hour grew late, her heart would thrill in anticipation of the time when he would take her in his arms, kissing her with a mixture of passion and tenderness that shot liquid fire through her veins. Reluctant to end their nights, they often stood holding hands and looking up at the stars that pushed their way through the black velvet sky like thousands of brilliant diamonds. Nicholas took great pleasure in pointing out the constellations and telling her the stories he had heard as a boy about the gods and goddesses, their turbulent lives and wondrous adventures.

Late one evening the first week in May as they strolled the outskirts of the camp, Nicholas stopped and pointed to the sky. "See the three stars, there, in a row?"

Lilyan followed his direction. "Yes."

"That's the belt of Orion, the hunter. If you look closely, you can see his upraised club." He drew an outline with his finger.

Lilyan squinted. "Not really."

Nicholas chuckled. "It's difficult to see." He paused. "Lilyanista?"

"Yes."

"You do know that I love you, yes?" He faced her, taking her hand in his.

"I believe I do." Her heart raced as his thumb traced circles in the palm of her hand.

"But do you realize how much?"

She leaned back, looking up at his face barely visible beneath the brim of his hat. "If it is only half as much as I love you, then your body cannot contain it."

He sucked in a breath. "The days we spent together traveling here from the DeKruifs, I watched you. The way your body comes slowly awake long before you open your lovely green eyes. I wake in the mornings remembering the way you stretch your arms to the side and arch your back. Do you realize how graceful your hands are when you braid your hair? Hair that looks like spun copper by firelight." He twirled a tendril of her hair around his finger. "I lay down at night wondering what it would look like spread across my pillow."

Tension coiled in the pit of Lilyan's stomach as the effect of his words swirled around in her body like warm honey.

He dropped his hands to his sides. "But what a terribly uncertain time to be in love. Yes?"

Lilyan pressed her other hand to his chest. "If I have learned anything over the past few months, it is this. Nothing in this life is certain. God has given us the gift of this day, not the promise of another. And I believe He expects us to live each hour, each moment, acknowledging and enjoying that gift."

He curled his hands around hers. "If that is so, I will wait no longer. Lilyan Cameron, will you do me the great honor of becoming my wife?"

Joy like none she had ever known soaked into Lilyan's bones as she stood on tiptoe and pressed her lips to the corner of his mouth. "Yes," she whispered, and then kissed the other side of his mouth. "Oh, yes," she managed to speak before he took her lips, kissing her sweetly and reverently, holding his passion in check, letting her know how much he too cherished the moment. When he finally released her, they were both trembling.

"There is one request I have." Lilyan hesitated.

He nodded.

"I want always for there to be a place in our home for my family. For Andrew, Elizabeth, and Callum."

She studied him, trying to read his expression, looking for a sign that would tell her if she had asked too much of him.

"This would make you happy?"

"Very much."

"Then I vow, aga'pi mou, your family is mine now, and we'll make a place for them wherever we are."

Lilyan pressed his hand against her cheek.

"I will find a clergyman as soon as possible." He kissed her again. "Tomorrow, I think."

"I should like that very much."

When they were finally able to part from one another, Lilyan returned to her tent to find Elizabeth already fast asleep. She wanted to wake her friend, but did not have the heart to disturb her. Lilyan curled up on her blanket, but barely slept. In the morning the moment she felt Elizabeth stir, she blurted out her news. As expected, Elizabeth was overjoyed, but more than a little anxious about how they were going to throw together a wedding on such short notice. When the other ladies heard the news, they expressed the same concerns, but were quickly drawn into the spirit of planning a wedding.

By late afternoon, in the midst of starting a portrait of Karen, Lilyan noticed Evelyn hurrying about the camp. A bubble of concern rose in her chest when the other ladies started running toward their tents, throwing sand on the fires, and grabbing the laundry that had been laid on the bushes to dry.

Karen, who had her back to the commotion, twisted her neck around to see what was going on. "Oh, dear," she said. "We must be moving again. Let me go see."

Lilyan grabbed a rag and wiped the paint from her brush. "I'm going with you."

They hurried toward Evelyn as Callum helped her up onto one of the wagons.

"What's happening?" Lilyan asked Callum.

"We're breaking camp. Moving north toward Camden, along the Congaree River."

Grim-faced, Evelyn waved to them, and they watched as she expertly positioned her wagon at the head of the others.

"But why?"

"Dunno know for sure. General Marion sent his sergeant to tell Mrs. Stewart to pull up stakes." He took off his cap, slapped it against his leg, and slipped it back on again. "You and Elizabeth gather your belongings and put them in that wagon there."

So it is not to be my wedding day after all.

She was sad more than frightened as she ran to get Elizabeth. It seemed to take only moments for the women to break camp and line up the wagons. Lilyan and Elizabeth climbed up to sit on either side of Callum in the third wagon from the end.

"How far are we going?" Lilyan's heart pounded.

"About twenty, twenty-five miles." Callum slapped the reins against the lead mule, rocking them forward. "And before you ask, traveling at the rate we'll be going, it should take us about three days. Maybe four."

"And Nicholas and Andrew?"

"They're long gone. Left sometime during the night. I wouldn't be surprised, the way Marion drives his men, if they aren't there already."

"Will there be a battle?" Lilyan did not really want to hear the answer. Finding it difficult to swallow, she lifted up a silent prayer, beseeching God to spare her beloved, her brother, General Marion, and his men.

"Aye. I suspect so," Callum replied gravely.

Therefore, they are no more twain, but one flesh. Matthew 19:6

Chapter Twenty-Four

$\mathcal{I}$T TOOK THEM FIVE DAYS to reach the Congaree; stopping twice to repair wagon wheels jarred loose from the ruts in the barely discernable track that cut through the thick forests and swamps lining their way.

Lilyan's spine ached as if someone had hammered on it. Every muscle in her body felt ready to cramp with her next movement. With the enemy so close, campfires had been forbidden, and her stomach growled in protest against the cold corn mush and biscuits that had been her meager diet. Still, she would not complain; conditions for the army were much, much worse. It angered and hurt her to know that some of the soldiers slept on the ground without even so much as a blanket.

One of Marion's scouts met them on the bank of the river with the joyful news that Marion and his men, along with Light Horse Harry Lee, had defeated the British at a plantation owned by a wealthy widow, Mrs. Rebecca Motte.

Gritting her teeth, Lilyan listened as the man described in agonizingly slow details how the British had driven Mrs. Motte and her family from her mansion, which served as a depot for convoys moving between Charlestown and Camden and destined for

Granby and Ninety-Six.

According to the scout, the British dug a trench around the main house and fortified the area so well that even the field piece General Greene had sent could not make a dent in the walls. After three days of fighting, not wanting to wait out the siege for fear that reinforcements might come, General Lee made a decision to set fire to the house. But before doing so, he asked Mrs. Motte for her permission, which she gave willingly. On the morning of May the twelfth, he sent an envoy to give the British one last chance to surrender. But they refused. One of the privates in Marion's brigade advanced toward the house and shot several flaming arrows onto the shingles. The British scurried up on the roof to put out the flames, but the cannons and Marion's sharpshooters drove them back inside. Not long after, the British hung out a white flag. By one o'clock the garrison had surrendered, and the prisoners were secured.

Callum slapped his knee. "That's what I like to hear. What about the lady's house?"

"They were able to save it." The man answered and then grinned. "Mighty fine woman, that one. Some say she even provided the arrows for Marion's man to do the job; fancy ones her brother brought back to her from India."

"You don't say." Callum slapped his knee again.

Her patience worn thin, her heart hammering, Lilyan finally jumped into the conversation. "And the casualties, sir? Were there many?"

The scout tipped his hat. "Anyone in particular you concerned about, ma'am?"

"My brother, Andrew Cameron. Captain Xanthakos and his friend, Samuel Harris. And our friends Herald and Gerald Snead."

"That's a heap of men to worry about." He rubbed the sweat from his brow with his forearm and slid his hat back on his head. "All Marion's men. Same as me. Far as I know they're all fine, ma'am."

The drumming of Lilyan's heart slowed, but she would not be completely at ease until she saw her men for herself.

Two hours later, Lilyan glanced around the temporary encampment as she and Elizabeth threw blankets across bushes to air them out. Except for the rumble of the nearby river, the campsite seemed the same as the one they had dismantled days before.

As Lilyan stood up, a heightened sense of awareness slipped across her shoulders, and she reached up to massage the back of her neck. She turned and, at the sight of Nicholas walking toward her, she whooped with glee and ran into his outstretched arms. As he swung her around, she clasped her fingers in his hair, knocking his hat from his head, and rained kisses all over his face.

As he held her in his arms, Nicholas smiled wide, and his golden eyes sparkled. He loosened his clasp until she slid down his body, bringing her eyes level with his. And then he kissed her. A kiss that turned her bones to putty and caused her body to melt into his.

"Harrumph," Callum muttered from somewhere behind them.

To Lilyan's dismay, Nicholas let her go. As her feet touched the ground, she felt her cheeks grow hot with embarrassment at her total lack of restraint. Mortified, she buried her face into his chest.

He chuckled, stepped back, and lifted her chin until he held her gaze. "Quite a greeting, my love."

She smiled, tamping the desire to rise up on her tiptoes and kiss the most inviting dimple at the side of his mouth.

Nicholas grinned. "I promised you a wedding. The gentleman standing to your right is a chaplain. How much time would you need to prepare?"

"I feel as if I have been preparing myself for you my entire life," Lilyan whispered back.

Nicholas pulled her into the crook of his arm and faced Callum. "With your permission, sir, I would very much like to marry Miss Cameron."

Callum's bushy eyebrows drew together, forming a line across his forehead. "Hoots, mon! This what you want, lassie?"

"Oh, yes. With all my heart."

Callum's piercing eyes could have bored holes in a lesser man, but Nicholas would not break the stare.

Callum nodded. "You'll take care of her? Keep her safe from harm? As best as you can?"

"With my life."

"I canna ask anything more than that." He stepped forward, shook Nicholas' hand, and clapped him on his shoulder. He reached for Lilyan, pulled her into his arms for a swift hug, and then stepped back. "I promised your da I'd watch over you. Now your husband has the first rights to that. But know this, your safety and Andrew's will always take priority, and will till I take my dying breath."

Elizabeth ran to Lilyan and put her arm around her. With tears swimming in her eyes she smiled at Nicholas and held out her hand. "God bless you, Captain Xanthakos, for the joy you have brought my Lilyan."

Nicholas kissed her hand in a gallant gesture. "It's Nicholas, please."

When Lilyan saw Elizabeth fluttering her eyelashes, she had to suppress a giggle. *What a way my Nicholas has. Even my level-headed Elizabeth has fallen victim to his charm.*

The rest of the camp followers, who had been watching the interchange with rapt attention, began to chatter about the wedding.

"I've the perfect dress. I wore it to my sister's wedding," said Karen, who hurried toward the tents.

"I'll bake a cake," said Linda, ticking off on her fingers the ingredients she would need.

Evelyn broke away from the group and, in her usual direct manner, asked, "How long do we have?"

Nicholas fixed his gaze on Lilyan and cocked his head. "This evening? After supper?"

So long, Lilyan wanted to wail, but instead she nodded in agreement.

Nicholas caressed her cheek. "Till then, my sweet."

Suddenly, the women swept her up and headed toward her tent. All the while Evelyn rattled off instructions. Fetch bath water. Find some soap. Anyone have lavender water or perfume?

Someone pulled off Lilyan's dress and took her shoes. Someone else loosened her hair. Soon she found herself resting on a pallet in just her shift with a cool cloth over her eyes while someone scrubbed her hands and feet and shaped her nails. They cooed over her as if she were a child, and she relished every moment of it. When they finally allowed her to open her eyes, it was to the delightful sight of a barrel, filled to its brim with steaming water.

Trying to keep her modesty from being completely shattered, she stared at Elizabeth, who read her silent entreaty and bade everyone leave. She disrobed, slid into the bath, and moaned her pleasure as the water caressed her skin like molten silk. She closed her eyes and wanted to purr like a cat when Elizabeth lathered her hair and then rinsed it with a bucket of warm water. Reluctantly, she stepped from the bath and into an enveloping blanket. Elizabeth directed her to sit on a stool while she dried her hair and brushed it with long, soothing strokes.

"Do you know … are you aware … of what is … expected of you?" Elizabeth asked.

Lilyan twisted her head around to find that Elizabeth's cheeks had turned rosy. She felt her own cheeks flush. "I have an idea. I understand that it will be painful at first. And then very … very … pleasant? At least that's what you told me the first time I asked."

Elizabeth's breath rushed from her mouth as she put the brush down on the stool next to Lilyan. "Good. Yes. Nicholas is a gentle man and he loves you so very much. Let him guide you, and all will be well."

Lilyan donned her chemise and allowed Elizabeth to lace her stays. *The next time this corset is untied, it will be by my husband.* Her pulses raced at the thought, and her cheeks felt like they were on fire.

"Did I fasten them too tight?" Elizabeth asked, fanning Lilyan's flushed face with her hands.

Flustered, Lilyan was searching for an answer when Karen stepped inside the tent carrying a sky-blue mantua folded across her arm. "I can't believe I found it on the first try." She paused to catch her breath. "Been saving it for a special occasion, and there's nothing more special than this."

Karen held the dress in front of her. "It might be a bit fulsome, but you can lace it up tight. And here's a kerchief to tie around your shoulders," she said, handing the dress and lacy blue scarf to Elizabeth, who draped the scarf over a stool.

Karen pulled a pair of slippers from underneath her arm and placed them on the ground. "These are from Brenda."

Lilyan reached out and traced her fingers across the silver colored daisies embroidered on the underskirt of the dress. "It's lovely," she said and gave her friend a hug. "Please tell Brenda how much I appreciate the shoes."

Karen, her eyes dancing with pleasure, dashed outside to wait with the others.

Lilyan stood and held up her arms while Elizabeth lifted the dress over her head and shifted it into place. She draped her hair across her breast as Elizabeth moved behind her. Soon her bodice was cinched as tightly as her stomach muscles. Elizabeth draped the kerchief around Lilyan's shoulder and tied it in a knot in front of her to cover the décolleté neckline.

Lilyan studied her friend's expression as she folded down the layers of lace.

"What are you thinking, Elizabeth?"

"Do you know the significance of this color for me?"

Lilyan shook her head.

"At the beginning of Cherokee weddings, the bride and groom wrap a blue blanket across their shoulders. At the end of the ceremony, after a holy man blesses the union and all those present, the couple sheds the blanket, and their relatives envelop them in a white one."

"It makes a lovely picture."

Lilyan smoothed her skirt around her hips and slid her feet into the slippers. She bent over to retrieve her clan Cameron pin from the top of a crate that served as a makeshift vanity, but Elizabeth reached it first and said softly, "Let me."

"Elizabeth?" Lilyan paused while Elizabeth attached the pin at her shoulder. "Do you have any idea how much I wish that you could find a gentle man too? Someone to cherish as much as I do my Nicholas?" She hesitated. "I know we agreed never to talk about it, but I cannot tell you how much I hate what happened to you—to us."

Elizabeth made no answer, her expression stoic.

"You never talk about getting married or having a family. Did that beast steal that hope from you?"

Elizabeth jerked up her chin. "I assure you, he harmed neither my body nor my spirit. And I have you to thank for that, dear one." She patted Lilyan's hand. "Please do not trouble yourself on my account."

She pressed a hand to her heart. "Many hopes and dreams are very much alive, here, deep inside. And I promise to share them with you one day, but right now, we have to get you dressed. Your Nicholas is waiting."

Nicholas is waiting.

167

Lilyan gulped as feelings of anticipation, fear, excitement, and curiosity took turns tumbling around in her stomach. Those same sensations kept her from eating any of the stew beef Linda brought for her supper. Finally, after much coaxing, she nibbled on a biscuit.

After what seemed like hours, Lilyan stepped from the tent to the applause and the oohs and ahhs of the ladies gathered outside. Lilyan clasped the skirt of her dress and made a deep curtsy. Her coppery tresses, flowing across her arms, seemed to catch fire in the lantern light. Her eyes misted when Izell draped a frothy white lace mantilla over her head. A lump of emotion prevented her from expressing her thanks for such a beautiful gesture, so she kissed the woman on both cheeks.

"Good news," Evelyn said. "Mrs. Motte has offered one of her farmhouses for your honeymoon."

"You'll sleep in a *real* bed tonight," Brenda exclaimed.

"If sleep is what you want." Evelyn winked, and several of the women giggled.

Lilyan stared at Evelyn, unable to absorb what she was saying, because of her new friend's complete transformation. Gone was the hard-driving, stalwart woman who seldom wore a corset under her linsey-woolsey shirts and sailor's breeches. In her place stood an attractive woman in a linen dress printed with pink roses on a green background. Her fiery red hair, usually scrunched underneath a battered hat, had been artfully arranged underneath a white gauze mobcap. Wispy curls framed her face and softened the lines that crinkled at the sides of her lively blue eyes.

In that instant Lilyan saw through the protective shell Evelyn wore in defense against a life that had not been very kind. Underneath it all dwelt a woman of character, of warmth, and charm, who had cherished and had been cherished in return.

Lilyan touched the lace that draped softly from Evelyn's elbow-length sleeve. "You look lovely."

"Thank you kindly." Evelyn yanked on the hem of her bodice. "We'd best get on with the ceremony, though. I can't bear this finery too long."

The ladies parted to make way for Andrew, who strode toward her in a uniform that had been freshly brushed and, despite a few tatters here and there, looked quite fine.

How handsome he looks, though still a bit too pale.

He swept off his hat and made a grand bow. "Good evening, Sissy." His eyes twinkled. "I have come to escort you to your groom."

Lilyan bobbed a curtsy.

"But before I do, I have something for you." He reached inside his coat, drew out a scarf, and presented it to her.

Lilyan immediately recognized the pattern of green squares against a red background; the Cameron tartan.

She unclasped the Cameron pin from her bodice and handed it to him. "Would you do the honors?"

With shaky fingers he draped the scarf across her body and pinned it at her shoulder.

Just then a man stepped from behind the women gathered around her. "Excuse me, ma'am. But I'm to give you this." He handed her a bouquet. "Compliments of General Marion."

Lilyan clasped the spray of moccasin flowers, sweet lady's tresses, and orchids.

"Picked 'em himself, he did. Scoured the swamps for hours for that one there in the middle." He pointed to the most beautiful white orchid Lilyan had ever seen. "Told me to express his regrets for not being here, but only the most urgent of business could keep him from the captain's wedding."

Lilyan stood on tiptoe and kissed the man's cheek. "Please, convey my deepest gratitude to the general. The flowers are exquisite, and I shall never forget his beautiful gift."

The man nodded, and as he walked away, Lilyan wondered if Marion's urgent business involved some plan that would take her Nicholas away.

Andrew held out the crook of his arm. "Shall we?"

She took his arm, and they walked toward the center of the encampment.

He patted her hand. "Ma and Da would be proud, Sissy."

Yes they would, she thought, as they approached Nicholas. His handsome face was lit with such love and pride, her knees suddenly felt weak. Elizabeth, Samuel, and the chaplain stood with him beneath an arbor someone had fashioned of willow branches entwined with crossvine flowers, the same brilliant red-orange color that now swept across the sky.

As her brother escorted her toward the wedding bower, the intimate gathering parted to make an aisle, their faces glowing with pleasure as she passed each of them. And then she spotted Callum near the front of the group. He stood with his hat held to his heart and his head ducked down. She slowed down as she neared him, and he glanced up revealing tears that had pooled in his pale blue eyes.

"You are a wonderful sight in your tartan, lassie," he said, his voice cracking. "I so wish your da could have been here."

Lilyan cupped his chin in her hand. "You combed your hair," she whispered.

She had seen him do that only once—when paying a call on a widow who lived in Charlestown.

He snorted. "I take to these doings like a dog in a dancing school. But, this is your wedding, lass, and I wouldna wish to be anywhere else."

She kissed his cheek and then turned to see her beloved shifting from one foot to the other, as if eager to get on with the ceremony.

The next hour passed in a blur for Lilyan. The signing of the marriage bonds, which would be recorded in the chaplain's home church, the vows, the toasts, the applause, and cutting the cake spun together in dream-like visions grounded only by a pair of golden eyes filled with so much adoration it made her shiver.

She barely felt Nicholas' hands span her waist and lift her onto his horse, but was happy for the warmth of his body when he mounted in the saddle behind her. She managed to wave good-bye to her well-wishers and blew kisses to Andrew and Callum and Elizabeth, who told her that her things had already been taken ahead to the farmhouse.

As much as she appreciated the efforts her family and friends had put into making the ceremony such a glorious occasion, she felt a deep sense of relief when she and Nicholas were finally alone. As they traveled a moonlit trail through the forest, her body melted back against his rock-hard chest, and she inhaled a deep breath.

"What is that lovely smell, Nikki?"

He chuckled. "Someone plaited Olympus's main and tail with crossvine. He was indignant at first, but decided to take it in his stride."

She stroked the horse's neck. "Olympus? That's your horse's name?"

"Yes."

"What made you choose …?" Lilyan twisted her head around to look up at him. "Surely not?" Laughter welled up in her chest.

He cleared his throat. "I know. It's silly. I thought it would be amusing to mount Olympus every day."

Their laughter echoed through the trees around them.

My husband has a sense of humor. My husband; how I adore the sound of that.

"You have a beautiful laugh, aga'pi mou. I must see to it that you do so more often."

How much time will we have to share more laughter? Is there someone out there in the night, hunting me, planning my capture, determined to take this time away from me?

She mentally shook herself. Where had that idea come from? It had been such a glorious day; she could not, she would not, let such ugly thoughts spoil her happiness. *God has granted me this wonderful time to love and be loved, and I will cherish it for as long at it lasts.*

She shivered, and Nicholas tightened his grasp across her body.

At the farmhouse, Nicholas dismounted and then took Lilyan by the waist and pulled her off the horse.

Still holding her up high, he said in a voice much deeper than usual, "The stars are shining above you, but there is not one that rivals you, my love."

Lilyan lifted her face to the gossamer black sky shot through with sparkling sequins and then gazed into her husband's glorious eyes. "Is this what heaven is like, Nikki?"

Nicholas swept her into his arms and made his way up the steps. "Not quite, agapimeni mou, my beloved." He carried her inside and closed the door behind them. "But we will know what it's like soon. Very soon."

[Love] beareth all things, believeth all things, hopeth all things,
endureth all things.   I Corinthians 13:7

Chapter Twenty-Five

IN THE FOLLOWING DAYS, Lilyan discovered what it meant to be as one with another—heart, soul, spirit, and body. Nicholas personified her every dream: passionate, attentive, gentle, solicitous, humorous, insightful, intelligent, charming, handsome . . .

Sitting on a blanket in the middle of a grassy meadow, with Nicholas' head in her lap, Lilyan smiled as she considered a dozen more words.

"That is a particularly delightful smile." Nicholas caressed her lips with his finger.

She thought he had been asleep, but as she was beginning to learn, Nicholas woke quickly and alert, unlike she, who remained fuzzy headed several minutes after dragging herself awake.

"Well, of course. I was thinking of you."

He stretched his arms above his head and then pulled Lilyan beside him, cradling her in the crook of one arm and resting his head on the other. "No wonder you were smiling."

She poked him in his ribs, and he grabbed her hand and slipped it inside his shirt. They fell silent until she began absentmindedly twirling his chest hair with her fingertips. He pressed her hand flat against him and turned onto his side.

172

"If you continue that, you'll have to pay the consequences."

Molten fire shot through the pit of her stomach at the thought of those consequences.

"Is that a threat, Mr. Xanthakos?" She sprang to her feet, barely escaping his hand as he grabbed for her ankle.

"It's a promise, Mrs. Xanthakos." He rolled up onto his knees. "And as you may know by now, I am a man of my word."

He smiled, his deliciously crooked grin exposing his sculptured white teeth. "Come here."

Lilyan glanced around for a way of escape. "I think not, Mr. Xanthakos. As *you* may know by now, *I* don't respond well to orders."

"We'll see about that."

Lilyan squealed, picked up her skirts, and dashed toward the house. But there was no contest. Nicholas caught up with her at the fence, lifted her up onto his shoulder, and dropped a soft whack on her behind. "There. So you will know who is boss in this family."

At that moment they both heard a horse approaching.

"It's probably someone bringing our dinner." Nicholas continued to stride toward the house with Lilyan still draped across his shoulder like a sack of flour.

Lilyan's friends had taken it upon themselves to bring the newlyweds all manner of treats over the past few days. With all their planning, preparing, and secretly delivering the tasty tidbits and sumptuous suppers, Lilyan knew the women were enjoying her honeymoon as much as she was.

Well, almost as much.

"Nikki, do let me down. This isn't dignified."

He whooped and popped her bottom again. But as the rider approached, Lilyan felt Nicholas' back muscles go rigid. He slid her to the ground and stood behind her with his hands on her shoulders.

"Afternoon, Captain. Madame." The man dismounted and doffed his hat to Lilyan.

"Corporal."

"Sorry about this, sir. But the general is asking for you."

Lilyan wanted to turn around and clasp her husband, but he clamped his hands on her shoulders.

"Tell General Marion I'll be there as soon as I can. Just let me escort my wife back to the camp."

"Sorry again, sir. But general says right away. Told me to see to your missus."

Nicholas turned Lilyan around to face him. "Please, go inside and start packing. I'll be with you in a moment."

She refused to look into his eyes for fear of bursting into tears. Instead, she nodded, stepped around him, and trudged up the stairs to the house. Inside, she methodically gathered their belongings. She was wrapping her things in a blanket when she spotted one of his shirts lying across the end of the bed. She picked it up, buried her face in it, breathed in his scent, and then folded it and slid it into his satchel.

She heard him come in and winced at the grim expression on his face.

"Marion won't be an independent partisan anymore."

"What does that mean?"

"Only that we'll be working closer with the main army from now on."

"What about me? And the rest of the women?"

"For now, you're to stay here. Once we find out where our main body will be, you may be attached to a brigade."

"How long will that take?"

"Lilyan, I don't know any particulars." He balled his hands into fists and held them to his sides. "You should know by now, the general is not one to share his plans."

Lilyan wrapped her arms around him. "I knew we wouldn't have much time, but—" Her voice cracked.

"Lilyan Cameron Xanthakos, you may not cry. You are a captain's wife now and you must act accordingly."

Lilyan sucked in a breath at the tone of voice she knew must engender respect from his men. But she resented his using that tone with her and was about to tell him so, when she looked up at his face. The sadness she witnessed there drew every ounce of resentment from her body. For an instant he had dropped his mask of self-sufficiency and had shown her a vulnerability that pierced her heart.

"Upon your orders, Captain." She gave him a lighthearted salute. "No crying here, sir."

"Thank you, Lilyanista."

They spent the next few minutes gathering their belongings and then stood at the doorway, looking around at their tiny paradise on earth.

"I will never forget this place … this time." Nicholas laced his fingers through hers and opened the door.

Lilyan stepped out onto the porch with him. "Come back to me."

"As soon as I can." He tipped up her chin, probing her eyes with his, as if searching her soul. "Courage, my love. God has blessed us. Has He not?"

She gulped, unable to form a response.

At the bottom of the steps, Nicholas waited for the corporal to mount and then helped Lilyan up to sit in front of him. He kissed her hand before letting it go.

"See to my wife, Corporal. Get her safely to the camp or there will be hell to pay. Do you understand?"

"I do, sir."

Lilyan disciplined herself from looking back until they reached a bend in the road. Unable to resist any longer, she glanced at the house only to find that Nicholas had already ridden away. Desolation crept from one end of her body to the other, slashing its way through her happiness like a scythe through a swath of dune grass.

At the campsite, she thanked the corporal for his assistance and hurried to her tent. Wretched with despair, she fell onto her pallet and despite her promise to Nicholas, cried until she could cry no more. She finally rolled onto her back to find Elizabeth sitting on the ground beside her.

Elizabeth took her hand. "I am here."

Lilyan could not bring herself to speak.

Elizabeth draped a blanket over her and tucked it under her sides. "Sleep now. You need the rest. I will be right here beside you when you wake."

The next morning, true to her word, Elizabeth was sleeping on the pallet next to Lilyan and awoke immediately when Lilyan stirred.

"Come," said Elizabeth, "let's eat a little breakfast and then go for a swim in the river as we used to do."

At the cooking fire, Lilyan made an attempt to eat the bowl of

175

mush and drink the ale Linda handed her, all the while accepting the best wishes of the other ladies and thanking them for their concern for her man. The fact that each one of them had a loved one in the fight did nothing to assuage her loneliness.

Elizabeth seemed so excited about going for a swim, Lilyan did not have the heart to tell her it was the last thing she wanted to do. The walk to the river turned out to be a pleasant surprise. The woods were rife with myriad colors of flowers popping up through the rich, loamy soil. Lime green ferns swirled in patches underneath dogwood trees bursting with their white and green blooms. When she stopped to study one of the lacy fronds, she thought she saw something moving among the pines. As she hurried to catch up with Elizabeth, she could not shake the sense that someone was following.

At the river's edge, Elizabeth had already pulled off her moccasins and was tugging at the hem of her skirt.

"Did you notice anyone in the woods?" Lilyan glanced over her shoulder.

Elizabeth shrugged. "No." She pulled off her dress and, wearing only her chemise, she touched her toes into the water. "Just right," she exclaimed and dove into the water, surfacing a few feet away. "Come on in. It's delicious." She paddled around and stuck her toes up out of the water.

It did not take long for Lilyan to disrobe and jump in, making a big splash that washed over Elizabeth, who came up sputtering. They played water war, giggling like children.

They had floated quietly for a few minutes when Elizabeth cleared her throat. "Lilyan, was it as we imagined?"

It surprised Lilyan that, for the first time since she had known Elizabeth, she felt the more mature, the more grown-up of the two. "It was nothing as I had imagined."

Elizabeth furrowed her brow.

Lilyan grinned. "We were right about one thing. It was very, very pleasant."

Elizabeth laughed. "I am happy for you. Nicholas is a fine man. Your children will be beautiful."

Stunned, Lilyan brushed her hand across her stomach.

Is it possible that we may have made a child? That thought pleased her, but was followed quickly by another frightening one. *If so, will the child ever know its father, and what chance would the babe have with a fugitive for a mother?*

Elizabeth touched her arm. "I have made you sad again. I am sorry."

"No, no. Don't worry." Lilyan headed for shore and sat on one of the rocks, drawing her fingers through her hair.

Elizabeth continued to swim for a while longer and then joined her on shore.

Lilyan yawned. "I am more weary than I realized. Are you ready to go back?"

"If we must. There really is quite a lot of work to do."

"Then let's get to it. Keeping busy will help keep my mind off Nicholas."

As she followed her friend back up the hill, Lilyan kept glancing over her shoulder. Try as she might, she could not to shirk the notion that someone was watching.

Have I not often told you that we came into this world but to prepare for a better! For that better life, my dear boy, your father is prepared. Instead then of weeping, rejoice with me, my son, that my troubles are so near an end. Tomorrow I set out for immortality. You will accompany me to the place of my execution; and when I am dead, take and bury me by the side of your mother." Isaac Hayne

Chapter Twenty-Six

OVER THE NEXT SEVERAL weeks, no matter how hard she worked, Lilyan could not stop worrying about Nicholas and Andrew. She longed for her dear husband with a yearning so strong it soaked into her bones and sapped her strength. Then one day they appeared at the camp, grinning, happy to be back, and all in one piece. For a time, Lilyan's despair melted away, until, without warning and without knowing where they were headed, her men left again.

June gave way to July and July to August. Lilyan's life became a series of waxing and waning emotions. Her greatest happiness came from cooking and sharing meals with Nicholas, shaving his beard and trimming his hair, mending his shirts, cuddling next to him in the evenings by the fire while Callum spun stories of his adventures in the backcountry. Her deepest pleasure came from sharing her husband's bed, waking next to him in the mornings, and watching his chest rise and fall. Sometimes to escape the sweltering heat, they would spend time swimming in the river, exchanging glances and touches as sultry as the torrid weather. She was still too shy to grant his wish to make love with him on the shore and appreciated his good-natured acceptance of her refusal.

Those enchanting times made his absences unbearable. As she watched him ride away, loneliness would steel over her like a candlesnuffer extinguishing a flame. She often wondered how she had ever lived before him.

It was also during those months that Lilyan began to sense a change in the way Elizabeth behaved in Samuel's presence. Her glares softened into shy glances, and her pansy-brown eyes often studied him as he ambled around the encampment. One evening, Lilyan caught her staring at Samuel as he puffed on his pipe, caught the smoke with his hand, and pushed it across the top of his head. Her gaze was so intent it was as if she was unaware of anyone else around her. When Samuel glanced up and locked his eyes with Elizabeth's, Lilyan had to stifle a giggle at the pure amazement on his face. When his shocked expression turned to puzzlement to a very knowing smile, the air seemed to crackle. Lilyan found the exchange fascinating and peered at the intimate group gathered around the fire to see if they were watching. When she looked at Nicholas who was seated beside her, his wink told her that at least he had noticed.

The next day, Lilyan attempted to broach the subject, but Elizabeth explained that she was not yet prepared to discuss it. The firm, but gentle, rebuff made Lilyan wonder if she had misread the scene at the campfire. But when they received news that their men had gone away again, the look of utter desolation on her friend's face confirmed her conclusion.

The bad news from the front only added to Lilyan's sadness. They learned that Banastre Tarleton had made a surprise raid on the Virginia legislature, capturing them all except Governor Thomas Jefferson, who barely escaped. A report came telling of a crushing defeat of forces led by the Marquis de Lafayette. Because Nicholas never spoke of the war, Lilyan found out from the Snead twins that he had been involved in an engagement with the British at Quinby Bridge near Georgetown after the British evacuated the town. But the Patriots failed to make the British retreat.

The second week of August brought news that stunned everyone in the camp. By order of Colonel Balfour and Lord Rawdon, after a short hearing before the board of officers in Charlestown, the British had executed Isaac Hayne. A state senator and wealthy planter from Beaufort, Hayne had fought with the Patriots, had been captured, and after he was assured that he would not be made to join the royal army, had given his oath of allegiance. But eventually, the British ordered him to join their forces. To avoid conscription, he left Charlestown and joined an American militia company. Subsequently he was recaptured, found in violation of his parole, and hanged, without a trial and with no examination of witnesses.

Will Andrew suffer the same fate if he is captured again?

Finally, in mid-August news came that the camp followers were to move, and from what Lilyan could gather, they would set up camp north of Georgetown. The women greeted the news with mixed emotions. They rejoiced to be closer to their men, but dreaded living in an area surrounded by swamps. Sweltering heat and the mosquitoes sometimes proved more formidable than the enemy.

Once they had packed their belongings and pushed them into the back of a wagon, Lilyan and Elizabeth decided to take one last swim in the river.

Halfway there, Lilyan stopped and glanced around, overcome with an uneasiness she could not explain. "Did you hear something?"

Elizabeth stood quietly, tilting her head to the side. "No. Nothing."

Lilyan rubbed the back of her neck. "I have this strange feeling."

"We can go back, if you want."

Lilyan shrugged. "No. No. I'm overanxious. Let's go enjoy our swim."

When they reached the river, they deposited their dresses on the bank and waded waist deep into the cool water.

"The current is stronger today." Elizabeth pushed herself closer to shore.

"They must have had rain in the mountains." Lilyan scooped her hands across the yellow-brown ripples and splashed the water up on her neck. "We could use some rain here. It's almost too hot to breathe."

After a while, Lilyan sloshed her way back to shore, sat on a boulder, and dangled her toes in the water. She loosened her hair and pulled her fingers through the long, tangled tresses.

"Mm. This feels so good. I hate to go back, but I think I left some of my painting supplies beside the campfire." Lilyan stood, dropped her dress over her head, and tugged the material across her damp skin. The water from her soggy chemise soon soaked through the dress, spreading dark blotches on the material. "Are you coming?"

"Not yet. I want to wash out my dress. You go ahead."

Lilyan leaned against a tree and shoved her feet into her shoes. "I should wait."

"No. Really. I'll be fine." Elizabeth swam to shore and, standing knee-deep in the water, she reached for her dress from a nearby rock.

Lilyan scanned the woods around them. "I'll go, but promise me you won't go swimming again."

"I promise."

Lilyan waved good-bye and trudged back toward the campsite. When she broke through the trees, to her delight she spotted Nicholas and Samuel standing by her tent. Forgetting her exhaustion, she sprinted toward them, but stopped when she heard a scream and then a *pop*, *pop* coming from behind her.

Nicholas vaulted toward her and threw her to the ground, covering her body with his.

"It's coming from the river," he shouted to Samuel.

"Elizabeth is down there!" Lilyan shrieked, struggling to get out from under him.

Samuel grabbed his rifle and bolted into the woods. Callum raced toward them and helped Nicholas grab her up, and together they practically carried her behind one of the wagons. Linda charged around the side of the wagon, brandishing a poker. Evelyn and several other women packed in around them, hurriedly loading their guns.

More shots rang out, and they all ducked.

"What in hades is going on?" Callum yelled.

"Not sure yet." Nicholas clamped his fingers around Lilyan's arm.

Lilyan struggled to free herself from his iron grip. "I left Elizabeth alone down there. I should have known better."

Nicholas stared at her. "What do you mean?"

"I don't know. I felt something ... sensed someone watching." She shivered. "I was so miserable, Nicholas, I forgot everything my father taught me about staying alert ..." The words died in her throat at the sight of Samuel trudging through the trees carrying a limp form in his arms.

"No!" she screamed, thrashing as Nicholas handed her off to Callum.

"Stay here," he commanded through clenched teeth and then raced down the hill.

As Samuel drew nearer, pain seared Lilyan's heart as she recognized the splash of red spreading across Elizabeth's body. With one desperate thrust she lunged away from Callum and scrambled her way to catch up with Nicholas, stumbling twice on the hem of her dress. Nicholas came to a sudden stop, and she slammed into his back, knocking the breath from her body.

He whirled around. "I told you—"

Dread seeped its way up Lilyan's throat as she gasped for air. She slipped around Nicholas and edged toward Samuel, fearful of what she would discover. A stream of blood oozed down Elizabeth's arm and dripped from her lifeless fingers. Lilyan looked into Samuel's eyes and saw in them a mirror of her own agony.

"She is dead," he said.

As if someone had struck her in the back of her legs, Lilyan fell to her knees. "It cannot be. It cannot be," she wailed.

She slumped to the ground. "Bring her to me, please." She pushed the words through her constricting throat.

Samuel came forward and gently lowered Elizabeth's body into Lilyan's outstretched arms. "My dear one. My dear one. I am so sorry. So sorry," she murmured, cradling her friend to her bosom, rocking back and forth.

She pushed back strands of Elizabeth's jet black hair, kissed her pale cheek, and wiped away the death beads already forming on her cool forehead.

Nicholas took Lilyan by the shoulders. "Come, sweeting. You must let her go."

She stared up at him, unable to focus through the tears swimming in her eyes. "But I wasn't there for her. I left her alone."

"Lilyanista …"

She allowed Samuel to pull Elizabeth away and felt Nicholas lift her up into his arms.

"How am I to live without her?" Her voice broke as if someone had grabbed her by the throat.

She pressed her face into his shirt. Bone-shaking sobs racked her body. Nicholas carried her into the tent and sat on her pallet. Holding her tightly in his lap, he made gentle cooing sounds until her crying subsided. A wave of grief welled up inside her, and she moaned from the agony of it.

Nicholas murmured words she could not understand, then kissed her flushed cheeks and forehead.

When he shifted his weight, Lilyan panicked and gripped his shirt. "Don't leave me. Please, don't you leave me, too."

"Shhh. I am here, my darling. I am here."

Five Thousand Pounds Reward!! His Majesty's Loyal Subjects are reminded that the above reward will be paid for the apprehension of Lilyan Allison Grace Cameron, and they are called upon to make every exertion to take her...

Chapter Twenty-Seven

THEY LAID ELIZABETH TO rest beside the river.

The chaplain who had married Lilyan and Nicholas and who had brought them such happiness presided over the ceremony. In a solemn, plain-spoken manner, he provided a gentle reminder of the ephemeral nature of joys on earth. Speaking from Matthew, he warned of storing up treasures on earth; treasures that can be damaged, destroyed, and stolen.

His words, like a flaming arrow, thrust themselves into Lilyan's heart and sparked a firestorm of resentment.

Yes, she cherished her family. What of it? What possible wrong could God find in that? She would sacrifice her life for her family. Was there no greater love than that? Was God so jealous that He had set out to take away her treasures one by one, teaching her some sort of horrible lesson? That notion struck fear into her soul.

"Sissy?" Andrew stepped closer.

"Courage." Nicholas pulled her into the crook of his arm.

"We're here for you, lassie," said Callum.

Yes, but for how long? Lilyan's body wilted from the grief that washed over her in sickening waves.

"Did not God tell Joshua that he would never leave him nor

forsake him?" The chaplain's question seized Lilyan's attention, and she wondered if he had read her thoughts.

"Most assuredly He knows our needs, and we are not to worry about tomorrow, nor about what we eat, what we drink, or what we wear. Our heavenly Father, who feeds the birds and clothes the lilies of the fields, knows our needs. But we must seek first His kingdom and His righteousness, and all these things will be given to you as well."

Lilyan had heard this message many times in her life. The familiarity reassured her, wrapping around her like a warm blanket. The meaning flowed through her like a healing balm, soothing the ragged edges of her heart. Though bolstered by this small comfort, she still could not bring herself to watch as the men lowered her dear friend's body into the ground. Instead, she turned away and, clutching Nicholas' arm, she made her way back to the campsite, vowing to return later.

Before entering her tent, Lilyan asked Nicholas and the others for some time alone. She spent an agonizing hour crying and pacing until she became so overwhelmed with loneliness that she rushed outside. She hurried to join Nicholas, Andrew, Callum, and Samuel sitting on makeshift benches circling a dormant fire. They greeted her with faces as bleak as her heart.

"Lilyan ..." Nicholas hesitated. "There is something we must tell you.

Lilyan wrapped her arms around her body. *What now?*

Nicholas nodded to Samuel.

"Elizabeth's death was not random," Samuel said.

Lilyan jerked up her head.

"There were three of them. Elizabeth killed one with her knife. One of them got away. The third I tracked down. Before he died, I made him tell me"—a muscle worked in Samuel's cheek—"why." He pulled a letter from his pocket, opened it, and withdrew a piece of paper tucked inside.

Lilyan stared the top half of the folded paper. "Pictures of Elizabeth and me? I drew them myself. They—they were at our house in Charlestown. I don't understand."

Nicholas unfolded the handbill. "Look. Here."

Wanted for the murder of Captain Remington Bradenton. Lilyan could feel the blood draining from her face. *Murder.* She shuddered, recalling the nightmarish event in vivid detail.

"That is not the worst of it." Nicholas handed her the letter. "Read this."

Lilyan scanned the flourished script penned by a London barrister to a Daniel Chambers, esquire, of Charlestown. According to the letter, Mr. Chambers, acting on behalf of the Earl of Bradenton, was to hire men to seek out Lilyan and Elizabeth and kill them. They would receive half of the money to buy provisions and the other half upon proof of their death.

Callum leaned over to look. "It's a king's ransom. Three, maybe four, times as much as any man here would see in a lifetime."

Shivering, Lilyan folded the picture and the letter and slipped them inside her dress.

"But what kind of men would do such a thing?" asked Andrew.

Callum shot a look at Samuel. "Outlaws."

Samuel nodded.

"But the Regulators wiped them out. Just before the war," Andrew blurted.

"Regulators?" Nicholas asked.

Callum folded his arms across his chest. "Back in the sixties, mostly in the backcountry, gangs of outlaws went around terrorizing the settlers. Thieving, killing, burning homes. Some of the worst were the Tyrrell brothers. Used to travel up and down the Broad River, all the way up to the mountains. You name something bad, and they did it."

Callum took a deep breath. "Well, God-fearing, law-abiding citizens got tired of waiting on the king to help. They banded together in what they called the Regulators, and set about ridding the country of those varmints. Lilyan and Andrew's father was one. That's how he was killed."

Callum unfolded his arms and slapped his thighs. "But enough of that. It's time we got down to it."

When Nicholas took Lilyan's hand, she searched his face. From the look in his eyes, she knew she was not going to like what he had to say.

"We are going to have to get you to safety—"

"No!" Lilyan jerked her hand away.

"Hear me out," Nicholas snapped. "There may be more of these

186

men out there. They know where you are. And for this amount of money, they will never give up."

"But I'm safe here. As safe as I could ever be."

"We've discussed this." Nicholas nodded around the circle. "And we've decided it's for the best."

Lilyan shot up from the bench. "You didn't discuss it with *me*, and I say I'm not leaving."

Nicholas eyed each person gathered. "Come, Lilyan, I need to speak with you alone."

"Fine. But it won't matter. I'm not going."

He took her by the arm, and they walked to their favorite spot on the edge of the camp. She sat on the bench he had made for them, while he paced back and forth until finally he knelt in front of her.

"Lilyan, I know the torment you suffer. For me, to watch you go through this ..." He held out his hands, palms upward. "I am without words."

Lilyan wanted to caress his cheek, but realized if she did, she would be giving away ground.

He clasped her hands and leaned so close she could see the dark brown flecks at the edges of his golden irises. "My reasons for wanting to send you away from here are purely selfish."

Lilyan started to speak, but he placed a finger on her lips.

"Please. All the time I have been fighting this war, working as a scout for Marion, I have had only myself to think about." He smiled. "And maybe Samuel. But he can take care of himself.

"Only now I have you, my darling. My Lilyanista." He caressed her cheek. "I must confess. Once, I enjoyed the exhilaration of outfoxing the enemy. The danger made my blood race. But that holds less and less appeal for me as each day passes. My days are measured by the number of hours I am away from you."

He pressed her hand to his heart. "You are so much a part of me. I wake wondering if you are still curled up on your pallet, so warm and sweet smelling. When I eat, I think about meals you will cook for me in our own kitchen. Instead of seeing trees as potential hiding places for the enemy, I think about how you would paint them in your beautiful murals.

"Simply put, my dearest, I do not concentrate as I should. Now, with this terrible bounty on your head, I would constantly worry about you. I cannot afford that distraction. It wouldn't be good for my men or me. I need to be cautious. I want so much to live, to love you, to make a life for us, to have babies. Don't you see?" He raked his fingers across his jaw.

With that, Lilyan did reach out and caress his cheek, and then she kissed the small scar at the corner of his mouth. "Where would you have me go?"

He rose and sat on the bench beside her. "Samuel suggests somewhere in the mountains. Callum says your father had many trusted friends among the Cherokee. Even though many Cherokee have fought alongside the British, Callum feels the loyalty to your father runs deeper." He hesitated. "He specifically mentioned the family of your Elizabeth."

Lilyan trembled. "She would have liked that. To know that I could find a safe place among her people."

Nicholas squeezed her hand.

Loneliness began to creep into her heart even though he had not yet departed. "Could you not go with me?"

"As much as I want to, I cannot. General Marion refused my leave request and Samuel's as well."

Lilyan hung her head.

"Do not distress yourself so. We *are* going to win this war. And we are so near the end. I can feel it."

"It's so far away, my love." She twined her fingers through his. "We would be parted for quite some time."

"It will be difficult, yes? But for now, I'd rather have you safe and far away than … than … I can't even bring myself to think it."

They sat quietly for several minutes.

"When will I go?"

"As soon as you can pack."

"Oh." Her heart sank. "How will I get there?"

He kissed her hands. "Marion has agreed to allow Andrew to accompany you. And Callum will go too, of course."

That news provided the only bright spot in Lilyan's living nightmare.

"Ah." He grinned. "To see that wondrous smile, even for a moment."

He stared at something behind her. "Callum is on his way. He probably wants to get away while there is some daylight."

Lilyan draped her arms around his neck. "So little time," she whimpered.

He drew her close. "But memories enough to sustain us for a while, yes?"

He brushed his mouth across her forehead, her eyes, her nose, and her cheeks and then captured her lips in a hungry and desperate kiss. They broke apart and, holding hands, walked back to the campsite.

After packing her belongings, Lilyan drifted to the river and stood alone by Elizabeth's gravesite; as alone as she could be with Nicholas, Callum, and Samuel lurking somewhere close behind the trees.

"I thought we would grow old together." Her lips trembled. "I envisioned our children playing—"

She pulled wildflowers from the grasses on the riverbank and clenched them in her hand. "I cannot remember ever telling you how much I loved you and how much I appreciated your coming to Andrew's and my rescue so long ago. We were so miserably unhappy and missed our mother so much. But in your gentle, patient, and caring way you made us a family again."

Lilyan lifted her face to the sky. "So there you are, somewhere in heaven. I imagine you are having a glorious time singing with the angels." She placed the bouquet on the rocks that covered the grave. "I refuse to say good-bye. We will be together again one day. Until then … "

She started for the camp, but paused a moment, looking back. "Somehow, I feel you are keeping watch over me still. And I will need watching over, dear one, for I do not know what lies ahead of me and I am frightened."

hello, o si yo
sister, u lv
husband, o ye hi
wife, o da li i
fawn, Awinita
warrior, di tli hi
horse, so qui li
seven directions- north, south, east, west, above, below, here in the
center

Chapter Twenty-Eight

BEFORE THEIR DEPARTURE, with foresight born of experience, Evelyn put together Lilyan's outfit—trousers, a homespun shirt with billowing sleeves, and boots covered with buckskin leggings. She instructed Lilyan to keep her stays unlaced underneath the shirt, and helped her don a vest that buttoned so tightly, it flattened her chest. Lilyan thought the results comical, but when Nicholas made a slow circle around her, eyes raking her from head to toe, she felt herself blush.

She tried repeatedly to confine her hair underneath her wide-brimmed felt hat, but it would not stay tucked in, and she stamped her foot. "I shall have to cut it."

His expression turned fierce. "You will not cut your hair. It is understood?" His tone left no room for doubt.

Lilyan bristled. "It will grow back."

Nicholas looked around at the others and then took her by the arm. "Come. Let us discuss this elsewhere."

Inside Lilyan's tent, she swung around to stare at him, jamming her fists onto her hips. "Why are you being so obstinate about this?"

He set his jaw. "Why must I explain myself? I am your husband."

"That's your reasoning?"

"It is all I need." He folded his arms across his chest and regarded her steadily.

Obstinate man.

"My hair is more important to you than my life?"

With that he began stomping back and forth, gesturing with his hands and muttering in Greek. The faster he paced, the louder his voice grew, stopping suddenly when Evelyn stuck her head between the tent flaps.

"Come with me, Lilyan. I think I have a solution." She winked at Nicholas. "We'll be back shortly, Captain."

When Lilyan entered the tent again, her husband's reaction to her transformation drained away whatever amount of anger she had left.

"You cut it." His expression was crestfallen.

"No." She could not resist cupping his cheek in her hand. "We stuffed my hair into a stocking cap and covered it with a wig. It belonged to her husband."

She pulled off her hat, reached back, and flipped the jet-black queue at the back of her head. "See, it looks like yours." She grinned up at him. "So, I have obeyed you, my husband. You are pleased, yes?"

"Most pleased." He swept her into his arms and kissed her so hard she had to clasp the wig to keep it in place.

Lilyan reluctantly stepped back and clamped her hands to her flaming cheeks. "This arguing. It is rather pleasant. Don't you think?"

His amber eyes held fire. "Most pleasant, aga'pi mou."

Evelyn, who stood just outside, cleared her throat. "Come, my dears, it's time to go."

Leaving her husband was one of the most difficult challenges of Lilyan's life. She cherished the newfound feeling of becoming attached to him as if by tender shoots of a vine, and she feared the painful tearing asunder of that delicate bond. She swore to herself she would not cry, but as he clutched her and whispered Greek endearments, the tears that swam in her eyes spilled over. They continued to flow as her friends took turns hugging her and offering their blessings for a safe journey.

At the end of all the farewells, she remembered that this time

Elizabeth would not be going with her. It was too much. She gulped a sob and clutched a hand to her heart. From the distress she read in Nicholas' eyes, she knew how hard it was for him to send her away. But she was also aware deep inside that her leaving was for the best. As she mounted her horse, she lifted up a silent prayer for strength, and even managed a tremulous smile as she glanced over her shoulder for one last look.

They had ridden an hour when Lilyan realized Evelyn had been right to insist she wear a pair of her trousers for the journey. The trail they followed narrowed in places, becoming almost invisible. Branches clawed at her legs from every direction.

Later, with the camp far behind them, plodding through thick patches of canebrakes, Lilyan forced herself to concentrate on their path and to store away the memory of her Nicholas standing with clenched fists beside an equally somber Samuel in front of her band of friends waving good-bye. But thoughts of Elizabeth soon crowded Lilyan's mind, so intense, so sad, that her body succumbed to the weight of them, and she slumped over in the saddle. The picture of Samuel cradling her beloved friend's body while the blood dripped off her fingertips had seared itself into her consciousness. She squeezed her eyes shut and tried with all her might to recall an image to take its place.

They traveled silently for the most part, Callum at the head, followed by Lilyan, and then Andrew, leading a pack mule. Sometimes they wended out of sight of the river, but never away from its rushing sound. Callum kept them moving at a steady pace for hours, until he came to a stop and ordered Andrew to lead the way while he doubled back to make sure no one tracked them.

"Follow the two notches," he said to Andrew before disappearing into the woods.

"Two notches?" Lilyan peered around them but couldn't spot notches in anything.

Andrew looked back over his shoulder. "I'll show you the next one we come to."

They had traveled about a half an hour, picking their way up and down steep bluffs carved into the land by the river, when Andrew stopped and waited for her to come alongside.

"There." He pointed to a giant elm.

She did not see anything at first, but after studying the trunk, suddenly the two short slashes carved into the bark became so clear, she wondered how she had not seen them at first glance. She was about to comment when she noticed Andrew concentrating on something behind her.

Nerves danced like sheet lightning up her arms.

"Calm yourself. It's only Callum."

She twisted around to watch her old friend until he drew up beside them.

"See anything?" Andrew asked.

"Nothing." Callum pulled off his hat, rubbed his arm across his forehead, and popped the hat back on his head. "Let's keep moving a while longer. You stay on point. We'll rest the horses and get something to eat soon. I could eat the back end out of a he-goat."

Callum turned to Lilyan. "Are ye faring well, lassie?"

Lilyan nodded, not about to tell him how chafed her thighs were.

"Good. Let's get going, then."

With each mile, Lilyan recalled more and more about her *wonder time* and the many things her father had taught her about surviving in the backcountry. They crossed an open area of knee-high sedges, stirring up grasshoppers as large as birds, which flew up around them and into nearby trees. Lilyan's horse shied.

"Easy," she murmured, patting the animal's neck.

She watched fascinated as a kestrel, its blue-gray wings and brilliant rufous tail blazing in the sunlight, swooped from the sky, crying *klee, klee, klee.* The miniature falcon captured one of the grasshoppers in its bill, and soared away. A dragonfly with pale blue wings drifted across her path. She studied its bulging aquamarine face and could not help smiling. *God must have chuckled while designing that creature.* She caught the sound of a woodpecker rapping out a tattoo and spotted it hammering against the side of a rotting loblolly pine.

"Become one with your surroundings," her father had told her. "Use all your senses, especially your sense of smell. For once it is fully developed you will discover that you can catch the scent of wild animals nearby."

Lilyan lifted her chin and drew in a deep breath through her nose. *Dirt. No. Mud. With a hint of overcooked eggs. We must be near a swamp.*

At that moment they broke through a thick patch of cane,

gaining an unobstructed view of the river. She scanned the moss-laden cypress trees lining the opposite shore.

I was right.

They dismounted, and Lilyan combed her fingers through her horse's mane, gently blew into his nostrils, and murmured her gratitude for a good ride. Andrew unsaddled the horses and led them to the water's edge to drink and then forage on the grass. Minding her sore legs, Lilyan eased onto a soft patch of moss and watched Callum pull their supplies off the mule's back and check its hooves. She leaned back against a tree while Callum watered the animal and then led it back up the embankment.

"Come over here, lass." Callum grabbed a handful of corn from one of the sacks. "So if you ever have to do this, you won't lose a finger."

Lilyan inched up off the ground, brushed the dirt from the seat of her pants, and stepped close to him. "He's not so different from a horse, is he?'

Her old friend gave the mule a baleful glare. "Nae, not much different from a horse weaned in Hades, that is. Hold your hand flat and move it toward his shoulder. Wait for him to step back and take the corn with his lips. Pay attention and keep your fingers out of the way."

Lilyan followed his orders, crinkling her nose at the wet, spongy feel of the animal's lips against her skin.

"Stroke his shoulder and tell him how much you appreciate his work today."

Lilyan did as he asked, remembering how her father had used that very phrase. She studied Andrew as he hobbled the horses and climbed back up the hill toward them. *He walks like our father.* But he looks tired … pale, she noted before sitting next to the saddles.

Callum offered her a biscuit. "This is all for now. Tonight we'll make a fire. Maybe cook up some fish."

He popped the cork from his wooden canteen and handed it to her. She took a deep swig of the tepid liquid and then another, realizing how thirsty she had been. Andrew devoured his biscuit, guzzled some water, and then stretched out on the ground, pulling his hat over his face. He was soon fast asleep.

Lilyan caught Callum's eye before he swung his head away.

He notices it too. Andrew's fatigue.

"Best we all sleep awhile." Callum flopped down and rested his head on one of the saddles.

Lilyan reclined beside him, wincing as she straightened her legs and making a mental note to find some salve once they stopped traveling for the day. She glanced at Callum, who huffed a couple of times before settling into a low-pitched snore. Try as she might, though, she could not relax; too many thoughts tumbled through her head. Would she see her beautiful husband again? Would the Indians really welcome her? Were all the outlaws dead or were more out there tracking them in the forest? Would she ever get beyond the bone-melting sorrow of losing her dear Elizabeth? The relentless questions disturbed her so much, she welcomed Callum's orders to mount and continue their trek.

Soon they left behind the ebony soil of the river-bottom forest with it stands of tupelo and cypress sloughs, the stirring of wind through the moss, and the constant chorus of tree frogs. The ground grew sandier. The mysterious, smooth flow of red-brown water turned to a golden green-brown that danced across rocks and boulders. Farther north they wound through open stands of pines, sugar maples, giant oaks, and hickory trees.

When they came to the juncture of two large rivers, Callum held up his hand. "This is where we'll camp."

Lilyan was faint with relief. Her bottom ached, and her legs had grown numb, but she did not know how much she hurt until she dismounted. It felt like a thousand needles pricking her feet as she made her way to lean against a tree.

"No rest for the weary," said Callum. "Andrew and I will take care of the animals and see if we can catch some fish. Ye'll need to gather firewood. Over there, underneath that oak. The dry branches and small logs. They'll burn hot but won't give off much smoke. Watch for snakes."

Lilyan limped back and forth between the tree and the camp, gathering several armloads of firewood and piling it beside the saddles. She dug into one of the bags in the mule pack and found a tin holding the flint and steel. Using some white moss clinging to one of the logs, she soon had a fire going. By the time she found green sticks to form a spit, the air cooled as the last rays of the sun skipped across the ripples in the river, turning them pink and orange.

She spread out their blankets and gathered tin plates, forks, and a sack of salt and placed them near the fire. Inside her bag she found her medicine box and removed a tin of ointment. Finally, she gave in to her fatigue and sank to the ground. She tossed off her hat and wig and massaged her scalp, then combed her fingers through the tangles. After loosely braiding her unruly tresses into a rope, she rose up on her knees to make sure that Callum and Andrew were still on the riverbank. Feeling self-conscious, she rolled down her trousers and gingerly applied ointment to the blood red bumps on the inside of her thighs. She had just finished the painful task and pulled up her clothing when Callum and Andrew approached the camp carrying a string of rockfish.

It took them no time to cook the fish and consume them. Afterward, strolling to the river to clean their plates, Lilyan thought she had never eaten anything so tasty in her life. At the river's edge, she dropped the plates, sat on her heels, and rolled up her sleeves. Light from the full moon revealed the scar on her arm, turning the shiny skin a milky white. She touched the jagged line and grimaced at the thoughts it evoked. The blemish was ugly, but not as dreadful as the memories of the two deaths that had scarred her soul, nor the irrevocable events that had led up to her flight through the desolate back country.

Forcing herself to focus on her task, she made quick work of scrubbing the dishes with sand and rinsing them in the cool water. All the while, the hairs on her arms tingled as she imagined men skulking through the forest, creeping nearer and nearer. She quashed her fears and made herself walk over to her horse. She bade him good night, rubbing her hand across his neck and haunches. Before gathering the dishes, she glanced up at the stars popping out overhead. It comforted her to know that Nicholas must be gazing up at the same sky.

"Can you feel my love going out to you, my darling?" she whispered and then raised her eyes to the heavens.

"Please, dear Lord, keep him safe from harm. Guard him from evil."

Back at the camp, she found Callum leaning against a tree staring at the river, and she knew he had guarded her every move. Andrew sat on a blanket with another wrapped around his shoulders. Callum and Lilyan joined him by the fire, now a pile of glowing, breathing embers.

Lilyan hunkered into her blankets and lay on her side. "How long will this journey be?"

Callum cleared his throat. "Barring bad weather and anything happening to our mounts, I'd say about seven more days."

A wolf howled in the distance, and the back of Lilyan's neck prickled. Heart racing, she rose up on her elbow.

"Don't let them bother you, lass. There's plenty of food out there for them to eat. Wolves are curious creatures, though, and may come close to check us out. But they won't attack. Our worries will come from two-legged animals, not the four-legged kind."

Lilyan eased back, willing her heartbeat to quit its racing.

"Since we'll be living among the Cherokee soon," Callum stated, "I think it best you and Andrew know how to talk to them."

That idea seemed to perk up Andrew, who had remained quiet for too long. They spent the next hour learning basic words and phrases. It puzzled Lilyan how changing the tone of a word could completely change its meaning, and she struggled with the strange language that had no *r*'s, *p*'s or *b*'s. Andrew picked it up right away.

"Lesson's over," Callum announced abruptly.

He stood and picked up his rifle. "I'll take first watch. Andrew, you take second."

Andrew nodded.

"We should be within a day's ride to Ninety-Six by tomorrow evening if we travel fast and steady," said Callum. "It's not much of a town, but there's a trading post. And that means we might start running into more people. We'll have to keep a look out.

"Lassie, if we meet anyone on the trail, keep that hat clamped on and your face down. You might want to smear some bear grease on your cheeks in the morning."

Lilyan crinkled her nose.

Callum chuckled. "Or maybe some of that river clabber would do."

He lumbered over to a tree and slumped next to the trunk. "Get some rest, and may God keep us safe through the night."

"God bless you both," Lilyan whispered.

LILYAN OPENED HER EYES to a gunmetal gray sky and shivered under the blanket clammy from the morning dew. The smell of rain hung heavy in the chilly air. An odd feeling crept over her; it seemed as if the birds, the insects, even the trees, had poised themselves for something ominous. That sense of foreboding increased tenfold when she heard Andrew cough, a crackling sound rising deep from within his chest.

She rose up and looked at him where he sat hunched over, a damp blanket draped around his shoulders. His white face contrasted starkly with his red hair.

"Are you ill?" Lilyan asked, jolted by the lump of panic forming in her stomach.

Andrew nodded. "I'm fine. Don't worry so much, Sissy."

Callum stood slowly, his joints popping and clicking with every movement. He groaned and massaged his knees. "I sound like the rigging on a ship."

Guilt, pervasive and stunning, swept over Lilyan as she looked at two people she loved more than her own life.

What had she gotten them into? Callum should be sitting by the fire at Mrs. Snead's waiting for her pies to come out of the oven. Her brother should be at home in his own bed drinking a cup of warm broth. Instead, they were here in the middle of a forest, putting their lives in danger to get her to a safe place.

Oh, Lord, there aren't enough words to thank You for allowing me to love and be loved by these dear people. Guide our path today and, please, keep us from harm.

"Let's get to it, then," said Callum. "I'll take care of the horses. Lilyan, you stoke up the fire a wee bit and make some coffee."

Andrew started to rise, but Callum put up his hand. "Dinna fash, laddie. I'll take care of things. You sit a spell."

Lilyan piled kindling pieces onto the embers and watched them long enough to make sure they caught fire. She grabbed the coffeepot and followed Callum to the river.

When she caught up with him, she tugged his sleeve. "He's not well, is he?"

Callum glanced at the ground and then stared straight into her eyes. "I'll nae lie to you, lassie. His wound, that rotten ship, scouting for Marion … they've taken their toll."

"Then why did you let him come?"

"No one could have kept him from it. He was that determined." He patted her hand. "He'll be fine. He's got more grit than ten men I know. Just like your da. He would have been proud of him, you ken. And you too, lass."

He glanced away. "Dinna fret over me either."

"But—"

"I ken you better than you think. Rest easy. I've got plenty more years left in me. Now, go fetch some water. I'm aching for a cup of coffee. And while you're at it, check over there"—he pointed to the water's edge—"and see if the varmints left any of the fish I had tied up. My mouth's watering just thinking about them."

They took their time eating breakfast, practicing their Cherokee, giving the dew a chance to dissipate and their bodies to warm by the fire. Lilyan suspected that Callum wanted to give Andrew more time to ready himself.

Sooner than Lilyan would have wished, they began the next stage of their journey, continuing up the bank of the Saluda River. Callum seemed more relaxed, leading them at a slower pace, for which Lilyan was deeply grateful. Though her skin had toughened and the biting rash had almost disappeared, by the end of the day her muscles still ached. That night it took her only seconds to fall asleep, but she awoke before dawn with painful cramps in her calves and had to jump up and hop about to work them out.

The terrain remained much the same, canebrakes closer to the water, stands of hardwoods, and long stretches of sandy soil farther away. Once, they came to a standstill to watch buffalo grazing in a lush field of grass. Lilyan thought the huge beasts magnificent, sensing that their tranquil air masked an underlying, awesome power. Callum told them how fortunate they were to see such a rare sight and muttered his fury toward the hunters who had practically driven the beasts from the Southeast not long before the war began. Andrew started coughing again, and they moved on. Farther along the trail Callum shot a rabbit, strung it on a rope, and slung it behind his saddle. The report of the gun rattled Lilyan's already fraying nerves, so she concentrated on the different ways to make stew.

Toward sundown, Callum suddenly twisted around in his saddle. "Stay back. Keep your head down."

August 26, 1781
Somewhere in the wilderness

Beloved,
I have a most marvelous tale to tell. I believe with all my heart
that God sent someone to heal Andrew and to minister to my Worried
mind…

Chapter Twenty-Nine

"Lo THE TRAIL," a man called out and then rode up close
to Callum.

Lilyan pulled on her hat and lowered her head. Callum started
talking to the man, but they were too far away for her to pick
out what they said. Andrew pulled up his horse beside her. He
started coughing again and, by the time he got it under control, his
face was flushed and his eyes watery. The stranger leaned over and
stared, first at her and then at her brother. He nodded at Callum,
dropped his rifle across his lap, and headed their way. When he
passed beside Lilyan, she raised her head, making contact with the
blackest eyes she had ever encountered. His gaze, so steady and
intense, seemed to bore into her soul.

Callum waved them forward and waited for them to come
alongside. "Gentleman there says a storm's coming. Told me
about an abandoned cabin about a mile up ahead. We'd best make
tracks."

Large drops of rain began to pelt them, and Callum signaled
to pick up the pace. Soon a slick layer of mud covered the path,
and rivulets of cold water slid down the floppy brim of Lilyan's hat,
spilling onto her arms and legs and soaking through to her skin.

Callum pulled off the trail, and by the time they found the cabin, the sky had opened up with such a deluge, Lilyan felt as if she were standing underneath a waterfall.

"Get the supplies and saddles in as fast as you can," Callum shouted over the raging downpour. "I'll string a tarpaulin over the horses."

Lilyan and Andrew scrambled to follow his orders. Inside, she noticed a pile of logs already stacked in the stone fireplace and, pushing some dry leaves under the kindling, she silently thanked the cabin's latest occupant for their kindness.

Could it have been the stranger who led them to the cabin, she wondered?

She searched through a haversack and found the small tin box that held flint and steel. As she struck the flint, sending a shower of sparks to ignite the char cloth, she struggled to ignore the darting movements in the dark corners of the room.

I'll be fine, she tried to convince herself, as long as they're mice and not snakes.

Nevertheless, she felt relieved when Andrew grabbed a stick, stomped across the dirt floor, and beat the varmints out the back door. That small amount of effort started another bout of coughing and wheezing that made Lilyan cringe. He pulled a dilapidated wooden bench closer to the growing fire and motioned for her to sit.

"No." She shook her head. "Not yet."

She scanned the one-room cabin and spotted a cot, which she shoved next to the bench. She laid blankets across the tattered rope-strung mattress and formed a pillow with a sack of corn.

"Come. Lie down." She patted the blankets.

Andrew shook his head. "Too much to do."

Callum lumbered into the cabin, stopping long enough to shake the water from his boots at the threshold. "Nae. It's all done. Do as she says, lad."

"Let's get those wet clothes off you." Lilyan grabbed the hem of Andrew's shirt.

Peeling the soaked garments from Andrew's body left Lilyan panting. Once she had him wrapped in blankets with his feet near the fire, she shuffled to the corner of the room, pulled off her vest and shirt, and slipped on a dry one she kept in her saddlebags.

While Callum skinned the rabbit, she draped the sodden clothes across the end of the bench.

"Callum, you should change too." She yanked the wig from her head and tossed it onto the bench.

"Ach. There's so much oil in this buckskin, the rain slid right off like water off a duck's back."

Lilyan found a pan and stuck it out of the hole in the wall that served as a window. She did not have to wait long for it to fill with water running from the roof. She watched Callum butcher the rabbit, put the carcass on a spit over the fire, and drop the rest into her pan, which she set on a flat rock next to the blazing logs. She seasoned the water with salt and sprigs of rosemary she kept among her small stash of herbs.

Andrew refused a piece of the rabbit Callum offered and said he was not up to it. Lilyan cajoled him into drinking as much of the broth as he could. He blinked often against the sticky mucous that filled his red-rimmed eyes. His nose was stopped up, and phlegm rattled in his throat when he breathed. He seemed to resent her fussing over him, so Lilyan waited until he fell asleep to check his forehead. It was warm, but she hoped it was from lying so close to the fire. She and Callum spent a while going over more Cherokee phrases and then held hands and prayed for God's healing for Andrew, and then they too succumbed to their exhaustion.

Lilyan jerked up out of her sleep. Disoriented, she glanced around, taking a moment to get her bearings and trying to sort out the strange sound assaulting her ears; Andrew's labored breathing. She crawled over to him and pressed her hand against his cheek.

Heavenly Father, please, please, was all she could manage.

"Callum," she called out. "He's burning up."

Callum woke immediately and joined her beside the cot.

"I think it's influenza." She hated speaking the dreaded words.

She hurried to the stack of supplies and found her medicine box, dug through the contents, and pulled out several hand-sized cloth sacks. "Hemlock bark, gum acacias, elm, blue flag." She ticked off the ingredients. "No cinnamon, cloves, or sage."

She held her hands out to Callum, who began to gather his gear.

"I'll fetch some from the trading post." He patted her shoulder.

"You can manage, lassie. I know you can."

"I'll manage," she whispered and watched with a heavy heart as Callum hurried out the door.

She had spoken with more confidence than she felt. Her bravado seemed even emptier when, just as the morning sun filtered its way through the canopy of leaves overhead, she heard a twig snap outside; a sound more fearful to her than the howls of a hundred wolves.

Lilyan snatched up the pistol Callum had left on the bench and inched her way across the room, keeping her body between Andrew and the doorway.

"'Lo the cabin," a vaguely familiar voice called.

Lilyan peeked around the doorjamb and spotted the man they had met on the trail.

"What's your business?" Her voice shook.

"I mean you no harm," the man answered calmly.

I'd like to believe him. But should I? Finally, she decided she didn't have much choice.

"One moment." She released the pistol and stuffed her hair underneath her hat. She wrenched her shirt out of her pants, letting it drape loosely to her knees. She slipped her arms into the vest and tried to button it, but her fingers shook too much.

"You may come in." She gripped the pistol once more.

The man had to stoop to get through the doorway. Inside, he doffed his hat, glanced at Andrew, and then looked at Lilyan with the ebony eyes she remembered so well.

"Don't be frightened. There's no need for the gun." His lips curled into a pleasant smile. "And no need for the hat either. Anyone with eyes in his head can see you're a woman."

"I—well—" Lilyan couldn't manage to form a sentence.

When the man walked past her, Lilyan caught the agreeable aroma of wood smoke and cedar.

He pressed his hand to Andrew's forehead. "He's very sick, ma'am."

Lilyan nodded, unable to speak from the lump that had formed in her throat.

He studied her again with his soulful eyes. "Will you trust me to help?"

She nodded again.

He pulled away the blankets Lilyan had tucked so tightly around her brother's body in hopes of sweating out the sickness.

"If we don't get his fever down soon …" He left the sentence unfinished.

Lilyan stared wide-eyed as he lifted Andrew as if he weighed no more than a pillow.

"Let's get him to the river."

She swept up the blankets and followed the man as he carried her brother along an overgrown path. At the river he strode straight in and stood waist deep, cradling Andrew in his arms.

She made to follow them in, but the man shook his head. "No. It's freezing."

Lilyan watched in awe as the stranger slowly, carefully bobbed Andrew in the water, sluicing him neck deep.

Andrew's eyelids fluttered and he moaned.

"Courage, young man. I know it hurts, but it's for the best."

The man's soothing tones echoed across the water straight into Lilyan's heart, massaging it and loosening the tight grip of panic. She breathed deeply, filling her lungs completely for the first time in a long while.

Later, once they had settled a much-improved Andrew back onto the cot, the man turned to leave. Lilyan clasped his sleeve and made an attempt to thank him, but he patted her hand.

"He should improve now. Try not to be so anxious, little one."

With that he strode out the door, mounted his horse, and rode away, leaving Lilyan shaking her head and wondering if she had dreamed it all.

"Sissy," Andrew murmured through cracked lips, "could I have some broth?"

Lilyan felt as if someone had socked her in the stomach, and she sank onto the floor beside the bench. She wanted to laugh. She wanted to cry. Instead, she folded her hands and lifted up a prayer of praise.

Finally, as the shadows of the trees lengthened across the ground and cast a gloom inside the cabin, Callum returned with the ingredients Lilyan had asked for. Knowing that time was critical, she mashed the herbs against the inside of a tin cup, added boiling water, and then spent a half hour spooning the mixture into Andrew's mouth, between his muttered protests.

THEY BROKE THEIR JOURNEY three days to wait for the weather to clear and for Andrew to gain back strength. To pass the time, Lilyan found the writing and painting supplies she had stashed among her belongings. She huddled near the window, pen in hand, poised to compose a letter to Nicholas.

She balanced the ink bottle beside her and turned to Callum. "What day is it?"

"Well, let me see." He brushed his fingers across his chin. "We've been on the trail six days since … since … Well, we buried … That is …" He cleared his throat. "By my recollection, it's August twenty-six."

Lilyan flinched at the grim reminder of Elizabeth's passing. Although, she mused, it was somehow fitting to calculate their place in time by the death of her dearest friend. Would the rest of her life be rooted in that pivotal moment?

Gripping the pen, she began to pour out to Nicholas her account of the stranger's visit. Some time later, she paused long enough to fix an evening meal and then finished the letter by firelight. She could have written so much more, but she worried about her supply of ink.

Could she use some of her paint pigments, she wondered as she curled up on her blanket before the fire.

The following morning she laid fresh wood and kindling in the fireplace for other travelers who might find themselves in need of shelter and then helped Callum fashion a simple frame of wood for Andrew to be carried upon, which they hitched to his horse. She entered the cabin to find Andrew slumped on the bench, exhausted from getting dressed. She put her arm around his rail-thin body and helped him shuffle to the doorway.

When Andrew spotted the makeshift conveyance, he roared, "I am not an infant."

Callum stood arms akimbo. "Nae, you're not. And that's why you'll be traveling on this."

Andrew stammered.

"Lad, you're as weak as a kitten. Too weak to ride without Lilyan and me worrying whether you'll fall off and break your neck. We can't stay here any longer. Our supplies won't last out. And we must reach the Indian town before the weather turns."

Lilyan looked up at her brother, pleading with her eyes.

"Fine, then." He slumped onto the frame, muttering fiercely at Lilyan as she covered him with blankets.

The following part of their journey proved grueling. Her brother's bone-rattling coughing spasms gave way to grumbling. He and Callum seemed to take turns mumbling their irritation. Nothing suited them, and their incessant complaining grated on Lilyan's nerves. As if to match her mood, the terrain turned rocky and steep, forcing their pace to a slow crawl.

Hanging onto the sides of the bouncing sled, Andrew even said as much. "I could crawl faster than this," he whined.

Finally, the situation came to a head. It was early afternoon, not long after they had veered westward away from the river and toward the foothills.

Callum had them stop to rest their horses, and he broached a subject that set off fireworks. "Trail ahead is going to be steep."

"Good." Andrew slammed his fist on the bamboo rails. "I've had enough of this."

Callum ignored him and talked to Lilyan. "I thought I might see if I could get a couple of Indians to carry him on a litter."

"What!" Andrew shoved away the blankets and crawled to the ground. "I can ride."

Callum guffawed. "Look at you. You can hardly stand."

"I don't have to stand. Just sit my horse."

Andrew inched toward his horse and tried to untie the ropes securing the wooden frame. But his body shook, and he dropped his head against the horse's haunches. He coughed, a barking, ugly sound.

"Enough!" Lilyan stamped her foot. "For three days I've endured you—both of you—carping until I could … I've lost my home, my livelihood, my dearest, precious friend. I had to leave my loving, wonderful husband. I'm wanted for murder. I'm exhausted from looking over my shoulder every step of the way. I'm sore and hungry for something decent to eat. Have you heard me say any of this?"

They stared at her, mouths gaping.

She whirled and faced her brother. "Andrew, I am sick of your stubbornness. You must be reasonable. You aren't well enough to ride."

Her voice broke, and she began to weep; something she had never done in front of either of them. She covered her face with her hands and cried from sheer grief, frustration, and fear until she was spent, and her sobs turned to hiccups.

Without a word, Andrew climbed back onto the frame. Callum, stunned, mounted his horse and waited for Lilyan to do the same. They rode the next few hours in complete silence.

That night as they huddled around the campfire, Callum announced, "I'll leave in the morning. See if I can find some help."

"Make sure they're sturdy fellows," Andrew mumbled. "I wouldn't want to be thrown off the side of the mountain."

A giggle erupted in Lilyan's chest, and she glanced at Andrew, who made a sour face at her. Callum chuckled.

Maybe we'll be fine after all.

The next morning after watching Callum disappear into the forest, Lilyan searched through her satchel and found the letter from the Earl of Bradenton's barrister placing a bounty on her head. While Andrew napped, she read the dispatch over and over. For days she had considered what she was about to do. She wanted to—needed to—communicate with Bradenton's family, to let them know how profoundly sorry she was and especially to plead forgiveness from his mother. Having lost her dearest friend, Lilyan could only imagine what it must feel like to lose one's son. It was a difficult letter to write. It evoked so many bad memories, she was hard pressed for the right words to express herself, especially when it came to explaining Elizabeth's death. She had just finished the letter when she noticed Andrew staring at her with a puzzled expression in his moss green eyes.

"Who is that to?" he asked.

"The Bradentons' solicitor."

He cocked his head.

"Would you like to hear it?"

He nodded.

Dear Mr. Chambers,

As I pen this letter, I am filled with such profound regret. I find it difficult to express myself regarding Captain Remington Bradenton and the ending of his life by my hand. I shudder with remorse at those terrible words.

I do not know how the circumstances of his death were portrayed to you, but I feel compelled to give you the true and factual account as I know it.

Captain Bradenton, my friend Elizabeth and I became acquainted at the home of Mrs. Melborne. It was there that the captain began to display an ungentlemanly and, I assure you, unwanted attention to Elizabeth.

On that dreadful evening, while searching the grounds for Elizabeth, who had sought escape from the captain's advances, I came upon the captain as he had begun a most savage attack upon her. I say savage because in attempting to subdue her, he had pulled her arm from its socket. In desperation and to prevent the captain from accomplishing his purpose, I picked up a statuette and struck him. It is a memory that has burned itself indelibly into my mind.

Elizabeth and I fled the nightmarish scene, thus beginning a series of desperate events, ending most recently in her death. My most beloved, most precious friend was killed by the very bounty hunters who carried your missive at the behest of the captain's family.

I have laid this terrible sin before my Maker and have received some solace in the blessed assurance that I am forgiven. Notwithstanding, my deed lays heavy on my mind and heart. So much so that I implore you, sir, in the name of Christian benevolence, please convey to the captain's parents my deep and abiding sorrow for having taken the life of their son. Tell them that I beg their forgiveness with all my heart.

I will leave it to you to determine how much of the details you wish to disclose to them, as I know it would be painful indeed to hear such a despicable report about one's beloved son.

I remain, your most abject and sincere servant,
Lilyan Cameron.

"It is a good letter, Lilyan." Andrew paused. "But shouldn't you let it lie?"

"No. Family is everything. Wouldn't you appreciate someone letting you know the circumstances of my death?"

"Even if that meant finding out you had died trying to commit something monstrous?"

Lilyan considered his question. "No one is perfect. Truth to tell, I imagine they must have some idea what he was capable of. This letter is more for me. I want them to know how sorry I am to have been the instrument of their son's death."

Andrew threw off his blankets. "Help me, will you?"

She did as he bade, stuffing a blanket behind his back as she helped him lean against a tree trunk.

"Sissy." He hesitated. "You remember how you used the chamomile to pass along messages in Charlestown?"

"Of course."

"Did you know that the Patriots call it 'the rebel flower'?"

She shook her head.

"They call it that because the more it's trampled on, the stronger it springs back. You're like that. You are one of the strongest people I know. When Ma died, you took on the responsibility of watching after me until Da brought Elizabeth to us. When Da died, you worked with the solicitor to sell his business and set up your own. When I was imprisoned, you refused to sit back and do nothing and joined the effort to free me. You didn't break when our Elizabeth died."

Elizabeth died. What pain those two words strung together brought Lilyan.

But ..." Andrew pursed his bottom lip.

Lilyan stiffened her back. "But what?"

He held up his hand. "Hear me out, please." He paused. "Do you know the source of your strength?"

"I believe I do."

"Then answer me this, how can you be so sure of the source of your strength and still be so full of fear?"

Lilyan could only stare at him.

"Remember when Mother used to read to us about King David? I thought it was exciting when he killed Goliath. But the more I know about him, the more I'm impressed with the way he reacted to being on the run. Hiding in caves, never knowing if he would live from one day to the next, he still called God his hiding place, his protector. God rewarded him for that. Gave him a deep inner peace. A sense of well-being."

His eyes bored into hers. "I watched you at Elizabeth's funeral when the parson spoke of storing up treasures on earth. It stung a little, didn't it?"

She bristled. "Yes. It did."

"I admire you so. I know you're strong, but I want to see some joy in you too. It's been a long time since I've seen you happy. Except maybe with Nicholas."

"Yes. He makes me very happy." She tilted her head. "You like your new brother-in-law?"

"Very much. Capital fellow. But back to what I was saying. I'm asking you to quit taking on the responsibility of everyone around you. And will you think about what you're asking in your prayers?"

"You're saying I shouldn't pray for the safety of my loved ones?"

"No, that's not what I mean. But maybe you could lift up your anxious feelings. Concentrate more on asking for joy. For contentment no matter what happens."

Lilyan sighed. "How did you get to be so wise?"

"Those weeks I was aboard the *Brixham*, an old man used to talk to us for hours about the Apostle Paul and the time he was in prison. There we were, in that black, stinking squalor, waiting to be shipped off to St. Augustine and only God knew what. But that man was so peaceful, so at ease, he made me want that too."

He glanced away. "And then there were all those lonely nights scouting for General Marion. So much time spent looking up into the black night—I couldn't begin to describe the effect it had on me. But it was freeing, comforting to know that God has a plan for each of us—not to harm us, but to prosper us."

Andrew snorted. "I didn't mean to preach."

"I appreciate the advice. I do. Because I know it comes out of love." She patted his hand. "And I promise I'll try not to be so anxious. But, as you above all know, I've practiced worrying for so long, it will be difficult." She studied his face. "Have you ever given thought to becoming a minister?"

"I think I should like that more than anything." His words broke up as another bout of coughing shook his body.

Lilyan pulled the blanket up around his neck. "No more talk, now, dearest. Try to get some rest."

In an unusual gesture of compliance, he dropped his head back against the tree and closed his eyes.

Waiting for Callum to return gave Lilyan plenty of time to contemplate their conversation. She wrestled with the idea of how to weigh her concern for the safety and well-being of treasured family and friends against the reassurances that everything that happens has a purpose, an eventual good, heavenly purpose. Could she find contentment in the awful situation she found herself in? She had to admit that she was weary of fretting all the time. Except for the short time she had been with Nicholas, it had been a while since she had experienced the deep, abiding joy God had promised her as a believer.

She finally determined that wiser minds than hers understood those complexities. That thought alone seemed to lift some of the heaviness in her chest.

Two days later, Callum still had not returned. To keep her mind occupied, Lilyan decided to sketch a picture of Andrew.

Sitting cross-legged on a blanket, she looked up from her drawing. "Tilt your head down a little, will you?"

He scowled, but grudgingly did as she bade.

"This is one good thing about your not being well. You can't run off—" The look on his face stopped her mid-sentence as he floundered for the pistol at his feet.

"Wouldn't do that if I was you," a voice snarled behind her.

The sorrows of death encompassed me
and the pains of hell gathold upon me.
I found trouble and sorrow.
Then I called upon the name of the Lord;
"Oh Lord, I beseech Thee, deliver my soul!"
Psalm 116:3-4

Chapter Thirty

BEFORE LILYAN COULD MOVE, an arm snaked around her neck and yanked her to her feet. As she slammed against a body, she felt the tip of a knife pushing up under her jaw.

"Put the gun down, boy." The man's voice was deep, gravelly, and deadly serious.

Andrew gripped the pistol tighter. Lilyan tried to catch his eye, but he stared unwavering at her attacker.

"I mean it. Bounty says dead or alive. I can take her back as she is"—the man pushed the knife into Lilyan's skin—"or I can cut her head off right here in front of you. Your choice."

Andrew released the gun, dropping it beside his foot.

"Now, send it over here."

Andrew kicked the pistol, and when it landed at Lilyan's feet, she curled her hands over the man's arm and pulled as hard as she could. He clamped her throat in a viselike grip that threatened to cut off her breath and rammed his face against the side of her head.

"Best not struggle, little lady." His rancid breath assaulted Lilyan's nostrils. "Good to see you got spunk, though." He chuckled. "Trip back to Charlestown might be more fun than I thought."

His insinuation drifted down Lilyan's arms like a giant spider web. Still holding the knife, he slid his arm from Lilyan's neck, down her breasts to her waist, and she gagged on the sour taste that filled her mouth. He stretched down, grabbed the pistol with his other hand, and aimed it at Andrew.

Panic drummed across Lilyan's rib cage, and she shrieked, "Please! Don't hurt him."

"Who's he to you?"

"My brother."

"Ah."

"Please. Can't you see he's ill?"

He shifted his arm from her waist, splaying his fingers across her stomach. "And just what would you do to save him?" He snickered.

"You dog!" Andrew shouted, trying to push himself up.

The man pointed the gun at Andrew's face. "Settle down or I'll blow a hole in your forehead."

Andrew slumped back, and the man relaxed his arm. "Where were we? Oh, yes. You were about to tell me what you'd do to save the lad."

Lilyan dropped her eyes, unable to look at Andrew. "Anything. I would do anything."

"Well, now. How can I resist such a bargain? I just might let him live. Sick as he is, he'll slow Callum down. Keep him from catching up with us."

His mention of Callum startled Lilyan. "You know Callum?"

"Used to trade together 'fore I found I could make more money outlawing. Heard he was the one takin' you somewheres safe after the Injun girl got herself killed."

A terrible thought wormed its way through Lilyan's mind. "You're the one that got away."

The man snorted. "You're a right smart one. I'll say. It was a close one. Me and Hank and Charlie had pretty much sniffed you out at Marion's camp. Charlie stumbled across you two at the river. But, damn his hide, he waited too long to signal, and you was already headed up the hill. That Injun girl shore did know how to use a knife. Gutted Charlie before Hank could get a shot off. Next thing we knew, that Catawban was bearin' down on us. Speakin' of which. Can't hang around here jaw-jacking anymore."

Before Lilyan realized what he was doing, in one swift movement

213

he let her go, sheathed his knife into his boot, and pulled a length of rope from his hip. "Hands in front, missy."

He stuffed the pistol into his belt, jerked Lilyan's arms forward, and lashed her wrists together. To Lilyan's horror, he slipped a leather cord around her neck and secured the end around his wrist. As if sensing her revulsion, he yanked on the noose, chafing her neck and making her gasp.

He stepped toward Andrew, pulling Lilyan with him. Nudging Andrew's leg with his boot, he sneered. "Guess there's no need to tie you up. You're weaker than a kitten tryin' to scratch its way out of a drownin' bag."

He tugged on the rope. "Come on, gal. Best be on our way,"

An overwhelming dread poured through Lilyan's veins chilling her through and through. "Andrew!" she cried out.

"Courage, Sissy!" Andrew yelled. "God go with you."

Lilyan strained to look over her shoulder, but the man snatched her head back with the tether and dragged her to the edge of the camp and the horses. When he shoved Lilyan's foot into a stirrup and tried to haul her up onto her horse, she swung her wrists out and shot him a glancing blow across his cheek. Snarling, he clasped her wrists with one hand and punched her in her stomach with the other. Pain radiated through Lilyan's torso and she doubled over.

He grasped the noose and wrenched her even further down. "Let's get somethin' straight. I could kill you right here and save myself a lot of trouble."

Nose to nose with him, gasping for air and with tears gathering in her eyes, she stared into the man's brown eyes—cold, feral orbs that held such contempt she believed his every word.

He shoved her back up. "So. You won't try nothin' like that again. Right?"

She shook her head. Afraid to look back for Andrew, she watched helplessly as her captor grasped the mare's reins and the tether in one hand and mounted his horse.

Dear Lord, will I ever see my family again?

She wasn't sure how long they had ridden before she came out of the daze that had held her in its relentless grasp.

Pay attention to your surroundings. Her father's warning swirled through her head. Forcing herself to concentrate, she took note of the lengthening shadows of the trees and soon reckoned they had been picking their way south through the dense forest for a couple of hours. Nightfall was not far away.

She stared at the bounty hunter, who rode beside her, a half a length ahead. Though he followed no discernable path, he kept a steady pace as if he knew the way well. Her heightened senses detected the murmur of a nearby rill.

"Water?" she managed to croak the words. "Please, could I have some water?"

"No," he growled without even turning around.

As they continued their trek, Lilyan desperately sought for a familiar landmark, something that would help her get her bearings. But the mid-evening sky cloaked the forest like a charcoal gray blanket, turning stands of bamboo and clumps of underbrush into lairs for hobgoblins.

Hobgoblins! Why consider such childish notions, when there's a real life monster not four feet away?

Gnats hovered around the welts raked into her arms from unseen briars. Branches slapped her face making her ears ring. One knocked her wig askew, spilling long tendrils of her hair down her back. If her hands hadn't been bound to the saddle, she would have ripped the loathsome thing from her head. She lifted her eyes in time to spy the first star punch its way through the heavens.

Father, please watch after Andrew. And me, Lord, will You watch after me too?

Lilyan finished her prayer and realized that, after a moment of eerie silence, the daytime animals—chirping birds, buzzing insects, scurrying squirrels—had turned over their domain to the creatures of the night. Bats darted overhead so closely she ducked. The faraway howl of a wolf echoed through the trees sending goose bumps rolling up and down her arms. She was also certain she heard the rushing of a river not too far away.

"We'll stop here." The man's voice shot through the night like a rifle, startling Lilyan so, she felt her heart clattering against her ribs.

He dismounted, snatched Lilyan's hands loose, and pulled her down. Exhausted, her legs buckled up under her and she fell to the ground. With fingers that felt like sausages, she grabbed her wig, snatched it from her head, and threw it as far as her aching arms could manage. Massaging her itching scalp, she heard the man hobble the horses and trudge over to her. Her back rolled up with tension when he dropped down beside her and nudged her arm.

"Here. It's jerky. Can't light no fire." His words pelted her in rapid-fire succession.

She grabbed the leathery strip of beef, wincing when she touched his callused fingertips.

He thumped her elbow with his canteen and popped the cork top. "Drink this first or you'll never get that down your gullet."

Lilyan swilled the tepid water so fast it spilled down the front of her shirt. She tore into the jerky with her teeth, choking at the briny smell. With each successive chew, the salty wad of meat seemed to grow until her jaws ached with the effort. Finally, when her stomach threatened to heave, she spit it out.

He guffawed. "Ain't meant to be gobbled down."

Lilyan gave up on the jerky and gulped some more water. She drew up her knees, wrapped her arms around them, and rested her head.

Suddenly, the man pushed on her side, knocking her over. "Get some sleep," he ordered and then stretched out beside her, not touching, but so close Lilyan's nose twitched at the sour stench of his clothes. Lying on her side, drawn up into a ball, her body began to complain about everything that had happened to it—the burning sensation in her shoulders, the throbbing in her wrists, the tingling in her fingers, the chafed skin on her neck, the itching bug bites, and the tightness of the scabs forming on the scrapes her arms. Mindful of her tormentor lying so close, she inched her fingers across the ground until she found a piece of tree limb. Enfolding the stick in her fists, she fought the sleep that began to steal over her. But it was a losing battle. She finally let go and nodded off, only to be startled awake by sinewy talons groping their way around her waist. She pushed at his hands, but the harder she pushed the more they seemed to roam over her.

"Don't fight me, gal. You ain't gonna win."

When he rolled her onto her back, she clutched the stick and rammed it into his stomach with all her might.

"O-o-o-of!" he screamed, letting go of her and gasping for air.

Lilyan jumped to her feet and took off, blindly racing through the moonlit woods, not knowing, not caring where she was headed, only that it was away from the monster. She tripped over a log and slammed headlong into a thick oak. She clasped her waist and when she could breathe again, sucked in deep gulps of air.

"You go ahead. Run," the man yelled, "as fast as you can. 'Cause you know I'll get you."

His voice seemed to come at her from all directions, and she raced away.

"Run all you want. I'm gonna get a coupla hours sleep. Then I'll track you down like a wolf. Aw-oo-oo! Aw-oo-oo!"

The menacing howl was followed by a maniacal laugh so full of evil that Lilyan sped heedlessly toward the sound of the river, scraping her arm against a branch and ripping the sleeve of her shirt. She ran until her legs felt like rubber, darting here, scurrying there, guided only by her instincts to get as far away as possible. Dodging her way through a patch of bamboo, she lost her footing and tumbled down a hill, rolling over and over until she landed with a thud, her check slamming against the dirt.

Spent and terrified, she clawed at the loamy-smelling earth and gave herself over to her despair, sobbing until her throat muscles clenched.

Dear God! I am so alone. So afraid.

She rolled over, and lying spread-eagled, she opened her swollen eyes and stared up at the full moon. A twig snapped nearby, and her stomach shook as unseen horrors stalked the night.

I am undone. I have come to the end of my strength. Lord of compassion, please, help me.

"Try not to be so anxious, little one." The words came softly into her head. Where had she heard them before? Puzzled, she sat up, inhaled a few shuddered breaths, and then she remembered. The man who had saved Andrew; he had spoken those very words.

You are there. My keeper. My refuge. Never slumbering.

Hope, like a daub of white paint splashed against a shadow on a canvass, came alive, casting a glimmer of light into the darkness.

Slowly, painfully, she stood, holding on to a slender bamboo tree. She waited for her head to stop spinning and then, step by step on dangerously wobbly legs, she trudged her way to the river, climbed down the bank, and drank her fill of the sweet, cold liquid. The hoot of an owl drifted across the rolling river. She scanned the tree line on the opposite shore, glanced up at the stars, and spotted Orion's belt, remembering the first time her beloved had pointed it out to her.

217

Nicholas. I have not spoken your name in such a very long time. But I feel you near.

She recalled some of the last words he had whispered to her. "Courage, my love," he had said. "God has blessed us. Has He not?"

Despite her newfound strength, Lilyan knew that her pursuer meant to track her down and, so far, she had left such an obvious trail, a child could find her. From now on, she must put into practice the things her father had taught her. She could almost hear his dear voice prompting her, "Traveling north, keep the river to your right. Leave a light footstep. Protect your feet and don't get your boots wet. Backtrack and cover your trail."

For an instant, she worried about what would happen if the bounty hunter caught up with her, but she fought back.

Lord, I am Your child, and no matter what happens, no one can take that away from me.

Feeling more attuned, more alive, she headed up river starting off at an awkward lope. Several times the skin on her neck would prickle and she would spy eyes peering at her through the underbrush. Once it was a raccoon, another time it was a bobcat.

Just don't let me come across a bear or a snake, Lord.

Pacing herself, she would walk a while and when she reached a clearing, she would break into a sprint. Walk, sprint. Walk, sprint. All the while praying that Callum and Andrew would appear around the next bend in the river. Finally, as a pale lavender wash made its way across the sky, waking the birds, Lilyan knew she had to stop and rest. Groaning so loud that she startled herself, she slumped down and leaned against a giant oak. Her eyelids grew heavy and she drifted off to sleep.

She awoke sometime later, fuzzy headed and thirsty. Stiff and sore, she plodded to the river where she spotted a log that had fallen, forming a bridge. While she scooped up a couple of handfuls of water over the sores on her arms, she formed a plan to try and elude the bounty hunter. First, she made very distinguishable footprints toward the log. Next, concentrating on keeping her balance and not on the water that flowed below her, she made her way over. She jumped from the log and took about twenty strides before retracing her steps, carefully walking backward, placing each boot into the prints she had made. After making the trip back across, she grabbed a branch from the ground and, as she made her way beside the river, she brushed it across the dirt, removing any trace of her presence.

She had walked about a mile when she came across a patch of blackberries. Ravenous, she dropped to her knees and snatched handfuls of the fruit and stuffed them into her mouth, swallowing some of the juicy morsels without chewing. She made herself slow down, until she felt she couldn't take another bite. She lay on the ground and, leaning on her elbows, she looked down at her purple fingers, tattered sleeves, and ravaged arms. Someone had told her once that blackberry leaves could be used as an astringent, so she pulled some from the bush, pressed and rolled them with her fingertips, then gingerly applied them to one of the cuts on her arm. It burned like the dickens, and she gasped. She took more leaves and wincing with pain, rubbed them up and down her arms.

"Turned out to be smarter than I thought." The rasping voice came at her from several feet away.

Oh, God. He found me.

Words of David, words her mother had once read to her, came crashing through her consciousness. "*I will not be afraid. What can mortal man do to me?*"

Fortified, she jumped to her feet, but not before he leapt across the ground and pounced on her. Grabbing her by the collar of her shirt, he hauled her toward the river, her heels digging in the dirt.

"Caused me a lot a trouble, missy. Almost fooled me with that backtracking trick."

Lilyan flailed her arms and raked her nails across his hand.

"You wildcat!" he yelled. "Now I'm gonna teach you a trick or two."

At the water's edge, he clamped both hands around her neck and shoved her face into the water. Eyes squeezed tight she floundered trying to pry his fingers from her neck. Desperate for air, her lungs burned and her head felt ready to explode.

Is this the end, Lord? Will I come to you now?

Suddenly, she felt herself being hauled up and dragged back up the bank. Gasping and choking, she fell to her knees. Her hair, partly gray from dirt, partly brown from mud and ragged with leaves and twigs, spilled down around her shoulders in thick ropes as she bowed her head.

"Learned your lesson yet?" he asked.

Lilyan parted her hair with trembling hands and looked up at him with all the disgust she could muster.

"I see you ain't."

She watched in horror as he undid his leather belt, folded it, and slapped the ends together making a cracking sound. When he raised the belt over his head, her mind screamed for her to flee, but her body refused. She could only cringe and brace herself for the pain. And then she heard a feathery *swish* and a squishing sound. To her amazement, the man faltered and, making a strange gurgle, he slumped to the ground, knocking her forward. She whirled, staring in shock at the arrow that had pierced straight through his neck, now gushing a steady stream of blood that soaked the ground around his head. Her glance slid from the dreadful sight, and she found herself looking into the eyes of an Indian standing only a few feet away. Followed close behind—dared she believe her eyes?— was the most wonderful sight of Callum racing toward her.

"Callum!" Lilyan cried out as he dropped down beside her and swept her into his arms. "Oh, Callum!" She buried her face in his chest.

"Canna leave you alone for a second, can I?" He awkwardly rubbed a hand across Lilyan's shoulder blades and waited for her bones to stop shaking. "It's all over, lassie."

Callum pulled away and studied her from head to toe. "Just look at what he did to you. Ach! I canna bear it. If he wasna dead already, I'd kill him again meself."

He stared into her eyes, leaned down and whispered, "Are you—? Did he—?"

Lilyan shuddered at his meaning. "No. Only the cuts and bruises you see."

Callum stepped away and nodded to the Indian, now joined by another who looked very much like him. "This here is Rider Smith and his brother, Smoke."

With her pulse still pounding in her ears, Lilyan studied the men who moved closer and stared back at her. They nodded when introduced but said nothing.

She leaned over and searched the woods behind them. "Where is Andrew?"

"He's fine. Back where you left him."

"Alone?"

"No, lass. He's with Golden Fawn. Rider and Smoke's sister. She's taking good care of him." He glanced over at the body and grimaced. "Get this vermin out of here."

Lilyan refused to turn around, but listened to them lift the body and haul it away. She tried to get up, but her legs threatened to buckle under her, and she fought a tide of nausea rising in her stomach.

Rider and Smoke returned, and so quickly that Lilyan surmised they had left the body out in the open to be devoured by the creatures that roamed the woods at night. That thought sucked the wind out of her and brought with it a deep sadness.

Yet another death.

It was then that the ground seemed to leap up and slam her in the face.

Yea though I walk through the valley of the shadow of death,
I will fear no evil, for thou art with me;
thy rod and thy staff, they comfort me.
Psalm 23:4

Chapter Thirty-One

LILYAN AWAKENED TO FIND herself riding on a horse, clasped tightly in Callum's arms.

"Where are we?" she asked, trying to blink away the sticky goop keeping her eyelids from opening.

"Still a ways to go. Go back to sleep. I've got you." Callum's chest rumbled against her ear.

Foggy headed, she floated away into a deep slumber. Once in a while she felt herself drifting up into consciousness, only to be lulled back into oblivion by Callum's comforting words and the rolling gait of the horse.

"We're here, lass. Time to wake up. Andrew's mighty anxious." Callum's voice broke through to her.

The mention of her brother's name brought her swiftly out of her daze, and to the glorious sight him being helped to his feet by an Indian woman.

"Sissy!" he cried out.

Smoke stepped close and held out his arms to help Lilyan dismount.

"Easy now," Callum ordered.

As soon as her feet touched the ground, she knew her legs

222

would not hold her weight, but in an instant Callum swooped his leg over his saddle, jumped down, and took her by the waist. With her arms draped across their shoulders, they practically carried her over to Andrew's awaiting embrace.

Her brother's body shook as he held onto her and kissed her cheek. "God is good."

She smiled up at him. "Yes. He is."

His eyes took her in, and he frowned at Callum. "Let's sit, before we fall."

Settled on a blanket, Andrew clasped her hands. "You look wonderful."

"And you are a liar." Lilyan chuckled, startling herself with the lighthearted sound.

A movement caught Lilyan's eye, and she noticed the woman who had helped Andrew.

"You must be Golden Fawn." Lilyan nodded at the tall, slender girl who bowed, moving with the grace of her namesake. "I cannot thank you enough for watching after my brother."

"You are most welcome." She flashed a smile that exposed beautiful white teeth and lit her nut brown eyes. She darted a shy, expressive glance toward Andrew, and a glow warmed her red-brown cheeks. "I know how it is with brothers."

Her accent was heavy and her tone nasal, but her voice was not unpleasant. Lilyan searched the young woman's face, trying not to stare at the pockmarks that marred her lovely skin. The girl, who looked to be about fifteen, seemed familiar, and Lilyan struggled to place her.

"You do not remember me?" Golden Fawn asked.

"I'm sorry—" Lilyan hesitated.

"Think back. You and your father, Fire Beard, helped us when the smallpox attacked my people."

"I do remember, now. You've grown up so, I hardly recognize you. You were five ... or six then? And very ill."

"Yes. But you were not much older. Our people still speak of Tsu la, Little Red Fox, who showed such courage and compassion."

"Little Red Fox. Did you hear that, Andrew? I have an Indian name and did not even know it."

Golden Fawn came forward and touched Lilyan's arm. "You have suffered much."

Lilyan closed her eyes, unable to respond.

"Come." Golden Fawn held out her arms, pulling Lilyan to her feet, and draping her arm around her. "We will get you to water."

"Smoke," she called out to her brother, "you will bring medicines. Yes?"

He nodded, walked across the clearing, and picked up a buckskin pouch.

"Wait," Andrew called out. "Here's a blanket and some clean clothes."

Smoke gathered the clothing and blanket and slung the pouch over his shoulder. Rider wrapped his arm around Lilyan and supported her as they followed Golden Fawn to the nearby stream. The young men left them alone at the riverbank, but indicated they would not be far away.

Golden Fawn gently removed Lilyan's clothing and, to Lilyan's amazement, she stripped off her own clothes and walked with her waist deep into the water. With a gentleness that Lilyan's battered body craved, the young woman cleaned her wounds with a sweet-smelling salve and then washed all the dirt and debris from her hair. Such tender ministrations dissolved all of Lilyan's inhibitions about bathing in the nude. They waded back out where Golden Fawn first helped Lilyan dress, then donned her own clothes. She spread out a blanket across a patch of sweet green grass and sat down.

"Come." She motioned for Lilyan to join her. "We will rest a while and let the healing begin."

Lilyan lay down and fell asleep the moment her head touched the blanket. Hours later, she awoke, astonished by the transformation in her body. She felt relaxed and most of her soreness and the stinging and burning were gone.

They returned to the camp, with Lilyan walking on her own, to find Callum, Smoke, and Rider packing the gear.

At Lilyan's puzzled expression, Callum explained that he felt it safer for them to renew their journey to the village.

It took the brothers no time to break down Andrew's litter and restructure it into one they could hold at waist height or rest on their shoulders. Impatient to get away, Callum barked orders at his troop until they had lined up and moved back onto the trail headed northwest—Callum in front, followed by the brothers carrying Andrew on the litter, then Lilyan, and behind her, Golden

Fawn on Andrew's horse with the mule tethered behind. Lilyan was sure that her brother resented his state of helplessness, but he kept any comments to himself, especially when they reached a stretch of boulders lining a waterfall that crashed down the mountain, spraying them all with a fine mist. The terrain became so rugged that Lilyan, Callum, and Golden Fawn finally had to dismount and lead the horses along a path ankle deep in slippery leaves.

Despite the rigors of their march, Lilyan could feel her senses coming alive. She sucked in deep breaths, filling her lungs with the crisp, cool, gradually thinning air. Each tree she passed vied with the next in myriad shades of green. Often the trail led them to precipices that opened out onto expansive views of rolling hills and valleys cut into swatches by meandering streams and creeks. Her fingers itched for her brushes and paints as she stored each successive image in her memory. Cedar branches and mountain laurels brushed across her shoulders, seeping their pungent aromas into her clothing. Several times they stopped to rest, and Lilyan drank greedily from the streams, sitting on the bank next to her horse, scooping up handfuls of the freezing, sweet-tasting water. Her newfound sensations were marred only by Callum's intermittent orders for Smoke and Rider to double back and make sure no one trailed them.

That evening they dined on roasted squirrel and trout along with sweet bread Golden Fawn made from cornmeal mush wrapped in green corn husks and baked next to the glowing coals. Andrew could not seem to get enough of the spongy bread, eating his portion and half of Lilyan's. When they finished their meal, Lilyan sat cross-legged on her blanket, studying the fire that breathed in and out, sending tiny sparks whirling overhead. She looked at Smoke, who peered at her across the camp. He said something first to Rider and then to Callum, who grinned and answered back.

Sensing herself the topic of their conversation, Lilyan asked, "What did he say?"

"He says that when he first saw you, your hair was black with mud, *gv ni ge*, but he likes it better now that it is the color of a fox, *gi ga ge*."

"It's still not as clean as I like." Lilyan ran her fingers across her braid. "You think it's safe to go down to the river to wash it again?"

"Aye," said Callum.

Lilyan rummaged through her satchel and found a bar of lemon soap and grabbed a blanket.

"But not alone." Callum nodded to Smoke, who joined Lilyan.

A brilliant moon hung in the sky, casting deep shadows and lighting their way.

As they neared the shore, Smoke came to a halt. "I will stay here."

Lilyan appreciated his regard for her privacy and made the rest of the trek alone. Once she reached the water, it took her three latherings before she could slide her fingertips through her tresses and hear the wonderful squeaking sound. Her scalp tingled and her skin pulsated from the ice-cold water. She sat on a boulder and rubbed her hair dry with the blanket, wishing with all her heart on the stars popping out in the sky that Nicholas could be there with her. She spotted Orion and lifted her finger to draw his outline, remembering once more the first time her beloved husband had pointed out the constellation to her and when she saw it again on her flight from the bounty hunter. She shivered at the recollection. Too soon her exhilaration waned, replaced by an encompassing fatigue that made her long for her bed.

Smoke met her halfway to the camp and followed her quietly, eyeing her hair as she lay on a folded blanket and covered herself with others.

He nodded and said something to Callum.

"He says that now you look like a daughter of Fire Beard." Callum poked the fire with a stick. "Lass, we've all been talking."

The hairs on Lilyan's arms tingled. *Where is this heading?*

"These outlaws. They're never going to stop hounding us. So, Rider here came up with an idea. We're only a half day's ride from a trading post, and we're going to turn you in. Claim the ransom for ourselves."

"What?" Lilyan shot up.

Callum grinned. "Knew that would rile you. Now, listen. We've got a plan. And a braw one, if I say so myself. Seems that Golden Fawn's father is the medicine man for her tribe, and she knows about a concoction that when you take it, it makes you seem dead."

Lilyan stared at him.

"You'll take the medicine, and then we carry you into the post on the litter. We'll get some witnesses to view your body, so to speak. Then, if nae goes agley, we'll ask them to sign a paper swearing that you are who we say you are. Hopefully, those folks will start spreading the rumor that you're dead and the bounty's already spoken for. We'll post a letter to the barrister in Charlestown. Word will get around in no time, and we won't be bothered anymore."

Lilyan pondered a few minutes. "What's in the medicine?"

Golden Fawn shook her head. "Do not worry. I would not harm you."

"What do you think, Andrew?" Lilyan asked.

Andrew furrowed his brow. "It might work."

Lilyan sat quietly a while longer until a terrible thought struck her. "But what of my Nicholas? What if he hears that I'm ... that I'm dead?"

"There's a good chance, with him running around in the swamps fighting for Marion, the news won't reach him. Don't see a way we could get a message to him for quite a while, either." Callum rubbed his chin. "Only thing is, if he does hear something—and I wouldna want to be the one to tell him—he's the kind that would want to find out for himself. And he knows where we're headed."

Callum scanned the others and then looked straight into Lilyan's eyes. "It's up to you, lass."

Lilyan had to force herself to say the next words. "When would we want to do this?"

"Tomorrow," Callum answered grimfaced.

Whether shall I go from thy Spirit?
Or whether shall I flee from thy presence?
If I ascend up to heaven, thou art there;
if I make my bed in hell, behold thou art there.
If I take the wings of the morning,
and dwell in the uttermost parts of the sea,
Even there shall thy hand lead me, thy right hand will hold me.
If I say, Surely the darkness shall cover me;
even the night shall be light about me.
Yea the darkness hideth not from thee;
but the night shineth as the day.
The darkness and the light are alike to thee.
Psalm 139: 7-12

Chapter Thirty-Two

WITHIN MINUTES OF SWALLOWING the bitter potion, Lilyan felt the muscles in her arms and legs grow stiff. Moments later, a chill began to settle in her bones. Her heart, which had been pounding in her ears, faded into a steady beat that grew fainter with each breath. Her eyelids felt heavy, and she fought to keep them open.

What if I never open my eyes again? She struggled against the panic that question evoked. *And what if I don't? Will not my beliefs open the doors of heaven for me?*

A comforting voice whispered through her soul, "Be not afraid."

At peace, she let go and drifted into unconsciousness.

LILYAN BURST INTO A FUZZY awareness with a headache so severe she felt as if her brain ricocheted inside her skull. Her eyes flew open, and she tried desperately to speak, but her throat closed.

Someone called for whiskey, and she soon felt the fiery liquid pass between her lips and slide down her parched throat. She coughed, and it was so painful, she grabbed her neck.

"Slow," Golden Fawn soothed. "You must go slow."

Lilyan studied her surroundings. *We're still at the camp. It didn't work. We failed.*

Golden Fawn and Callum vigorously rubbed her arms and legs until Lilyan felt warmth seeping into her muscles.

"Please," she rasped. "I want to sit up."

They helped her, propping their arms against her back, but she immediately regretted it when her head began to swim and nausea roiled in her stomach.

"Have more whiskey." Callum pressed the bottle to her lips.

She took a sip and felt it burn a path all the way down her throat. Her eyes watered when it slammed into the pit of her empty belly. "How long was I …?"

"Long enough to get this." Callum waved a piece of paper in front of her.

Can it be?

Andrew took the paper from Callum. "You are officially deceased as of today, September 4, 1781." He grinned at her, his eyes full of mischief. "How does it feel?"

Lilyan groaned and held her head. "I'll let you know when this headache is gone."

Golden Fawn smiled. "I have something for that."

Lilyan arched her eyebrow.

Golden Fawn giggled. "I promise it will taste much better."

"No matter. I think the whiskey has burned all the taste from my mouth."

"Lassie, I wish I could give you more time to recover, but we must be on our way." Callum put his hands under Lilyan's armpits and pulled her up.

"You walk around a wee bit while we get the animals ready," he said and then started barking orders at Smoke and Rider.

It took an hour for Lilyan to move about without trembling. Once Callum was satisfied with her condition, he mounted his horse and pulled her up in front of him. Relief flooded through her as she leaned back against his solid chest, and she was glad of his arm that wrapped like a steel band around her waist.

As they headed northwest toward the steeper mountains, Callum described to Lilyan what had taken place. The post they had taken her to, a cluster of three buildings—a combination tavern and store, a barn, and rustic sleeping quarters—catered to trappers and Indians within a fifty-mile radius and was usually packed to capacity. Callum could not believe their good fortune, for he and Smoke had arrived at a time when most of the patrons had left to set traps or hunt. The owners, Rhonda and John Baker, had not liked the looks of either of them, especially when they heard their purpose for coming to the post. Mrs. Baker especially had scowled at Callum when he threw back the blanket from Lilyan's face.

"Thought she was going to hit me with her broom when she got a good look at you," said Callum. "Instead she threw her apron up to her face and started to give me a tongue thrashing the likes of which I've never heard. 'How could you harm such a lovely thing?' she yelled."

He harrumphed. "Ach. I tell you, when she offered to prepare you for burial, and I said we dinna need her to, it was all I could do to head off an apoplexy. Had to do some quick thinking. Told her we already found a spot. She wouldna sign until I promised we'd put you someplace the varmints couldn't get to you. Feisty woman. I liked her."

He eased them past a branch that draped across the path. "I got about five people to sign both papers, wrote a letter to the barrister in Charlestown, and put one copy inside. Saved the other one for you." He snorted. "Thought you might like a keepsake."

Lilyan slapped his arm playfully.

"Anyway, Mr. Baker promised it would go out with the next posting. By the by, I posted the letter ye asked me to."

Lilyan remained silent while Callum picked their way across a shallow stream.

"Callum, once we've arrived at the Indian town, do you think we could get Smoke or Rider to find Nicholas? Tell him I am well?"

"I'll do my best, lassie. But I can't make any promises."

It took two days to reach the lake near the village that was to be their new home. Ordinarily, it would have taken half as long, but they stopped often for Lilyan and Andrew to move about; her to shake off the effects of the drug, and Andrew to test out his stamina. Lilyan recovered quickly, but Andrew, to their great disappointment, did not.

Lilyan drifted away from the others to stand at the edge of the lake and soak in the magnificent prospect before her. Like a fine mirror, the serene ebony water reflected the trees rising, layer upon layer, stretching up to the mist-covered mountains and to the cotton white clouds floating across the azure sky. Occasionally a dragonfly would zoom too close and a fish would pop up out of the water and drop back in, sending ripples rolling across the glassy surface. Wind whispered through thick patches of cattails and grass, reminding Lilyan of home.

Home had a much deeper meaning now. It was no longer Charlestown, but it was wherever her beloved abided. *My dearest, I miss you so.* Fighting melancholy, she returned to the group.

Callum had decided that Lilyan and Andrew would travel across the water with Golden Fawn and Smoke, while he and Rider took the long way around the lake and over the mountain with the horses and mule.

Lilyan watched the young men rummage through a pile of branches and grass to uncover a canoe that seemed to appear from nowhere. Soon she sat huddled inside the dugout with Andrew in front of her, burrowed beneath a pile of blankets. Smoke stood at the bow and Golden Fawn at the stern, each plunging long bamboo poles into the water, pushing them forward across the lake. They skirted the shore, avoiding the stronger currents, and eventually glided close enough to some huge rocks that Lilyan could have brushed them with her fingertips. Without warning, they cut sharply between two moss-covered boulders that loomed above them.

"Duck," Smoke ordered as he crouched low to avoid being knocked down by limbs that formed a thick covering overhead.

They passed underneath the cedar canopy, and to Lilyan's amazement, a deep, black hole loomed in front of them, reminding her of a giant's mouth ready to swallow them whole. Smoke and Golden Fawn pulled the poles from the water and slid them along the sides of the dugout. Almost immediately, Lilyan felt the tug of a very strong current. At the edge of the entrance, a ray of sunlight shot through the trees, turning the water around them a bright lime green and illuminating a cavern with shimmering pinkish tan, turgid objects that jutted out of the water and hung from the roof. Lilyan's imagination soared as she studied the curious shapes that looked more and more like menacing trolls with bulbous noses and swollen cheeks. She leaned over to drag her fingers across the water, shocked to find it ice-cold. Bobbing along with the current, she realized that the light behind them was growing fainter, turning the trolls into misty gray lumps. Before long, darkness engulfed them, as black as any she had ever known. She held her hands inches away from her face, but could not see them. All was silent except for the occasional *drip, drip* of water falling from the bamboo poles. The sound reverberated around them, sending a chill across her shoulders. She shivered and pulled her coat up around her neck and felt for the blankets to tuck them tighter around her brother.

Lilyan was reminded of David hiding in the caves from Saul's seneschals. She remembered the Bible verses where David spoke with such confidence of the reassurance that God was ever-present. He had no doubts that God would abide with him even if he rose up to the heavens or descended into Sheol.

Is this my Sheol? And are You with me, Lord?

I will be with you, even to the ends of the earth, came the response in her mind, lifting her spirits. Calm again, she sighed. She realized that Andrew was reaching back searching for her hand, and she clasped it.

"How are you faring?" he asked.

"Fine."

They both had whispered as if in church. *He must be as affected by this as I am.*

They had drifted awhile when Lilyan spotted a faint light ahead. Soon she could pick out the sides of the cavern and Smoke's outline as he took hold of the pole and pushed it into the water. When they broke out through the tunnel, she squinted against the brilliant sunlight. Her eyes watered and she blinked to clear them only to discover the most breathtaking scene she had ever witnessed. Craggy, steel gray mountain peaks, sprinkled with lush green forests, formed a complete circle around the lake. Cabins nestled near the lakeshore and lined a rambling path heading up the mountainside. Gentle swirls of smoke wafted from the roofs of the cedar-log structures that were held together with pink-tinged mortar, making them look like striped confections. Men, women, and children stopped what they were doing to stare. Some hurried to the shore, waving their arms high.

"*Seo. Seo. Seo,*" they called out, their faces bright with welcome.

Lilyan noticed a cluster of men and women who held back; their expressions wary and worried. *Not everyone is happy about our arrival.*

In no time, Golden Fawn had introduced Lilyan and Andrew to everyone, instructed several giggling women to help with the belongings, and enlisted the aid of two strong men to lift Andrew from the dugout.

What a happy caravan we make, Lilyan thought, mingling with the crowd as they filed behind Golden Fawn, who led them to a cabin set far away from the others.

"Welcome to your new home," said Golden Fawn, who pulled back the deerskin draped across the entrance.

Thou art all fair, my love;
there is no spot in thee.
He is altogether lovely.
This is my beloved, and this is my friend
Song of Solomon

Chapter Thirty-Three

DURING THE FOLLOWING MONTH, Lilyan made so many discoveries she could scarcely take them in.

She found the Cherokee to be among the kindest and most giving of any people she had ever met. Many mornings she would awake on the rope-sprung cot in the cabin she shared with Andrew and Callum and pull back the deerskin door to find freshly baked cornbread at the threshold. The woodpile stacked against the wall never diminished, no matter how many logs they burned for cooking or to keep them warm through nights that grew ever colder. One morning she found a bundle outside that held a long cotton skirt and a persimmon-colored blouse as well as rabbit-skin coats sized to fit herself, Andrew, and Callum. Although many of the women laughed at Lilyan's attempts to speak Cherokee, they good-naturedly corrected her and seemed to genuinely appreciate her efforts. Some of the villagers, though, glared at their guests or avoided them all together. Those people, Callum learned, maintained a fierce loyalty to the British, but would not harm them as long as the chief granted them sanctuary.

Several of the men about Andrew's age came by each day to help him from his bed and encourage him to walk. When they finished exercising, they would sit around the front of the cabin and show Andrew how to make arrows for their bows and darts for the blowguns they used to kill small game. The men earned Lilyan's undying gratitude, and she lifted them up in prayer every night. Her brother still had bouts with weak and wobbly knees and shortness of breath, but she could see his stamina improving. His conversations grew more animated. A new light shone in his eyes.

Golden Fawn became Lilyan's best friend. Andrew insisted that she teach Lilyan right away how to make the corn-and-bean-batter bread she had cooked for them on the trail. Lilyan became a willing pupil, learning how to grind corn before each meal, finger-weave cloth, and make clay pots for carrying water and storing dried fruit and nuts. They spoke part of the time in English and part in Cherokee. Sometimes Andrew would join them and often showed off how quickly he was mastering the language.

One day as they sat before the cabin, Golden Fawn revealed that her mother was Elizabeth's aunt. "Even though I was very young when it happened, I remember the day Fire Beard took Elizabeth away. My mother was showing me how to make *kanuchi*."

"Kanuchi?" Lilyan asked.

"We grind hickory nuts into a fine paste and roll it into balls until we are ready to use it. When you boil it in water, it makes a light cream that we add to hominy." She dropped the basket she was weaving. "It was one of my favorites, and I was sad to think that when Elizabeth got to Charlestown, she would not be able to have it again. To brighten my spirits before she left, Elizabeth told me the story of how the red bird got his color."

This chance to share a pleasant memory of her dear friend lifted Lilyan's own spirits. "And how is that?"

"Long ago, when the world was young, raccoon began to tease wolf so much that wolf became angry and chased raccoon through the woods. When they reached the lake, raccoon ran up a tree and onto a branch. Wolf searched for raccoon, saw his reflection in the water, and jumped in to capture him. Wolf looked for a long time until he nearly drowned. He grew so tired, he fell asleep on the riverbank. While wolf slept, raccoon snuck up to him and began to cover his eyes with mud and then ran away laughing."

She rubbed her fists against her eyes as if crying. "When wolf woke, he started to cry, 'I cannot see. Please, someone help me.'

Little brown bird heard the wolf's cry and flew to him. 'I am just a little brown bird. How can I help you, brother wolf?' Wolf answered, 'Please help me to see again. If you do I will show you the magic rock that drips red paint, and I will paint your feathers.'"

Warming to her story, Golden Fawn raised her eyebrows. "Brown bird picked away the dried mud from wolf's eyes. Grateful, wolf told brown bird to jump onto his shoulder, and they ran through the woods to the rock. Wolf pulled a twig from a tree and chewed on it until it was like a brush. He dipped the brush into the paint and began to paint the feathers of brown bird. When wolf was done, red bird flew away to show his family and friends how beautiful he was."

Lilyan studied the young woman who reminded her so much of Elizabeth and felt great relief that she could finally think of her dear friend without wanting to weep. "What a sweet story."

"Elizabeth had a way of knowing when someone felt bad and she often told such stories to us."

Lilyan stood, wrapping a blanket around her shoulders. "If you don't mind, I think I will go for a walk."

Golden Fawn stood. "I will see if I am needed in the fields."

Lilyan chose a steep path that eventually meandered alongside a wall of shale striated with so many colors and textures it looked as if an artist had brushed horizontal stripes of gray, shimmering silver, and rust brown along the surface. Near the top, she squeezed between massive boulders where, to her delight, she ferreted out a hideaway, a ledge that displayed a view so perfect it brought tears to her eyes. A symphony of colors burst forth across the valley in shades of vermillion, lavender, fiery oranges, vibrant yellows, soft apricots, and purples. Distant peaks rose up to the sky covered in a thick mist.

That place became her own special haven she visited daily. Dangling her legs over the edge or sitting cross-legged, she would draw charcoal portraits of the women and children of the village or simply gaze at the layers of rolling hills that reminded her of the ocean, a thought that made her homesick for Charlestown. Sometimes in the evenings, with only the brilliant moon and stars to light her way, she would climb to the perch and stand with her arms flung open.

"Do you sense my love, Nicholas?" she would say. "I'm casting it out into this magnificent night, hoping, praying that it will find its way to your heart."

Her sanctuary also served as a place of contemplation and prayer. It pleased her to discover a new depth, a maturity of spirit in her prayers, which no longer consisted of desperate, fearful pleas for the safety of her family. Instead, her times with the Lord seemed more like conversations, opportunities to share her hopes and dreams for the future, but always with the calm, blessed assurance that no matter what happened, her heavenly Father would work all things to good. Keen anticipation and hope began to well up inside her. The sense of expectation puzzled yet exhilarated her.

And then one day as she and Golden Fawn followed the path to the lake, carrying pots for water, the air seemed to fairly tingle with excitement. Lilyan heard the chattering of the villagers rise and fall as news of seeming import wafted through the town. They started to point and then run down the hill, as they had done when Lilyan and Andrew first arrived.

Continuing at a leisurely pace, Lilyan cupped her hand above her eyes to block out the sun's glare. She watched several of the men pull a dugout from the water and greet a tall, lithe man who slid his legs over the side and jumped onto the sand.

The moment he took a step, she knew him. "Nicholas!" The pots slid from her hands and shattered to pieces at her feet.

Nicholas looked up, spotted her, and took off running toward her. Lilyan raced so fast she barely felt her feet touch the ground. With her heart tripping, she scanned him from head to toe as he came closer and closer and then swept her into his arms.

"My beloved. My beloved." His body trembled.

Locked in his warm embrace, she buried her face into his neck, delighting in the wonderful, familiar smell of him. They clung to each other, neither of them moving. He released her only to clasp her head in his hands and to place hungry, desperate kisses on her face—her forehead, her cheeks, her chin.

"My Lilyanista. I knew you were not dead. My heart could not have continued to beat if that was so," he muttered between kisses.

He claimed her mouth, and she ran her hands up his arms, stood on tiptoe, and twined her arms around his neck, knocking off his hat and burying her fingers in his hair. He swept her up against his chest and twirled her around, staring into her face with such adoration that she laughed —a sound echoed by the crowd gathered around them.

"You found me." Lilyan cupped her hand to his jaw, now covered in a thick, curly beard.

He swallowed hard. "Yes. I did."

She rubbed her thumb underneath his eyes glistening with unshed tears. He slid her hand to his mouth and kissed her palm.

"Come," she said, "Andrew and Callum will be delighted to see you."

"Wherever you lead me." He wrapped his arm about her and matched his stride to hers.

"I was so worried that you might hear of my death. But it was the only way we could think of at the time to stop the outlaws. I wanted to spare you, but there was no way to get word to you. I pleaded with the chief to send a messenger, but he would not allow it. And I simply couldn't ask Andrew or Callum to go alone. ..."

"I know. I know." He pulled her closer.

They stopped when they saw Golden Fawn hurrying to meet them.

Lilyan gazed up at her husband. "This is my Nicholas. Nicholas, this is my dear friend, Golden Fawn. She is Elizabeth's cousin."

The young woman nodded, turning her face away as if once again self-conscious of her scars.

Nicholas tipped up the girl's chin with his fingertip and looked her in the eyes. "I'm honored to meet you."

She smiled back at him and stepped aside to let them pass.

At the cabin, they came upon Callum carrying a sack in one hand and propping Andrew up with the other.

He dropped the bag to the ground and clapped Nicholas on the shoulder. "'Tis good to see you, lad."

Andrew grinned and reached out his hand. "Mighty good to see you again, Brother."

Nicholas clasped his hand, pumping it up and down. "You've been ill?"

Andrew nodded. "Getting better each day."

Lilyan glanced at the gear leaning against Callum's leg. "Where are you two going?"

Callum cleared his throat. "Thought we'd go stay with Smoke and Rider. But I do want to hear your news, Captain. Find out how the general's doing."

"We'll catch up soon, old friend."

Callum picked up the sack from the ground. "You look like you could use some rest right now, lad. You two go on inside. Sun will be down soon, and it's getting colder by the minute. I stoked the fire up for you."

Lilyan kissed Callum's cheek and then hugged Andrew. "You'll be well?"

Andrew rolled his eyes. "No more worrying. Remember?"

"I remember." She ducked under Nicholas' arm as he held back the deerskin curtain.

Inside, a cheery fire had turned the room into a cozy haven. Lilyan pulled off her coat and hung it over a hook. "Here." She held out her hand. "Give me your coat."

She watched him peel off his buckskin jacket, but when he started to hand it to her, she could not resist stepping forward, burying her face in the open folds of his shirt, and resting her cheek against his heart. He dropped the coat on the floor and wrapped his arms around her.

She clasped his shirt in her fists. "You are here with me. I prayed and prayed for this. And now my prayers have been answered."

He captured her lips in a kiss that set a river of molten lava swirling through her stomach. When he finally released her, she looked up into his beautiful golden eyes so full of love she could hardly bear it. His eyelids were swollen; the rims were bloody red, and his eyes looked as if someone had smeared charcoal underneath them.

She dipped a gourd into the water bucket and handed it to him. He drank heavily, dribbling the liquid down his chin and onto his shirt.

"When is the last time you slept?"

He looked nonplussed.

"Come, my love." She took his hand. "Why don't you lie down?"

She led him to the bed and noticed that someone had pushed two of the cots together. The fresh cedar bows she had placed on top of them that morning had been rearranged and covered with blankets.

"Only if you lie with me." He slumped onto the bed, never

taking his eyes from her.

When he reached for his boots, Lilyan knelt in front of him. "Let me help you." She unlaced his leggings and pulled off his boots.

Nicholas leaned closer and pressed his face onto the crown of her head, and breathed in heavily. "Umm. Your hair smells wonderful."

I cannot say the same of your feet, she wanted to say, but she could not bring herself to tease him. There would be time for teasing later. Besides, after what he must have endured to find her, she refused to acknowledge any fault in him.

They cuddled on the bed, Lilyan pressing her back into his chest. He tucked his knees up under hers and draped his arm across her stomach.

"Tell me about it. How you found out about me," Lilyan spoke in a hushed voice.

"It was Snead. He heard about it and came to tell me. I wanted to die. But even though there were witnesses who swore to your death, there was a part of me—small, buried deep inside—that would not accept it."

Lilyan caressed his arm.

"I was desperate. I had to know the truth. And then if it was true, God forgive me, I wanted to hunt down and kill whoever did it. I went to General Marion and told him I was leaving to do just that, with or without his permission."

"Oh, my. What did he say?"

"He said he understood. He had wanted to do the same when the British killed his young nephew, Gabriel. Gentleman that he is, he gave me leave. Samuel and I headed immediately for the Baker Trading Post."

"Samuel came with you? Where is he?"

"Not far away." Nicholas chuckled. "We thought it best that he stay away from the Cherokee."

"He loved Elizabeth, didn't he?"

"It's not something we ever spoke of. But, yes, I believe he did."

Lilyan sighed, and Nicholas tightened his hold on her.

"Well. My hopes came alive the minute I spoke with the Bakers, and they described the man who was supposed to have killed you. I knew it was Callum. I wasn't sure what had happened. I had not figured out your plan yet. All I can tell you is, being told you were dead, but trying not to believe it, nearly drove me mad."

Lilyan's heart ached to think of him suffering so.

"Before you left, Callum told us you'd be heading for this village. Samuel and I searched out some Cherokees and asked them the way. They were suspicious of us at first, but I convinced them I was only looking for my wife."

He yawned, pushing his chest into her back.

"And then you found me," Lilyan finished his story.

"Yes, aga'pi mou, I found you." His voice drifted off, replaced by a low, steady snore.

Lilyan sighed. *I am home. My beloved is mine and I am his.*

She lay there awhile before his body relaxed enough for her to slip from his embrace. She slid onto the bearskin rug that covered the dirt floor. Staring into the fire, she poured out her thanks to God for allowing her to be with Nicholas again. She drew her knees up to her chin and drank in her husband with her eyes. He lay on his side facing her, and her gaze traveled the length of him from his toes, up his long legs to his muscled thighs, to his golden brown forearm, and the dark curly hair exposed by his open-necked shirt. She considered his coal black beard. *That will have to go soon.*

She heard a rustling noise outside and peered around the deerskin curtain in time to catch Golden Fawn's eye as she deposited a pot on the ground. Her friend waved and then stepped away. Lilyan reached out and pulled the pot inside, wafting the delicious aroma of corn, beans, and squash.

Nicholas stirred and then opened his eyes. "Hello."

"Are you hungry, Nikki?"

His mouth curled into a smile as sensuous as the movement of his body as he stretched his arms over his head.

"Yes. But only for you, my love. Only for you."

Therefore do not be anxious for tomorrow…

Chapter Thirty-Four

THE FOLLOWING DAY LILYAN, Nicholas, Andrew, and Callum stood together on the ledge of Lilyan's hideaway.

Nicholas joggled a mirror in his hand, catching a ray of sunshine and reflecting it across the valley. A few moments later, they witnessed a flash of light from the facing mountain.

Lilyan cupped a hand over her brow. "Is that Samuel?"

Nicholas grinned at her. "Yes. He is showing us where to meet him."

"By my reckoning it should take us about two hours to reach him," said Callum.

"Then how many days to your land?" Andrew asked.

"Three days." Nicholas dropped the mirror into the pouch draped over his shoulder. "I'm hoping the snow will hold off another two or three weeks until we can build a cabin."

Lilyan twirled a piece of fringe from the front of her husband's jacket around her finger. "One large enough for all of us?"

He pulled her to him. "I gave you my promise. There would always be room in my home for the ones you love."

Callum harrumphed. "It's going to have to be a mighty big one. What with Smoke and Rider and Golden Fawn coming along.

I want my bunk as far away from those two men as I can get. Didn't think I would ever get to sleep last night. Thought I was in the middle of a thunder storm."

Andrew snorted. "Only rumbling I heard was coming from your side of the cabin."

"Ach. That's some way to talk to your elders, laddie. Come along, we've got things to do."

Callum and Andrew left to make their way back to the village. Lilyan could still hear Callum even after they passed between the boulders and away from sight.

She laughed, twined her arms around her beautiful husband, and rested her head on his shoulder. "I'm glad the chief agreed to let Golden Fawn and her brothers come with us. They will be safer, I think. What did you tell the war chief?"

"I told him feelings are running high with the some of the Patriots. And they're talking about getting even with the Cherokee for taking sides with the British. He thanked me for the warning. The situation doesn't look good."

They stood quietly for a few minutes.

His body tensed. "I'll have to go back, you know. After I get you settled in."

Her heart seemed to drop into her stomach. "I know."

He kissed the top of her head. "It shouldn't be long, now, before the fighting is over. When I was at the trading post, word came that Cornwallis had surrendered his troops."

"That is good news."

"America will have independence. There are many promises ahead."

"If there's one thing I've learned through all of this, aga'pi mou, it's that we are not promised tomorrow. Only today. We have to make the best of each moment. God will provide the rest."

"That He will, my love. That He will."

Author's Notes

I HAVE BEEN PASSIONATE about history since my seventh grade teacher, Miss Lucia Daniel, introduced me to South Carolina history and brought alive the people who took part in it. After her class, I knew that people in history books existed—really lived—and weren't a series of annoying lists I was obligated to memorize. I discovered that Francis Marion, who is revered by many, romanticized by some, and totally unknown to others, was a diminutive, unattractive, shy but brilliant leader of men, who kept his word. One poignant detail of his life that touched my thirteen-year-old heart was that he was childless and planned to bequeath his belongings to his young cousin, Gabriel, of whom he was quite fond. But the British killed Gabriel when they discovered his relationship to Marion. a tragedy that greatly saddened the general.

Marion's devotees hold an annual meeting, The Francis Marion Symposium, in Manning, S.C., dedicated to his exploits. There's usually a dinner theatre where attendees wear colonial garb. It's really quite an intriguing event; you should attend. I mean it. You'll have fun, meet other history buffs, and learn about the Revolutionary War.

My passion for history makes it imperative that I get it right. Consequently, for various projects I've worked on over the past twenty years I have spent hundreds (maybe thousands) of hours in various libraries scrolling through microfilm, handling precious handwritten documents, filling copy machines with quarters, and scribbling legal pads full of notes (which, now that my handwriting has gone to the dogs, even I have trouble reading), and squeezing maps, photographs, pamphlets, and brochures into three-ring binders, meticulously including footnotes and references. I've spent countless hours on the Internet and have had fascinating conversations with experts in the field of Indian medicine, Colonial American cooking, botany and biology, wallpaper design, paper and silk production, indigo planting, mixing paints, the Gullah language, and the proper care of horses. I cannot tell you how much I appreciate re-enactors. Now, there are some people who want to get it right!

Because I realize that I can never use all the information I have gleaned, I have posted it on my website, *www.susanfcraft.com*. Feel free to visit and take away whatever is useful to you.

There are a few things in The Chamomile that might cause careful historians to pose a question or raise an eyebrow. The following list, which is in alphabetical order (as good as any way to order it, I suppose) is my attempt to clear up any misunderstandings.

Blacks Serving in the Revolutionary War

The status of blacks at the Revolution was quite different (and better) than it was by 1820. Most of the blacks serving with the army in South Carolina were probably servants of white soldiers but they carried weapons and fought. Before the fall of Charleston, servants of officers had to serve in the line in case of emergency or a fight so we may assume they trained with the soldiers even though they were not paid.

(by historian, Karen MacNutt)

(see more at *www.susanfcraft.com*)

Brixham

I couldn't have the rescue take place on any of the three real prison ships docked in the Charleston Harbor at the time, because of the meticulous ships' logs and rosters of prisoners. For the same reason, I didn't want to use the name of any from a list of Revolutionary War British prison ships. I needed a fictitious name. Many ships were named after coastal towns so I settled on the fishing village/port of Brixham. I liked all the history associated with it -- Francis Drake's ship the *Golden Hind* docked there -- plus it was near Torbay, the name of one of the real prison ships. I searched British maritime and War Department records for a real ship named *Brixham* and found the *H.M.S. Brixham*, a Royal Navy minesweeper in service from 1940-48. So I named my little schooner the *Brixham*.

Cherokee Village

This picturesque village and the way Lilyan gets there through a cave were creations of my imagination. So sorry about that. My editor, who was sorely disappointed that the village is fictitious, insisted I include this so we don't have people combing the Blue

Ridge Mountains, asking the locals where the village might be.

Fishing Negroes

Some slave watermen used their skills to supply their masters and others with fish. By the early eighteenth century, an identifiable group of "fishing Negroes" had emerged in South Carolina, particularly in Charleston.

(Slave counterpoint: Black culture in the eighteenth-century Chesapeake, by Philip D. Morgan)

(see more at *www.susanfcraft.com*)

Golden Cheese Rounds

The First American Cookbook: A Facsimile of American Cookery, 1796, contains a recipe for cheese — "The red, smooth, moist-coated, tight pressed, square-edged cheeses are better than white coated, hard rinded, or bilged. The inside should be yellow, and flavored to your taste. Deceits are used by salt-petering the outside, or colouring with hemlock, cocumberries, or saffron, infused into the milk."

Mock Death Potion

Golden Fawn could have used a concoction with pennyroyal (also called lurk-in-the-ditch, mosquito plant, pudding grass, run-by-the-ground, squaw balm, squaw mint and tick weed) to bring about Lilyan's "fake death." As an easily-made poison, early colonial settlers used dried pennyroyal to eradicate pests. The Royal Society published an article on its use against rattlesnakes in the first volume of its Philosophical Transactions (1665). A mixture that contains pennyroyal may cause loss of consciousness, coma, low blood pressure or slow, irregular heartbeats; and may reduce the urge to breathe.

Oath of Allegiance

Lilyan's Oath of Allegiance is a compilation of oaths I found during my research, including one that Benjamin Franklin was asked to sign. (see more at *www.susanfcraft.com*)

Paper Mill

The first paper mill in Charleston, S.C., was built in 1806.

Mr. Pierre Dessausure, the fictitious proprietor of my mill, runs a "cottage industry" where he experiments with making paper and dabbles in wallpaper.

Violet Plantation

This is a fictitious place, although the place where I locate it is real — Haddrell's Point, an inlet on the northeast side of Charlestown Harbor.

Wallpaper

A wood block was carefully prepared in relief, which means the areas to show "white" are cut away with a knife, chisel, or sandpaper leaving the characters or image to show in "black" at the original surface level. Artisans would apply ink to the block with a roller and bring it into firm and even contact with the paper or cloth to achieve an acceptable print. The content would print "in reverse" or mirror-image. Multiple blocks were used for coloring, each for one color. Often, a simple design was block printed, and an artist embellished the design by hand. The earliest known fragment of European wallpaper that still exists today was found on the beams of the Lodge of Christ's College in Cambridge, England, and dates from 1509. In 1785, the first machine for printing colored tints on sheets of wallpaper was invented, and a patent was registered in 1799 for a machine to produce continuous lengths of paper.

Finally, but most importantly to me, The Chamomile is an inspirational novel about someone who faces adversity and survives it through faith. My intent was to portray a woman who maintains a genuine, abiding relationship with her creator and who really struggles to live by that faith, but makes a mess of it sometimes. (Don't we all?)

Historical Figures Who Appear in *The Chamomile*

(For more information about these historical figures and about the Revolutionary War in South Carolina visit www.susanfcraft.com)

Lt. Colonel Nisbet Balfour (British Commandant of Charlestown, South Carolina)

After British troops occupied Charlestown in 1780, Balfour became Commandant of the city. According to General William Moultrie, Balfour had a "tyrannical, insolent disposition" and he "treated the people as the most abject slaves." David Ramsay, a patriot placed in exile in St. Augustine, Florida, stated that Balfour displayed "all the frivolous self-importance, and all the disgusting insolence, which are natural to little minds when puffed up by sudden elevation, and employed in functions to which their abilities are not equal." Other, more generous, observers say that Balfour was understandably unyielding towards the revolutionaries and scrupulously carried out the commands of his superiors in regard to policies in Charlestown.

Francis Marion (Col. Continental Army, Brig. Gen. South Carolina Militia: 1732-1795)

Contemporaries acknowledged him as one of the top heroes of the American Revolution. Born to a planter family on the Carolina frontier, Marion distinguished himself as a lieutenant in the Royal Provincials during the Indian Wars. He was commissioned in the Continental Army at the beginning of the Revolution where he gave competent, but not remarkable, service between 1775 and 1780.

When the British took Charleston in 1780, Marion evaded capture. He reported to the American forces in North Carolina. Sent ahead to organize the militia, he was not present at the disastrous American Army defeat in August of 1780. While many "sunshine patriots" surrendered to the British, Marion organized the only continuously effective resistance to the British occupation of South Carolina between August of 1780 and the spring of 1781.

Unable to destroy Marion, the British called him a "damned old swamp fox" in frustration. The American news papers, starved for good news, began publishing Marion's weekly reports of success thereby creating the nationwide Marion legend.

When the Continental Army re-entered South Carolina in the spring of 1781, Marion, with the help of LTC Harry Lee, captured Ft. Watson and Ft. Mott. This ended British ability to support their forces in the interior and forced their eventual withdrawal to Charleston. Marion's greatest achievement came at the end of the war.

In 1782, South Carolina had the same spirit of vengeance that marked the reign of terror after the French Revolution. Marion used his power as commander of militia, as well as his status as a folk hero, to advocate forgiveness for British sympathizers. By doing so he was threatened and acquired political enemies. Marion would not be intimidated.

Physically, Marion was a small man, probably between 5' to 5'2" tall. There was, however, nothing small about his character or courage. His intellect, his force of character, his dedication to the ideals of the American Revolution, and his magnanimity were instrumental not just in wining the war for independence but in establishing the frame work for a just government after the war.

The war destroyed his personal fortune but he rebuilt. In 1786 he married his cousin and lived as a country gentleman, loved by his friends and respected by his enemies, until his death in 1795.

(Sincere gratitude to historian Karen MacNutt for this information and to Carole and George Summers, coordinators of the annual Francis Marion Symposium in Manning, S.C., for their assistance)

Rebecca Brewton Motte (1738-1815)

In January 1781 after her husband died, Rebecca Motte, who lived in Charleston, S.C., was granted leave from the city's British occupiers to go with her daughters to her Mount Joseph Plantation home in Calhoun County, S.C.

The plantation became a principal supply depot for the British campaign in the South. It garrisoned about two-hundred soldiers and became known as Fort Motte under the command of Lt. Donald McPherson. American forces sought to destroy the British interior chain of military posts, including Fort Motte, to gain control of everything within thirty miles of the sea.

Before General Francis Marion and Lt. Colonel Lighthorse Harry Lee attacked the plantation on May 8, 1781, the Motte family was asked to retreat to a farmhouse nearby. When American forces failed to take the fort, they decide to burn the British out. Mrs. Motte encouraged the Americans to set the main house afire in order to dislodge the British. She herself is said to have provided the arrows used to ignite the roof. (One firsthand account of the siege says that Nathan Savage, a private in Marion's brigade, made up a ball of rosin and brimstone, to which he set fire and slung it on the roof of the house.) The British surrendered when the fire broke out, and tradition has it that both sides assisted in putting out the fire, saving the house. Following the successful American siege, Mrs. Motte graciously hosted a dinner for officers of both armies.

General Sir Banastre Tarleton (1754-1833)

Tarleton joined the war against the colonies in May 1776. His initial efforts in upstate New York, Pennsylvania, and New Jersey, were successful, and he won much acclaim.

He became the commander of the British Legion, a mixed force of cavalry and light infantry also called Tarleton's Raiders. In 1780 he proceeded to South Carolina, rendering valuable services to Sir Henry Clinton in operations which culminated in the capture of Charleston.

The short, stocky, redhead became known for his ruthlessness and viciousness during the many battles and raids throughout the Southern colonies.

He was known for waging total warfare, burning property and destroying crops as he went. He acquired a reputation for brutality after the battle of the Waxhaws in 1780 where he faced Virginia Continentals led by Abraham Buford. According to American accounts, Tarleton ignored the white flag and mercilessly massacred Buford's men.

Another account of that battle says that, as the Americans surrendered Tarleton's horse was struck by a musket ball and fell. This gave the loyalist cavalrymen the impression that the rebels had shot at their commander while asking for mercy. His men, thinking he was dead, became enraged and stabbed the American wounded where they lay.

The British called it the Battle of Waxhaw Creek, while the Americans called it the "Buford Massacre" or the "Waxhaw

Massacre." Tarleton became known as the "Butcher of Waxhaw" and "Bloody Tarleton."

The Waxhaw massacre became an important rallying cry for the revolutionaries. "Tarleton's quarter," meaning "no quarter," became a rallying cry for American Patriots for the rest of the war especially at the massacre by American troops of loyalist forces at the Battle of Kings Mountain, October 7, 1780, where all the participants save for one British officer were colonists.

CPSIA information can be obtained at www.ICGtesting.com
Printed in the USA
LVOW060958291011

252647LV00002B/4/P